The Waste Gun

by

John Lars Shoberg

Dedication:

To Trudy

ISBN 978-0-9863301-3-1

Print 1 - November 2019

Table of Contents

Prologue

Sunrise was creeping into his rear view mirror as Jeff was looking forward to finishing up his rotation of graveyard shifts. After this load of timber, he would have four glorious days to lay around and re-adjust to the sunlight before he began a month of day shifts. He would be able to see and talk with Laura and Ginnie again. Working rotating shifts was tough, but with the pay differential and the Baxter Tree Farm's contribution to his on-line tuition, it was worth it. He only had a little time left before he finished classes. And they were his passport out of the middle-of-nowhere Oregon and back into the real world.

Sunlight reflected into Jeff's eyes before he ever saw the actual chain stretched across the road. He yanked on his jake-brakes to slow the trailer and pumped the cab ones to bring his rig to a halt. He had to react quickly yet carefully; there was no room on this company road for a jack-knifed vehicle. In fact, one little slip would send him and his rig plunging 200 feet down into the lower valley. Fortunately, you don't travel very fast on dirt roads, and Jeff came to a complete stop inches before touching the State Patrol sign hanging in the middle of the chain.

He breathed a sigh of relief.

Next he looked around for the troopers responsible for barricading the private road leading to the company lumber mill.

The reddish glow of the morning light highlighted the two individuals who were approaching his truck. He was sure they weren't there a moment earlier. In fact, this road was so narrow that Jeff couldn't see where their patrol car could be parked.

One of them motioned for Jeff to get out of his cab. The adrenaline Jeff had needed to stop his load safely was wearing off, making him too slow in wondering why they wanted him out. Normally, troopers wanted you to stay inside your vehicle. He opened the door, grabbed hold of the ladder, and climbed

1

down.

He was forcing back a yawn when something bit him in his left shoulder. He reached for it with his right hand while his left arm began to go numb. He lost his grip with his left hand just as he finally succumbed to the sleep he had been fighting off for the last hour.

One of the two men jumped the chain and ran over to the semi. Not in time to catch the driver's body before it hit the ground, but at least he stopped the man's head from thumping against a large rock on the roadside.

"Damn it, Carlos, couldn't you have waited another second? At least let him get down before you shot him? You could've hurt the guy." Nathaniel Sollinsky had agreed that the loggers had to be stopped. Especially in this case, when they were again cutting into the natural forests, violating their pledge to use only the trees specially grown for logging purposes. But despite the violence of what they were planning, no one was supposed to get hurt. Destruction of criminal property was one thing, but life— Life was sacred. Life was what Eco-Now was all about.

Putting the dart gun back in his concealed holster, Carlos simply replied, "Sorry."

"Sorry! All you can say is 'Sorry'?" Nathaniel was amazed. How had this man become so callus all of a sudden? Carlos had come to their group full of exuberant idealism. He had been the driving force that propelled Jason Conrad's plan forward.

He must have been more focused on the mission than even Nathaniel had realized.

Focusing his own efforts on moving the body, Nathaniel was glad he was two inches taller than this driver; his weight-training efforts didn't hurt, either. "This guy could use a diet," he mumbled to himself. Managing to get the driver safely over to the woods, he propped him up against one of the thicker trees.

"We're not here to hurt anybody, just shut this mill down," he said as he approached their barricade.

"That is so," Carlos replied dryly as he rolled the chain out of the way and threw it into the forest. A forest that Baxter Tree

Farms had purchased just this year in the hopes of filling their ever-increasing production quotas. Last year had seen another explosion in new home construction, especially in the newly developing parts of Mexico. Lumber was bringing a good price again, a very good price. Production was outstripping the resources that Baxter had available in their planted acres. Eco-Now, the group Nathaniel and Carlos represented, was fine with harvesting trees that had been specifically planted for lumber production, but 'Old Growth Stands Must Stand', as their slogan stated.

"We're doing this before the regular shift starts coming in to avoid casualties. That means we have to be careful with the people working the graveyard shift."

Slapping his hands together, Nathaniel picked up the satchel he had hidden behind one of the trees and brought it over to the stack of pine logs neatly arranged on the trailer heading for the mill. Opening it, he removed bundle after bundle of dynamite sticks and placed them deep between those logs.

Carlos had a similar satchel and was working on the other side of the trailer. Only Carlos worked at a faster pace, placing two bundles for every one of Nathaniel's. Also, the bundles that Carlos placed were not the same as Nathaniel's. About half of them were incendiary gels, to ignite the logs carried on the trailer; the rest were military ordinance, a much more powerful explosive than mere dynamite, and formed into shaped charges. Once the logs caught fire, the explosive would blow them into any structure on the left side of the truck. They both connected their detonators to the bundles and ran the wires to the cab of the tractor-trailer.

"Where's the timer?" Nathaniel asked as he leaned over Carlos' shoulder, looking at the black box Carlos was hooking up.

"I chose a radio-detonator," Carlos stated. He made the final connection of all their wires into a black rectangular connection box. He pulled a smaller version out of his coat and toggled its green switch to the up position. A red light appeared on the connection box. Carlos smiled and toggled the switch back down;

3

the light slowly faded away. Using duct tape, he secured the wiring box under the driver's seat and covered over all the exposed
wires.

"That's a good idea. We'll have better control over when it
goes off. We can explode it when nobody is in the vicinity. I'll
call Jason and let him know we're ready."

"No," Carlos barked. "Radio silence. No calls." He turned
on his friend, and the fire behind his words made Nathaniel step
back just a little.

"Okay. Look. I, ah, got to take a leak. I'll be right back."
Nathaniel quickly walked back into the woods. Jason had not
really said to call when they were ready to drive the truck into
the mill, but something about Carlos was really bothering Nathaniel, and he wanted someone else's opinion before going any
further with Carlos' changes.

Nathaniel found a very thick tree and stood behind it as
though he were going to pee. He pulled out his cellular phone
and speed-dialed Jason's number. It rang once before he felt the
sting in his left shoulder. He heard Jason answering as the phone
fell from his hands and he blacked out.

"Hello. Hello," came from the phone as Carlos picked it up
and disconnected the call. He then dumped the phone into another of his pockets. Even though Carlos was shorter and slimmer
than Nathaniel, he easily lifted the sleeping man onto his shoulder and carried him back to the cab. Nathaniel was dumped in
the space behind the seats. Then Carlos went over to the sleeping
driver and carried him back to the cab. He boosted him into the
passenger seat and discreetly taped him into a sitting position,
making it look like he was taking a nap.

Carlos had no trouble driving the rig the rest of the way to
the mill. Being early and in the middle of nowhere had certain
advantages. As he approached the gate, Carlos could see only
one guard barring his entrance into the work area.

"Haven't seen you before," the guard said as Carlos brought
the rig to a stop on the security scale.

"New trainee," Carlos said in a much more friendly voice

4

than he had used earlier. He handed the guard the forged ID that Eco-Now had provided him, as well as the regular papers from the pouch in the driver's door.

"I see Jeff's training you **real hard**," the guard smiled at his jest. Carlos grimaced internally but he knew seeing someone he could recognize would put the guard at ease. "He already show you where to take this load, Mr. Ra-mer-ez?"

"Yes, I promised to wake him when it was parked. It's been a long shift," Carlos hated every minute he had to spend talking to this company pig-dog, but had enough training not to let it show.

The guard went into the scale house and came back with the weight ticket for the load. Handing it to Carlos, he added, "Okay, but wake him up before any of the other boys see him. Mr. Lonigan just fired Henry Jackson for sleeping on the job last week."

"Sure thing." Carlos wished he could add this bloated fool to the pile of corpses he was going to signal the world with. He put the rig into gear and drove toward the unloading dock.

But that was not where he planned to leave this load of ill-gotten trees. He parked it next to the building where these fat capitalists were planning to get something useful out of their rape of the Earth, the lumber mill. It was then that he noticed the safety office across the road. He would pay that pig-dog back by getting the main tool of the plant and its safety department at the same time. He moved the rig directly between them.

Jumping down, Carlos looked to the fence, a mere ten yards away. He pulled the wire cutters he had brought out of his pocket and took exactly two steps towards it.

He stopped.

He thought for a moment and smiled as he began walking back toward the guardhouse.

He managed to get in through the back entrance without the guard seeing him. Using the wire cutters, he cold-cocked the old man while he was sitting down reading last night's newspaper. He waited until the whistle clock was about to go off, then he flipped the green switch again and pressed the first button, just as the shift change whistle blew.

The dynamite exploded, sending both logs and shockwaves into the safety office. Carlos' special explosives also went off. Their roar preceded the inward collapse of the mill's walls and dropped a large section of roof; the incendiaries ignited a fireball that engulfed several buildings in the area. Carlos believed he could actually hear some the workers scream. "A just retribution," he proclaimed to only himself.

This would get the national coverage that Eco-Now wanted. Carlos hoped that the added death toll would ensure the world-wide coverage that **he** was looking for.

But enough fun. He pressed the second button and placed the radio-detonator in the fallen guard's right hand. "You pig, they will think that you were knocked out by the blast from the explosions that you yourself set off." Carlos laughed at the justice he had wrought for Gaia as he escaped into the woods.

He was through with Eco-Now. They had just become too small for Carlos Rondonate's vision.

Chapter One

"Indulge me. You **have** got this thing working, right?" Leo Dayton, the CEO for Nuclear Recyclers, the company he was trying to get off the ground here today, asked. The question was more to distract himself from the ominously empty conference room he and his partner now occupied. Whether the things Peter kept building would really work never concerned him. But he was worried that none of the venture capitalists he'd invited today had arrived yet. And it was only twenty minutes until the announced starting time for their presentation.

They had rented one of the technology-enabled conference rooms of the Hyatt Regency Los Angeles. It was just minutes from LAX, where Leo had paid for a small fleet of cabs to wait

walked into the room.

"Is this going to be another toy show?" the newcomer said.
He was definitely not as worried as Leo was about letting
the gray of his hair show, nor did he have to concern himself
with it thinning. He had the look of someone who knew exactly
what they were about, except that he was trying to find a place to
hang his overcoat. While it wasn't exactly chilly in LA this time
of the year, Mr. Alan Hoffman had just flown in from Minneap-
olis, where it was extremely cold right now.

Leo turned from the model and hurried over to take the coat
for him. "Not this time, Mr. Hoffman. This is just the model of
what we plan to build."

Peter could see his partner visibly relax. This was Leo's element, working the money men, getting the financing for whatever project he was organizing. And as more of the financiers
that had been invited walked into the room, Leo began his joyful
dance between them. Getting one situated at the table, another
couple of them started on the buffet line, hanging up yet another's coat, and doing that small talk thing which puts people at
ease and hopefully gets them ready to understand a highly technical presentation when what they really wanted to know was
how this was going to make them money.

Peter's presentation! Yeah, the model had worked, but how
many dozens of times had they tested that piece of the puzzle?
Peter went back over to his laptop that was residing on the
room's electronic podium. He had installed it into the hotel's
projection system and wanted to check it yet again. Just to make
sure everything was running correctly and the line to the Internet
server was secure. Fiber optics, at least the connection would be
a fast one. As long as the servers were up and the net itself
wasn't overcrowded.

That was something he couldn't control, and when people
counted on him to get the job done, that lack of control worried
him. Since it was still a few minutes before the scheduled start
time, and he could see Leo was still waiting on a few more people to show up, Peter decided to check net traffic. Hopefully

9

there would be no major events creeping up that would grab web users' attention and cause massive net congestion, tying up the lines he needed to get to his server back at their New Orleans office.

The lead story on the news was the press conference called by FBI Agent Corsair about the bombing of a lumber mill somewhere in Oregon and the destruction of the same company's corporate offices in Sacramento. A group calling itself Eco-Now was taking responsibility for the mill, while at the same time denying any knowledge regarding the office bombing. This despite the identical taggents—plastic pieces with microscopic codes used to identify where the explosives were manufactured—being found at both bombings and on the lumber mill's security guard, who was being charged as part of the conspiracy, owing to him having been found in possession of the triggering device for the Oregon explosions. Nothing really big, the Internet should be clear if he needed to pull down replacement representations to cover any drive failures. One thing that embarrassing dissertation defense had taught him was to always have a backup plan.

"Peter," Leo had walked up behind him and draped an arm around his shoulder. "Everything ready?"

Peter stood up and looked over the lectern where he'd been working, to see fifteen of the twenty potential investors that Leo had invited sitting around the conference table ready for him to get started. Leo reached into the podium and fingered the touch screen monitor built into it, moving the seating arrangement displayed there to match how he currently had everyone situated. At least Peter would know the names of anyone asking a question.

Finding the remote for the projector, Peter pressed the on button twice, turning it on. It would take only a moment to warm up. "Let's do it, then," he said, just low enough for Leo to hear.

Leo began, "Gentlemen and Ladies, I welcome you to this business proposal for Nuclear Recyclers, soon to be Incorporated. I think we have an exciting project for you today. One that should, no, will corner a service niche that no one else will be able to duplicate. But to really explain what I am talking about, I would like to present to you the brains behind this operation, Dr. Peter von Scorio," he announced. He pointed with his left hand to Peter, began applauding as a cue for the others, and took the seat just south of the lectern as indicated on his revised electronic seating chart.

Studying the controls attached inside the podium, Peter found the ones to dim the room lights, cut their luminance in half, then saw that the projector was set for 'Video 1'. He rapidly found the input selector, switched to computer and got the opening screen of his presentation.

"Ladies and gentlemen, the United States—no, the world— is continuously generating hundreds of tons of radioactive waste every year." He switched from his title slide through several types of nuclear waste generators until he finally got to the underground storage site in the salt mines of Nevada. "Radioactive waste that will either have to be placed in a secure storage facility for tens of thousands of years before it can be safely handled and disposed of, or..." He let the word hang for a minute as he switched to a cross sectional picture of the Earth's interior. "...or be returned to the fiery cauldron from which it originally came. In its simplest terms, what we are proposing to do is to send that dangerous waste to a recycler that can actually do something with it. Send it back to the Earth's core." The next slide was an artist's rendition of the waste gun shooting a waste container into a volcanic ridge.

"This project would have the merits of containing the buildup of radioactive waste; not needing to safeguard it from either terrorists or innocent future generations who might happen to stumble upon it." He had an animated slide that had first shown the number of canisters in the storage cave increasing, then decreasing. "But more importantly, this is a niche opportunity, a market that nobody has yet been able to tap." The slide changed to projected revenue spreadsheet that Leo's accountant friends had produced. "And if we can get there first, we will have it to ourselves. The immense amount of proprietary designs and huge startup costs will exclude competitors from trying to enter this field." A slide appeared of the waste gun immersed in water and a number of different animated submersibles swimming around it. "There are only a few locations on Earth where what I propose is possible." A map of the underwater volcanic Atlantic ridge came on the screen, followed a minute later by film footage shot of the ridge. "And the first one there will have almost exclusive use of it. As for the continued earnings potential of this venture..." Slides of third-world hospitals and reactors followed in succession. "The rest of the world is waiting for us to find a way to deal with the nuclear poison. Once we have standardized their transportation system, everyone will be able to utilize our facility. The entire world will need the services we can provide." Stopping on the slide of the (proposed) Nuclear Recyclers, Inc. corporate logo, Peter ended with, "Instead of locking up both resources and land to control our radioactive waste, we would be recycling it, giving it back to the Earth. Allowing it to be converted back into the raw material that future generations will have available, while at the same time saving resources for us and our children."

There was a spattering of applause as Peter finished and Leo got back up to take the podium. "Thank you, Dr. von Scorio. It was about a year ago that I heard about Dr. von Scorio's idea. Believe me, it wasn't easy to find out about it. The thesis work he had done was considered farfetched and deviated from the 'shrinking resources' dogma that's going around college campuses these days. But I had a friend who had a friend who knew somebody—" he paused as some around the table chuckled, "—who had heard about Dr. von Scorio's idea. Fortunately, the web page he had built to facilitate his thesis presentation was still available on the university server, and I was able to locate it. I've researched the financial aspects of this venture for the past six months. You will each find in front of you our business plan and revenue projections." He held up a green-covered business plan folder and a blue-covered financial folder (both having the proposed logo on them) to emphasize which one was which.

"I think you will find that we have a very large market niche here, with great growth potential once the world sees what we can do."

Harriet Laughlin broke in before Leo could go any further. "We've heard a lot of rhetoric here. And your numbers are, well, numbers. A good accountant can make them say whatever you tell her to make them say. I, for one, want to know how you're going to make this project a reality. How does this gun thingy actually work?"

That was one shrewd lady, Peter thought. *Dangerously beautiful. One could easily overlook the fact that a quick mind lay behind that face. She had made her fortune in these kinds of deals, made it in less than ten years, made it in an industry where you didn't stay in this business long unless you could pick the real winners from the wannabes.*

She had also offered them the perfect segue into their technical presentation. Much quicker than the speech Leo had practiced on him all during yesterday's flights.

"This is where I come in again, Leo," Peter stood back up to the podium and gently moved his partner aside. His laptop had Leo's presentation queued up. So Peter simply dropped the cursor to the bottom of the screen and closed it out. Then opened his Technical Proposal presentation file. This change in plan was going to slow down the remainder of their presentation, but hopefully their audience wouldn't notice. Peter had to close the master file that linked all the individual files making up the presentation and would have to open each one up individually, as they were needed. But these people were ready for the fun stuff.

"I will be more than happy to go deeper into our plan with anyone who wants to, after I have finished this basic demonstration. But for right now, I intend to Keep It Successfully Simple.

"What we intend to do," as he spoke, he clicked from one computer slide to the next, dramatizing his points, "is construct a linear accelerator under the ocean, right above the Mid-Atlantic ridge. Then we are going to launch canister after canister of nuclear waste at a forty-five-degree angle into the gap between the two tectonic plates there. We plan to launch the canisters with enough force to punch them through the flowing lava and under the Eurasian plate. Once it has gotten below the plate itself, the canister will be caught in the underground magma flow and be pulled further away from the opening. This will allow it enough time to melt into the molten core. Once melted, the contents will disperse amongst all the other minerals waiting to be given back to us."

"But why do it underwater?" asked a man in a dark blue suit. Peter checked the seating chart, Frank Walsh. He had a green star by his name, Leo was counting on his support. "Working at the depths you would have to, what, 500 to a thousand feet down?"

"Fifteen hundred," supplied Peter.

"Okay, fifteen hundred feet down is a bit risky. Couldn't you set this accelerator thingy up on land somewhere? Like over an active volcano?"

"There are a couple of reasons we couldn't do that," Peter explained. "First, a volcano is a vent from the Earth's core to the surface. We would have to punch all the way down that vent and under the plate anyway to get the canister to stay down there. The underwater sites we have in mind allow us to only have to punch a short distance through the lava. And secondly, the design for the accelerator is too heavy to use on land. We need the buoyancy of the ocean to support our structure."

"What about regulatory red tape?" asked a lady across from Mr. Walsh. Peter looked down, Cynthia Holridge, a blue star meant she was a hopeful. "The federal government isn't just going to let anybody infringe on their monopoly!"

"We have on retainer the law firm of Holden, Riley, and Franklin to smooth out any regulatory difficulties we might run into. They are preparing international briefs on our behalf, since we expect this will go before the United Nations." Well, at least Peter knew Leo had them on retainer and they let him know all the problems they were going to have.

"You make it sound really easy, young man." Peter looked

at the seating chart again. The elderly man in the green-stripped polo shirt was Lawrence Radcliff. Leo had put an orange star by his name; not easy to convince, but worth the effort. If he could be brought on board, a lot of the others would follow his lead. Leo had told Peter that Radcliff had a reputation for picking winners and people watched where he was investing to put their own money. "And if it is so easy, why hasn't the government been doing this?"

"Frankly, Mr. Radcliff, that's because I haven't invented everything that will be needed to do this yet," Peter replied with all honesty.

"You don't have everything you need developed to make this work?" Radcliff asked as he looked around the table at his fellow investors.

Peter didn't apologize; if it wasn't new, someone else would have already done it. Everybody here knew that. "Most of what we will be needing is off-the-shelf technology, but as with everything, the devil is in how to put them together. In addition to my geophysics Ph.D., I hold an engineering certificate from Kansas State University. I am fairly certain I can tinker together anything we might need. Also, Leo has promised to hire me the best people available. Right, Leo?"

Peter noticed that Leo was getting nervous again. Everything had been planned out, rehearsed. He never liked Peter's ad-libbing. "But there is one piece of this system I came ready to demonstrate." He came out from behind the podium and made his way to the foot of the table where the model of the gun was waiting. "Here you see a working model of the actual gun. A concept demonstration model, so to speak." While running through the steps to fire the model again, Peter narrated, "We plan to drop the waste transport canisters the US DOE currently uses to the ocean floor. With submersibles, we'll capture them and place them inside the first of a series of magnetically-locked rings. Alternating the polarity of the electromagnets in each ring, we plan to accelerate the canister through the structure until it has enough speed to drive itself one quarter mile through liquid rock and under the Eurasian plate." As he said plate, he flipped the red switch and the beer can again hit the pillow with a re-sounding *whump*.

That caused a few of the listeners to pick up the financial reports and look over the figures. Others dug into the green book for the technical specifications there. Only Mr. Hoffman leaned back in his chair and waited for the rest.

Of course this made Leo nervous, so he did the only thing he could think of, he got Mr. Hoffman another cup of his favorite cappuccino, fat-free French Vanilla, and came back to see what he could do for him. Offering him the drink, Leo asked, "What do you think, sir?"

"I know that this is beyond my depth to understand and assess its viability," he began, then took a sip of the drink Leo had brought. "Thank you," holding up the cup then sipping from it again. "If you don't mind, I would like to take these booklets home with me and have some of my people go over them." He began pushing his chair back to get up.

"Please do," replied Leo. "Then you are interested in the project?"

A silence fell over the room as everyone heard the question and wanted to see how one of their numbers was going to jump.

"Let's just say that I'm intrigued. Your idea has merit, but I need to know if you have the ability to pull it off. Do what you say you can do. Now, if I may take my leave, I have a plane to catch back. I don't care how much money you have, they still won't hold up flight schedules for you. Thank you, Mr. Dayton." Turning, he looked across the room as he said, much louder, "And you too, Dr. von Scorio. You'll be hearing from me."

Two more were getting ready to follow Alan Hoffman out the door, but they were definitely not carrying the material Leo had for them. When he tried giving copies to them, they simply said they were not interested in science fiction stunts.

Of the remaining dozen, half were still reading one or the other of the reports, three were with Peter looking over the model, Frank Loranzo and Abigail Martin were on their cell phones, and Lawrence Radcliff was coming up behind Leo.

Radcliff tapped him on the right shoulder while waiting to his left. Leo turned to his right and Radcliff got his laugh. "Fell for it again, eh, Leo?"

Leo responded with, "I'm just a bit nervous about how you guys are viewing this project. Peter's got good ideas and all we need..."

Radcliff held up his hand to stop him. "He does, old friend. But it will not be his ideas that will bring us around. We've all seen you enough in these deals to use you as our barometer. You've put more effort into this than any of your earlier projects. That will carry this a long way. I am going to need a few copies of your materials, and should my people say your findings are sound, you can count on my support."

Leo gratefully shook the older man's hand, grabbed the binders that James Fellows had left behind. He hadn't counted on Jim anyway, but Lawrence Radcliff! "Yes, sir. Please review them and let me personally know if there is anything else you need." He pulled one of the new SD business cards from his suit pocket and handed it to Radcliff. "One of my new cards. My numbers are on it and in it. Just plug it into your phone and the card can either dial my number or connect an e-mail to me."

"Well there is one thing. If I fund this project, I would like you to consider a nephew of mine for a job with your company. This stuff is right up his alley and would give him something productive to do. Doesn't seem to be able to stay in college." Then he added more to himself than to Leo, "I'll have to show this stuff to Jacob."

Relieved, Leo would have taken the man's dog on as VP at this point. "Send him around, I'll see if we can use him."

"I think it might be better to have him talk to your friend, Dr. Scorio." Leo could just feel Peter wince at the shortening of his name, assuming Peter heard it. The *whump* Leo had just heard meant he was probably too wrapped up in his demonstration. "We talk business and that would just bore Jacob. Ah, but Dr. Scorio talks his language, Dr. Scorio could talk to his interests as neither you or I could." Patting Leo on the shoulder, he concluded with, "Have him talk to the young genius." Then Lawrence took the folders from Leo and left the room.

* * *

Nuclear Recyclers was going to be cash strapped if none of the investors they'd talked to came through with financing. In fact, after all their guests had left, Leo and Peter grabbed several plates of food off the buffet to stash in the refrigerators back in their adjoining rooms. Later, Leo was sitting on the bed in his room, finishing off one of those plates, watching the nightly news, as Peter was hooking back into the Internet to check on messages.

"President Oswald today announced," Peter heard from behind him, "the freezing of Eco-Now, Earth First, and several other eco-terrorist groups' assets in response to this week's bombings. Several members of Eco-Now's eco-round table were also arrested. The President said that America's hands would never be tied by fringe groups who didn't care for the pain of their fellow man.

"In economic news today, the government issued new industrial activity figures showing the twelfth straight month of reduced output. The stock markets dropped another 2 percent while the Federal Reserve met in emergency session."

Peter tuned out the rest of the broadcast as he got his connection made and began retrieving his e-mail. Mostly junk mail that he fed to his removal program to get him off their lists. One from Janet that he would save for later tonight. He had several replies to the data requests he had out. Those he filed away for later review. The one from Aqua-Machinists had the last part of information he needed to finish the design work on the Caissons. One of the investors who had been at the meeting today, Harvey MacGuyer, must have sent Leo an e-mail, since Peter was getting a carbon copy. Harvey apologized that he was not going to be able to participate in their growth, but wished them luck.

He also had one from an investor who had not been at the conference at all. He hollered over for Leo while it was opening.

To: ldayton@nuclearwaste.com
cc: vonscorio@nuclearwaste.com
From: anonymous
Subject: Investment
Dear sirs;

I took the liberty of downloading your presentation, business plan and financial statements today. I like what I see. I don't make face-to-face contact, so don't ask. I am willing to donate one hundred million dollars to get you started. I think what you are doing is very important to the human race and want to do my part. Please forward your financial institute's routing information, and I will wire you the money.

Sincerely; M.A."

"Well, what do you make of that?" Peter looked up at his partner, who was reading the message over Peter's shoulder.

"A donation. Damn, that means we don't have to pay it back."

Peter turned away from his computer screen to face Leo. "But why a donation? We're not a non-profit group. This guy could simply make it an investment. That's what we're asking for, not charity. I know we'd be able to get his money back. Something doesn't seem right with this, Leo."

Leo pivoted over to sit on the edge of the bed. "So I suppose you want to give the money back?"

"We haven't even accepted the money yet! All we have to do is ignore this guy. It can't be legit."

"But all we have to do is send him Citizen's Bank's routing information. If he comes through, he comes through. If not, then what's the harm?" Leo asked, spreading his arms.

"I don't know," Peter replied, pulling on the ghost of the beard he had just shaved off last month after having it all through his college years. "And that's what really bothers me."

"Okay, then we just ignore him." Leo got up, leaned over to Peter's computer and pushed the delete button on the e-mail he had open. "There, it's gone. Besides, once we get Hoffman and Radcliff on board, a few more will want to jump in. We should have no problem raising the one billion dollars we need to get through the trials of the system.

"No problem. Listen, I'm going to hit the sack. You should, too. We have an early flight in the morning."

"Okay, good night, Leo." He left, shutting the connecting door without any click of its lock. It was going to be a long day tomorrow, but even longer after that. His next step was going to be actually building the first of the Deep Caissons. Hopefully, somebody would come through with enough money to get that started.

Chapter Two

Alan Simmons checked his watch once again as another patron entered the Coffee Shop who was not this Carlos fellow. The man was already thirty minutes late. Another jingle as the door opened again, and in walked an average height, medium built, olive-skinned man, dressed completely wrong for this java-based bistro. Instead of heading for the counter, he scanned the seated customers as though he were looking for someone. Alan stood up and waved him over to the wall table he had held for this meeting.

"Carlos Ramerez?" Alan asked, offering his hand to the newcomer.

The newcomer took that hand and bore down on it. "And who is the one asking?"

Alan motioned for him to sit down, retrieved his hand and

massaged blood flow back into it. "My name is Alan. And I represent a small group of influential individuals who are supportive of your work. If you are the man we have heard about? And if you are, we would like to assist you. Are you Carlos Ramerez?"

"I have gone by that name," he replied. "Order me a coffee, Jamaican, black, large."

Alan used an app on his phone to place Carlos' request. "So what do we call you, then?"

"Carlos will do. Alan," he replied with a noticeable absence of last names.

"Very well, Carlos. What are your plans going forward?"

"You may know me, but I have no idea who you or your 'influential individuals' are. Maybe you're FBI?"

"We both know that you would have screened out that possibility long before you walked through that door."

"I don't have all resources..." Alan raised his hand to cut Carlos off as the barista brought their drinks to the table.

After the man had left, Alan pretended to sip his too-hot drink. "I think we can help your lack of resources." He took a phone from his pocket and slid it across the table to Carlos. "That's a secure line with the latest encryption software. Uses a satellite uplink rather than conventional towers. You will be able to get a hold of me anywhere on the planet."

"Wi-Fi?" Carlos asked.

"Plus, you are hooked into several secure databases for your research on potential sites. The passwords are already stored in the device.

"But that is just the beginning. If you agree to attack a few targets of our choosing, we can supply you with money and munitions."

"And you get what out of this deal?"

Alan took a long pull on his latte, "You mean aside from the altruistic benefits of improving society?"

Carlos nodded.

"Yes, the targets we suggest will benefit our group financially, as well as bringing us political influence. We expect to reap

21

more than sufficient dividends to pay for your services, Mr...?"

"Rondonate, Carlos Rondonate."

"I'll just key that into my phone. Expect a text before the end of the day. I think you will find the subject rather explosive."

Chapter Three

Special Agent Neil Corsair had been with the bureau for ten years, always a team player backing the lead of other agents. So he had to think about the assignment Supervising Agent Alan Turner had just dropped in his lap. "Special Agent Matheson said it was your work on the Philly terrorist club that brought them all in. I need that expertise again. Only this time, I want you in charge. I have a feeling the Oregon lumber camp bombing is going to turn out much bigger than this report from the Portland office. Domestic and military explosives; I don't like it. Put together a team, establish an action plan, and let me know what resources you need."

It had taken him almost eight years to get assigned field work, now only five assignments later, here he was leading his own team. Well, he would be once he picked them.

Explosives was what had called Turner's attention to this case, so an explosives expert. He logged into the FBI personnel database and searched case files. Harold Fellows' name appeared in several Explosives Unit (EU) reports. Every time with a positive commendation from his Supervising Agent. He had his explosive man.

He would need someone with more profiling experience than he had. Special Agent Martin Hughes had been with the bureau for almost twenty years and had done hundreds of accurate profiles. Neil dashed off an email offer to join his team.

He sat back in his chair and thought for a moment. "I'm going to need legs on the ground." Standing up, he walked over to

Lawrence Brown's desk.

"Hey, Larry." The Special Agent set down his copy of the Chicago Tribune and looked up at Corsair. "You got anything going at the moment?" Neil asked.

"Just researching new leads on bad guys. You got something?"

"Turner handed me the Oregon bombing case. Thinks it might turn out to be something bigger than reported. Interested in being part of my team?"

"After what you did on the KC sniper case, count me in." He stood up and stuck out his hand.

Finalizing his friend's participation on his team, Neil asked, "You have anyone you would recommend?"

"Paul St. Martin knows a thing or two about bombings."

"Have him come by the third floor conference room this afternoon and we can get this investigation started."

Chapter Four

Peter felt just a little nervous sitting in the back seat of the submersible prototype they were calling Deep Caisson. Yes, it was meant to become the workhorse of Nuclear Recyclers, Inc. And yes, he had already spent weeks building and testing this prototype. But this was its open-water trial. And he had no control over it, he was just the passenger.

David Wong, his old California Institute of Technology roommate, was piloting the vessel. If anything went wrong, Peter could only offer advice, and under the rules of the test, he wasn't even supposed to do that. Under normal operating conditions, the pilot would be the only person in the submersible and would have to handle any problem by himself. But Peter just had to be here for his baby's maiden voyage.

"All clear," radioed the tugboat captain as he switched off

the magnetic line connecting the two boats. "Have a good trip. We'll wait for you at 29 degrees 10.0 minutes north by 87 degrees 20.0 minutes west at 1400 hours."

"Roger that, *Iron Maiden*. See you guys in a couple of hours," Wong responded. He leaned his head back towards Peter to say, "Just like old times, aye, Pete?"

No, not like old times, Peter thought. *This time it's my vessel, which just happens to be a brand new design with over a million dollars tied up in it.* But he said, trying to hide his nervousness from the new hire, "Yeah, I guess so."

"Then let's drop to fifty feet and do some cruising." The pilot reached over to his control console and flipped the two ballast tank switches to open and entered fifty feet, zero inches into the submersible's computer. For any depth they wanted to maintain, the computer could immediately calculate the necessary amount of water needed to carry as ballast, factoring in all the variables its hull sensors measured. The idea was to give them precise control over their depth. They would need this to do the precision work they planned. As Deep Caisson dropped below the surface, Wong angled the diving planes down and she descended even faster. "Just like in the simulator," Wong said over his shoulder.

Both he and Peter had spent dozens of hours over the last two weeks tuning their skills in a mockup of this cabin. Wong to understand the controls, Peter to redesign those controls to make them more ergonomic or user-friendly, then Wong to learn everything all over again. If something did happen today, Peter knew exactly what to do to get them home. And if both of them were incapacitated, Leo could press the return button on the tugboat and all the ballast tanks would dump their water, raising her to the surface, where he could hunt them down.

Having built the cabin to accommodate someone of Peter's own size, six foot two, David's five-foot-four made it look quite spacious. More than the room they had back in college, inside David's two-man submersible they'd used every chance USC would give them. The black-haired, gray-eyed Wong had been pursuing an oceanography degree while Peter was getting his

24

bachelor's in Physics.

"Still a good hundred feet from the bottom," David announced as he leveled off at their first scheduled stopping depth.

Something flashed past the viewing window in front of David. "What was that?" Peter asked, not even trying to hide his concern.

"Sonar shows multiple contacts coming up from behind. Not strong enough to be metallic. I'd say—" Before he could finish, the contacts passed the view window and were perfectly pictured in the low light display screen just above it. "—it was a school of fish," Wong finished. "Just like the schools we joined off Catalina Island."

"Okay," Peter said with relief. "Let's get our readings and move on to the bottom for the next set of tests." He swung his seat around to the right and activated the computer console there. He read off the checklist of gauges and sensors he wanted checked and entered the readings as Wong announced them.

Everything showed nominal. "Okay, that's the last of them. Prepare to take us down."

"Aye, aye," David replied as he entered their new depth choice into the computer and adjusted the dive planes.

Peter watched through the portholes on either side of his seat, rear portholes that were here only because of this test; Peter had no intention of including them in the working Caissons when they were built. A working Caisson was going to be a one-man vessel, there'd be no need for passenger windows.

He noted the temperature drop as they passed through the thermo-cline. It had always amazed Peter. It was like passing between two rooms, one being as much as ten degrees warmer than the other. And they never mixed. It was always warmer above the thermo-cline and colder below it.

Peter leaned forward to look over Dave's shoulder. It was getting darker now, except where the lights from their ship hit things; colors were being washed away. Reds first, then yellows and greens, blues would be the last to go. And when they were gone, there would be no light at all. Thankfully, the heads up display used a low light imaging system to extend the range of the operator's vision. They were going to need it at the depth they planned on working. The green details of the bottom were shown by the system long before Peter could actually see it.

"Bottom ho," announced Wong. He set the submersible gently down and engaged the treads to move it over to some debris that had been thrown overboard by a passing ship. He brought her to a stop. "Ready for the second checklist."

Again they recorded all the readings that Peter needed to proclaim the Deep Caisson seaworthy. It was when they had the last reading that David switched off the engines and spun his seat around to face Peter.

"Okay, Pete, what's the matter?"

"What are you talking about?"

Wong looked at his old friend and now boss, fixing his glare on his eyes. A glare he saw Peter pull away from. "What gives? In all the time I've known you, you've never been this quiet during a dive." He folded his arms in front of his chest, emphasizing that they weren't going anywhere until David got his answer.

"Nothing's the matter," Peter tried. When he glanced back at David's face and saw his ex-roommate's stern expression, he knew that response wasn't going to cut it. "Okay, I'm nervous. That's all, really nervous."

"It's not like we haven't done this kind of thing before," David pushed further.

"Yeah, but this is this ship's first real test. In the remote trials, if something had gone wrong, no big deal, we could just throw more money at the problem. Now it's our lives on the line."

"Your ship is hardly untested. Aside from all the tethered trials we ran, the Coast Guard ran enough of their own to certify her ready. If you'd asked them, they would have pronounced her seaworthy after yesterday's trip." He looked at his friend sitting in the back seat. Then it came to him; Peter's undergraduate behavior, his constant worry about grades, it all finally made sense. "You've never trusted yourself, have you? Never really had any confidence in your own conclusions. You always had someone to check your answers against. There was always some professor to validate them while we were at school. That's why you kept having me proofread your papers? You were getting better grades, but you still needed me to not find any mistakes."

Peter didn't know what to say, embarrassment reddened his face.

"And those were just academic exercises. This is the real world. There's no one around anymore to tell you if you're right or wrong."

"I know," Peter mumbled, then with much more force, "My answers are no longer just academic. The problems we face are real. The consequences of my answers are real. If I make any mistakes, we're going to have to live with them. Right now, if anything..."

Wong jumped in, "Quit that! There aren't any. And you can't let doubts ruin this trip." David had been lighthearted up to this point, but as he looked deeper into his friend's face, he continued. "I know you well enough to ignore them, others won't. The rest of Nuclear Recyclers is looking to you for leadership. Right now, there's dozens of people who believe in your vision. Before we're done, the whole world's going to share it. But you have to keep up a front, show the world that **you** have no doubts. None! Keep them private. Discuss them only with friends, friends who know you. Don't let them kill this dream. This thing's too important. They'll keep you on your toes. Keep you from actually making any of those mistakes you're so worried about. Which-if you'll remember-we could never actually find. So don't let them show."

"I guess, there were lots of people checking my numbers. Maybe I..."

"See?" David stopped him before Peter could bring on the self-doubt again. "Everything's taken care of. You're just along for the ride. So sit back, fasten your seat belt, lock your tray table in its full upright position and leave the driving to me." He swiveled his captain's seat back to its forward position and brought the Caisson's engines back up to speed.

Peter reached out from his chair and squeezed his friend's shoulder. "Thanks, David." Thanking him more for keeping Peter's secret than for his show of confidence.

"What are friends for? Other than getting each other good jobs, that is." Which was David's way of thanking Peter for the call last summer asking him to pilot one of the new submersibles. "Let's check out these arms you built and get this garbage cleaned up."

The Deep Caisson had several different types of arms built into it. There were several different jobs it would have to do. The main job was collecting the six-foot-diameter travel canisters off the ocean floor once they'd been dropped, then positioning them in the first ring of the gun. But there was nothing big enough here to actually test them on. Wong tested the smaller arms by collecting the debris that was littering this part of the ocean floor. Aluminum cans, plastic bottles, even an old fishing pole he picked up easily with the smaller arms, then he placed everything into the collection bin mounted on the port side of the submersible.

On the starboard side was a tool locker. Inside was a series of tools the Caisson would need to fix things between dives. The tools were held magnetically to the side of a box, with a chip in each to let the pilot know which one he was about to pick up. Once the pilot had the one he wanted, he could bring it out and screw it in place with the tool attachment arm. Out of the series of ten tool trials, David only fumbled one of the valve wrenches, and had to pick it back up and stow it before they were ready to move out over the continental shelf for their deeper tests.

Wong used the treads to bring the Caisson to the edge of the continental shelf, then disengaged them and propelled his ship back into free fall. He allowed the submersible to descend another thousand feet to a final depth just shy of what their normal working depth would be. They left the reef environment of the Pinnacles and descended into the gloom and sandy bottom of the deep Gulf. David could feel Peter shiver behind him. "Piece of cake. She's handling better than my sub ever did." He waited for a second to get some response from his friend, then added, "You okay, back there?"

"Yes, but it's getting blacker and blacker."

"That's why you installed these guidance and enhanced visual systems for us poor defenseless pilots. Bottom coming our way. I'm about to set her down." The submersible handled so well, he was able to bottom her without even a slight bump. "There we go. I have her down at 1315 feet below the ocean surface."

Okay, Peter thought, *what was the next thing we were to do? Oh, find the canister that the Iron Maiden was going to drop. It's so dark though, is David going to be able to find it?*

"Hey, Pete, turn on the locator. We need to find your test weight's homing signal," the pilot called over his shoulder. Peter knew that David could easily turn his chair and engage the locator himself, he was just giving him busy work.

They had to locate a fifty-five-gallon drum and return it to the tugboat to get a ride home. A radio transmitter buried in the sand weighing down the drum was supposed to lead them right to it.

"Got it," David acknowledged almost as soon as Peter had switched on the locator. "About one mile to starboard. It must have drifted a bit on the way down. We should be directly under the tug now." David lifted the Caisson off the bottom and turned right. Engaging the twin engines to maximum thrust would have them covering the single nautical mile in about five minutes.

The green outline of the drum silhouetted itself on the overhead display and Wong made the necessary course correction to place it directly in front of the submersible before he grounded her. Peter could now see the drum in the lights he had provided, once it was only one yard in front of them.

David extended the large arms of the Caisson and opened the pinchers to accept the diameter of the drum. They had been designed to encircle a cylinder over five times the diameter they were currently practicing on. It was like holding a toothpick with both hands. Once he had the claws around the drum, Wong magnetically locked them together and pinched them closed. One of the things they were testing for was if the recovered cargo could slip out once the arms had locked onto it.

"Okay, I've got it,' announced David. "Looks like it's time to head for the lady who's taking us home." According to new regulations, submersible operators were to maintain atmospheric pressure in their cabins whenever possible, this allowed divers to work eight-hour underwater shifts without the need for lengthy decompressions. All of Nuclear Recycler's submersibles were designed to meet this standard. Peter and David wouldn't need decompression when they got back to the surface. Still, David took them up slow and gentle, not wanting to drop their load of simulated waste. It took them just over twenty minutes to make the assent, with David correcting on the way up for the distance they had to travel to locate the drum. Sonar showed he was going to bring them up just off the starboard side of the tug. But it also showed a couple of much larger vessels flanking their ride home.

Chapter Five

"Corsair," barked the speaker on his desk. "In my office now!"

He had barely gotten in the door this morning; his cup of coffee from downstairs was still burning his hand as he switched it from his right to his cooler left hand. He shook off the accumulated heat and acknowledged the summons, "Yes, Sir." He rapidly walked by the other agents' desks, down the main aisle to the glass-encased side office of his boss. He knocked twice, then let himself into his boss's office.

The identically blue-suited man sat behind a desk twice the size of Corsair's, grabbed a fax sheet off the top of a pile of report folders and handed it to Neil before Neil even had time to drop into his usual seat.

The fax message contained a single sentence. "The recent Eco-Terrorist attacks are connected."

"I.T. checked the posting phone number. It's the Ramada downtown," Turner said after giving his agent a moment to take in the message. "Here's the address," Turner gave him another sheet of paper. "Get down there and find out who sent this. Then start connecting the dots on those cases your team is investigating. If there is some black operation behind them, I want it found and closed down."

"Yes, sir!" Neil was closing the office door just five seconds later.

He stopped at his computer long enough to start a search of all eco-terrorist cases for the last five years and call across his desk to Brown. "Call down for a BuCar, Larry. We're going to the Ramada." He held the elevator as Special Agent Brown finished pulling on his jacket and jumped in.

* * *

The door to the Ramada Quantico's Manager's office emitted a feeble noise and slowly opened. Franco Lane, the desk clerk who had been on duty the night that the fax was dated, had been called in early today.

"Franco, please come in," Roger Martin, the General Manager of the Ramada, said from behind his desk. "Come in and have a seat. These gentlemen would like to have a word with you."

"Franco Lane," the first man addressed the young man as he walked up to Mr. Martin's desk. Lane was wearing a white button-down shirt with the hotel name stitched on it, red tie and dark blue trousers; he came in prepared to work an extra shift. Roger Martin had simply worn a red pullover shirt with brown jeans, his customer contact was much more limited. "Special Agent Neil Corsair of the FBI," Neil held his badge out for the clerk to inspect. "And this is Special Agent Lawrence Brown." Special

31

Agent Brown held his out, also. "We have a few questions we'd like to ask you."

"Have I done something wrong, Mr. Martin?" Franco looked from the two agents back to his boss.

"No, Franco," answered the fortyish man behind the desk. "They are only inquiring about one of our guests."

"We understand you sent out a fax for someone earlier this week," Neil jumped in. "Tuesday from the time stamp on the message. Can you remember anything about the person who asked you to send it?"

"I don't want any trouble, Mr. Martin." Franco had never taken the chair his boss had offered and now began to move his right foot slightly back and forth while standing there.

"I promise you are not in any trouble, son," Martin came around from behind his desk and draped his arm around Franco's shoulder to reassure him. He softly asked, "Do you remember sending it and who you did it for?"

Franco looked down to the floor's carpet and took a couple of seconds before answering. "He was not a hotel guest. Mr. Martin, I know your policy. I follow your policy. But he offered me five dollars. I didn't think it would be a problem. It only took me a minute away from the front desk. Helena was covering. I didn't see no problem. I am sorry, Mr. Martin; it will not happen again."

"Franco. Son," the hotel manager took Franco by both shoulders, turned the boy to face him and looked him straight in the eyes before commending him. "You helped someone, never feel bad about helping a potential guest. But Special Agents Corsair and Brown, of the FBI, they need your help now in finding the man you sent it for."

"The man who had you send this fax..." Neil held the fax sheet out to Franco, "...may hold information vital to National Security. And as you were willing to help a stranger, I know you want to help your country. Can you tell us anything about him?"

Roger ushered his employee to one of the guest chairs in front of his desk and encouraged him to sit down, to relax.

"He was well dressed, Mr. Martin, sir. Nice, neat suit, dark blue with pin-striping, red tie, very polished shoes. He was slightly shorter than I am, even though he stood tall to my humble bearing."

"You're five eleven?" asked Brown.

"Yes, sir. But I try to stand at whatever height the person I am serving is. I couldn't stand low enough for this government man. He was about..."

"Government man?" Corsair leaned forward in his chair as he interrupted Franco.

"Si." Franco shrunk down in his chair against the glare lashed upon him. He continued in a quieter voice, "He arrived in a black SUV with U.S. Government plates on it. I didn't get a good look at the numbers. He got out on the right side, so I do not think he was the driver."

"Any impressions would help, Mr. Lane. Anything you can think of," Larry encouraged, handing the clerk his business card.

"He looked to be just slightly younger than you are, Mr. Martin. But that is all the description I can remember. If you are taller than the man you wish to serve, it makes him nervous if you look him in the face. I have studied many carpets because of my height."

Chapter Six

David had always loved jumping whatever he was piloting right out of the water. Bank it at a forty-five-degree angle, rev up the engine, and let loose. He could almost get the submersible in college airborne. Not a Caisson, though. It shed ballast evenly as it ascended, and while the bow planes were giving some lift, they could not be angled steeply enough for this maneuver. Peter had designed the Caissons with David in mind. It was designed to give a smooth stable ride in all conditions, especially when carrying cargo. They broke the surface as horizontally as they'd cruised the depths.

While David locked the submersible's controls, Peter released the hatch and pushed it back. They would need to get that drum secured right away, then hoist the Caisson into her docking cradle before they could move on to their next test site.

As he stuck his head up into the Caribbean daylight, he noticed the two ships flanking their tug, two U.S. Naval vessels, and not small ones. One looked like a light cruiser and the other a guided missile destroyer. *Now why are they out here?* Peter thought.

The deck crew of the tug sent over a triple-folded and quilted canvas strap to wrap around the drum. They encircled the drum twice with it, then threaded one of the looped ends through the other and connected it onto the hook of their lifting crane.

Peter stretched out on the deck and stuck his head back into the Caisson's hatch. "Dave, slowly release the claws." Gradually they opened, and the canvas cable tightened as it took up the weight. As soon as he could see it was swinging freely, Peter rolled over onto his back and gave a whirling hand motion to the winch operator to let her know that she could lift the load. The drum was hauled back aboard the Iron Maiden, where it would be set into a holding cradle, metal rings used to bind it to the side of the control cabin, and then it would be released from the straps that had brought it home.

Peter got up from the deck and was beginning to climb back into the Deep Caisson for a ride back to her towing rack when Captain Harris stepped out of the Maiden's bridge and motioned Peter to join him.

"Dave, the Captain wants to see me about something. You okay getting her back into towage?"

"Sorry, no can do. I got a sand pebble in my shoe," Wong hollered back through the still-open hatch. But before Peter could respond, "Just close the hatch, you're letting all the warm air in."

Peter pulled the hatch back into place and gave the locking wheel a quick spin, not enough to really secure it but enough to keep it from bouncing open while rounding the ship. One of the deck hands threw him a rope, which he grabbed to steady himself as he stepped from one vessel to the next. Once Peter was aboard the tug, one of the other hands tapped the Caisson stoutly with a boat pole. David moved the Caisson away from the side of the ship and around it to the back, where he could secure it for its trip to the next site.

Peter didn't give this procedure a second thought as he climbed the steep stairs leading to the bridge and the waiting skipper. It wasn't until he opened the door that he noticed the naval officer on the bridge with Captain Harris.

"Dr. von Scorio, I'm glad to have you back aboard," began the man who looked too small to actually challenge the Atlantic Ocean on a daily basis. But Leo had checked all his references out, and this man's skill was greatly respected. And his crew was considered top notch, even if he overpaid them to keep other skippers from stealing them away. "I'd like to present Commander Ben Wallace to you. It appears the Navy has heard about our little trip today."

"Good afternoon, Dr. von Scorio." The very tall and slightly-rounding navy man in the immaculately pressed double-breasted blue suit offered Peter the hand he wasn't adjusting his hat with.

This guy has to be about my age, Peter thought as he shook the officer's hand. *Not a day past thirty.* "Glad to meet you, sir," he said. "But I have to wonder why." Despite looking like he was putting on weight, the navy man had a very firm handshake.

"Right to the point," the Commander began. "Very different from your partner. Took us a while to get him to drop the small talk and tell us where you were." He dropped his arm back next to his body; it stopped in position and seemed to lock itself there.

"So Leo sent for you?" It would be just like him to try and get extra news coverage by having the Navy around.

"Actually, Mr. Dayton didn't contact us. We contacted him. It seems you have caught the attention of some officials in Washington. People who would very much like to see you succeed. They have asked my superiors to provide your company with a little military support. With my experience with deep recovery operations, I have been assigned as your liaison. Whenever you're out to sea, for any reason, the U.S.S. *Halsey* and the U.S.S. *Vella Gulf* will be going with you." He pointed out the bridge window at each of the two naval vessels flanking the *Iron Maiden*. "But only surface support. You will still have the freedom you need to build your systems and operational freedom to deploy them. I want to tell you that I am personally fascinated by this prospect."

"And just what do you think we are doing out here, Commander?"

"Why, developing an underwater nuclear storage facility. And as such, we can't allow just anyone access to it. I intend to help you develop the security for your site."

"Ah, Commander, we're not going to be storing any waste. We're going to actually dispose of it." Peter looked at the surprised expression of the navy commander and explained exactly what they were planning to do. "Once the cylinders have been driven under the continental plate, they will disintegrate, along with their contents. The Earth's core will do all our recycling for us."

"There's no half measures for you guys!" the commander responded, after taking a moment to absorb Peter's entire plan. "I thought a land-based facility was better for storage. But recycling, as you suggest, is preferable to any storage. It will be an honor working with you.

"I have a favor I'd like to ask," the navy man went on. "I have been in a few submersibles in my time, and I'd like to take a look at yours, if I could."

David would be just climbing out of it, so there would be plenty of room for him to look around. Besides, he might find something Peter could improve. "Okay, let's go." Then he led the way off the tug's bridge and back to where the Caisson was docked.

David had stowed the Caisson's arms back in their slots along the side of her hull before bringing her into her parking position. This gave the submersible a stubby cigar shape with her rack of ballast tanks built into the underside of her hull. There was no conning tower to obstruct her lines; she had been built to fit inside the waste gun's rings should the need arise. Jet engines provided her propulsion. They needed only two circular openings in the bow and two more in the stern. This ability to back water could, as David was so fond of saying, allow him to stop on a dime. It would also allow him to reverse course very quickly when needed.

Commander Wallace was fascinated with the ship. After David had walked onto the tug, Wallace climbed out on the towing harness for a closer look. "Stowing the arms inside her lines! Must boost her speed, right? What is her top speed, anyway?"

"We haven't done any speed trials. She's not a racing vessel," Peter defended.

"I've had her up to twenty knots without topping out," stated Wong. Peter turned and presented his friend with a puzzled look. "Hey, the Coast Guard pilot wanted me to open her up. Unfortunately, we had to slow back down when we began pulling away from their cutter."

"Twenty knots. I didn't build this thing for racing." Almost as an afterthought, Peter brought his hands up and placed them on his hips in an indignant stance.

At least, he thought he was being indignant. He heard a chuckle from the naval officer behind him, looked back at him— whereupon Wallace stopped—and turned back to catch Wong smirking also. "Okay, you two, what's so funny?"

"You're just not the hard-ass type, Pete," David said, now actually letting go with a small laugh. Behind him, Peter could see the deck hands fading away.

Dropping his arms back to his side, Peter looked from his friend to his naval escort. "But..."

"I know she's important to you. She's your baby. But we have to find out what she can really do if we need something in a pinch. Don't worry, I won't break anything you can't fix." Moving past Peter and out onto the other side of *Deep Caisson*'s towing harness, he began talking to Commander Wallace. "Want to see the inside?"

"Sure," came the excited response. So Wong began un-dogging the entry hatch to show off his toy.

Chapter Seven

"Oil, crude oil, Bakken crude oil. A thick sludgy pollutant that is transported across our country on rail cars. Until they build another of their leaky pipelines," Charles Roscoe told the members of Save America that were huddled around the small conference table in the cold shack in central Indiana. "We need to stop this flow now. We need to demonstrate to America the dangers this stuff represents. Just how risky it is to fuel our energy needs with this dirty sludge."

Pointing to a topographical map of the rail system running through the suburbs of Indianapolis, Indiana, he continued. "We will place a thousand charges shaped to blow upward under the northern rail of this strip of track. When the oil train passes over them, we shall not only blow her up, but we will send that vile liquid into the Middle Class suburban homes along its southern boundary. Then we ignite the oil and those Earth rapers, ah, those homes become a beacon to the excesses that are killing the Earth."

"All very well, Charley. But we can't do the damage you are suggesting with Ammonium Nitrate bombs. We would need..." said Jason Arnold, the bearded, slightly bulging, overall-wearing founder of Save America.

"Military grade explosives? Like Semtex?" Charles cut him off before he could spread doubt about his plan. "It just so happens that my sponsor, ah, I acquired a large supply of the stuff last week. Yes, without the right explosives, we would never be able to launch our vendetta." *Yes, I will have to pick just the right*

38

hill to watch this spectacular conflagration, he internalized.

* * *

Finally, around three in the morning, just as the local weatherman had predicted, clouds began rolling in and covering the light shining down from the full moon. As the blanket of darkness spread over the valley, members of Save America swarmed out onto the BNSF tracks. Teams of two began working to secure the explosives at just the right angle and connect their detonators.

Over the last week, the group had prepared around 600 shaped charges to go between every third tie under the left rail. They were expecting at least one hundred cars in this oil train, over two kilometers of crude. The charges were arranged to drive the left side of the cars skyward while rupturing their tanks, spilling the crude all over the quiet Indianapolis community. Then Arnold himself would ignite the oil with a flair pistol, burning the community to the ground.

And Carlos would sit away from the carnage on his hilltop perch, watching it unfold. There was no need for him to get his hands dirty in this operation. If he could inspire men to do the right thing, his work would be accomplished that much quicker.

They had two hours to complete their preparations. But that should be more than enough time for his dozen volunteer terrorists to finish and clear off the scene.

Just after 5 AM, as everyone was clearing the tracks, a train whistle announced it was coming to the last of the road crossings before entering their little valley.

"Too early," Carlos said as he swung his night vision binoculars around. "The train is arriving too early." Yet there it was; a double engine diesel locomotive was heading their way, picking up the speed it had dumped before crossing the road for safety reasons. "It can not be the oil train. Not this early."

As the rail cars finally came into enough light for Carlos to see, they were a mixture of boxcars and flat cars, none of them loaded with the cargo crates they were designed to carry. Defi-

39

nitely not the rounded shapes of oil tankers. "It is an empty train. Not the prize I am looking for."

He reached into his pocket to call Arnold and tell him to hold off. Nothing was there. *I ordered everyone to leave their phones behind*, he remembered. With everyone's cell phones left at the house, Carlos had no choice but to physically get to his people. He ran down the hill, waving to get their attention. But the train was faster than he was and closed the distance before any members of Save America could see Carlos coming.

As the train passed over the explosive-lined track, Jason Arnold triggered the explosives. The train flew up on its left side and smashed through the noise reduction wall the rail road company had erected to preserve the little community from the unpleasant sound of passing trains. As the first of the cars crashed into the homes on the other side, Jason aimed his Verey pistol towards the crashing sound and fired his flare in that direction.

Its light sped forward until it exploded into the underside of one of the boxcars, igniting nothing. When it burned out, darkness again descended on the tranquil Midwest community. First car alarms, then moments later police sirens began going, screaming into the night.

Carlos stopped his run half way down the hill. There was nothing for it now, so he headed back to where they had left their cars. *Incompetents*, he thought as he got into his blue cargo van. *Americans are completely incompetent. So much for training independent warriors in this fight. No, next time I will have to take a more direct hand in my operation.*

Chapter Eight

"Agent Corsair, it's good of you to get here so quickly," said the stocky yet not paunchy blue-suited agent who greeted Neil as he walked into the local Sheriff's offices in Indianapolis.

"Can I assume you are Agent McCarthy?" Neil responded,

taking the man's offered hand and checking the federal badge hanging from his suit breast pocket. He had looked the man up on the federal database after getting his e-mail and memorized his photo. It was slightly out of date; Ronald McCarthy had been working out since it was taken. "The case you described made this an urgent matter for me. I'd like to introduce you to Special Agent Martin Hughes and my explosives expert, Special Agent Harold Fellows."

"This is Sherriff Browning of Marion County." The slightly shorter man rose from his chair behind his desk and offered his hand to Neil.

"Pleased to meet you, sir."

As Neil took the officer's hand, McCarthy continued. "Jake's department was among the first responders on the scene. They have several members of Save America in custody. The ones who hung around to watch the mayhem." Sheriff Browning gestured for everyone to have a seat. "They also recovered several pounds of unexploded Semtek from the scene and, with a little help from me, are preparing a warranted search of what we believe to be the group's headquarters. I thought you would want in."

"When do we go?" Neil asked as he rose from his chair.

*　*　*

Early the next morning, Sheriff Browning, Neil, Martin, Fellows and Agent McCarthy were huddled around the command van for this operation. Two dozen sheriff's deputies were making their way around the large Victorian mansion described on the judge's warrant. A SWAT team from the Indianapolis police department was ready to breach the entrance. One officer had a battering ram he was hoisting around like a small wooden log, another officer was armed with a riot shield to breach the entrance for the four assault officers, armed with M-16 rifles.

"Agent McCarthy, the last of the deputies is in place, sir," was radioed from the spotter they had stationed in a 100-foot, utility company man-lift a few houses down Park Avenue.

McCarthy, who had turned away to take the radio call, turned to Browning and the FBI agents. "Everyone's in position."

"Then let's go before anyone is spotted," announced Browning.

Neil nodded to the Sherriff's logic.

Agent McCarthy keyed his radio. "All Units. Go, go, go!"

The SWAT team members burst through the wrought wire gate surrounding the property and ran up to the front door. It took a single swing from the battering ram to throw inward the decaying front door. Then the shielded officer ran through the entry way, followed by his four comrades. the first officer dropped his battering ram and drew his service pistol, while the shield man set down his shield and did the same. Two by two, they secured the bottom floor of the house.

As they reassembled at the foot of the main stairs, two men emerged onto the upper balcony.

"Down on the ground!" The officers ran up the stairs, pushed the men fully to the floor, and cuffed them. The two officers with service weapons then escorted them out of the house as the remaining four conducted their room-by-room search of the second floor.

"First floor is secured," Officer Anderson told the command staff. "These two must have been woken up when I broke the door. Jenkins, Reilly, Martin, and Taylor have begun a search of the second floor."

"Hand them over to the Prisoner Transport Officers and join us inside," commanded McCarthy. "I, for one, want a look in their basement." He turned to the FBI men, "I assume you want to join me?"

Before they took two steps towards the mansion, an explosion rocked the foundation of the building. The upper floors with the remaining officers just dropped into the cloud created by the ejected grains of concrete and brick.

Everyone surrounding the home had been knocked to the ground. Maybe not all of them by the actual force of the blast, but by the unexpected reality of it. As they got back up, Sherriff Browning remembered the SWAT team. "Those men! Get Fire and Rescue over here now!"

* * *

Agents Corsair and McCarthy looked into the interrogation room through the window in its door. The only two men they had recovered from their raid on the Save America headquarters sat cuffed to the center table. Neither of the men looked comfortable. Both men were a little shorter and plumper than the orange prisoner jump suits had been built for. One began talking to the other, who was making pains to ignore the first. At least for a couple of minutes, then he snapped at him to "Shut up!"

"Give them a couple more minutes," Agent McCarthy said without turning his head away from the window. "They look just about ready to separate."

"Good cop, bad cop?"

"No, I want to run a bluff. Then you take Mr. Silent in there to Interrogation Cell 2. I should be able to get Mr. Talkie in there to sing."

After another few minutes of Mr. Talkie's jabbering, his partner violently raised his hand to the end of his tethers, as if to strike him.

"They should be ready," Agent McCarthy said as he unlocked the cell and opened the door for Neil. "I just got off the phone with the hospital." Agent McCarthy said to the two men in the room.

How? We've been standing by the door for the last half hour. Neil kept to himself.

"Those sheriff deputies aren't doing as well as you guys. If they take another turn for the worse... Well, you know the respect 'Cop-Killers' get around here."

"Or for that matter, what 'Environmentalists' get in prison." Neil understood the bluff.

"And the guard outside says you two aren't getting along, so

43

it looks like we are going to have to separate you." Agent McCarthy bent down and undid Mr. Silent's cuff, slid it out of the loop in the table and recuffed his wrist. Then he handed the chain to Neil, "See what this guy has to say."

Cuffing his prisoner into the table of Interrogation Cell 2, Neil took a seat in the chair opposite him and sat there for a minute. Then he got up and left the room, returning a moment later with Martin. He then took some papers from inside his suit and set them on the table, spread them out, straightened a few creases, lifted them up to line them all up nice and neat, set them on the table and smoothed them out again. Martin just sat there, staring at their prisoner.

"What would Mr. Arnold think about you two now?" Neil began asking.

"He'd tell us to shut up and let him do the talking."

"I hope for your sake your buddy in the other room feels the same way. I hate it when I have to sift through different testimonies to decide which one is the truth and which is a lie. Too damn much work."

Mr. Silent tried to fold his arms, but the chain wouldn't let them reach until he leaned on the table.

"That's probably for the best. If you don't say anything, you won't contradict your partner next door."

Neil folded his papers and put them back into his suit's inner pocket. As he stood up, he added, "By the way, Jason Arnold was killed in the explosions last week. He won't be coming to bail you out of this. And since we only found you and your friend in that house last night, you'll be the ones on the hook for any fatalities."

"We had nothing to do with last night's explosion or the oil train derailment."

"Oh," Neil said as he sat back down. "Do tell."

"No, Charles said we couldn't be trusted with the Semex..."

"Semtex," Neil prompted.

"Yeah, that stuff. Stuff felt like clay, can't be no real explosive. I told him so, so he benched me and Jurgens to watch duty over the safe house. Only I guess it wasn't so safe, cause I guess that stuff actually works."

"Charles?"

"Charles Roscoe. Speaks real clearly like he has to think about every word he's saying. Doesn't like fools, one slip up and you're off sweeping floors instead of doing the good stuff."

"The good stuff?"

"You know, working to save America from itself. Stopping oil companies from killing the planet. But Charley was more intense than any of us regular guys. We just wanted to stop them. I had the feeling he wants to destroy them."

"But wasn't Jason Arnold in charge?"

"Not by looking at how he treated Charley. Took all his advice, let him plan our missions, and eventually order us guys around all the time. No, Charley was running things those last few weeks."

"Do you think he was killed in the explosion last week?"

"No, he came by the house three days ago and took several crates out of the basement. When I asked why, he just said he was done with unsupervisable fools."

Chapter Nine

The *Damocles* arrived at the test site at 1000 Central Daylight Time. She held the first five of the magnetic rings to be constructed in one hold, stored two DeepWorkers in another and towed a Deep Caisson in its towing harness. She was designed as an all-purpose vessel during the trials, but once Nuclear Recyclers commenced operations, she would become their Nuclear Waste Transport Vessel.

It was just last week that they got around to naming her. In fact, it was the new electronics operator, Jacob Helman, who had come up with her name. "This thing is going to hold all the cylinders on the surface. Above our heads, as it were. It's going to be hanging above us, just like the Sword of Damocles."

Leo frowned a bit, since he didn't know what this fresh-out-of-school kid was talking about. "What Sword of Damocles?"

But Sid Merek, the draftsman knew. "The Sword of Damocles. It's from Greek mythology. You see, Damocles was a courtier to Dionysius the Elder, the guy who ruled Syracuse about the fourth century BC. Well, Damocles would flatter the old man so much that he decided to give a party in which Damocles would switch positions with Dionysius. Damocles thought this was great fun, until he looked above his head and saw a very large and very sharp sword suspended above by a single thread of hair from a horse's tail. Realizing the dangers that come with great power, Damocles begged to be released from this seat of honor."

It was Jacob's idea, and he wasn't going let Sid have all the fun, so he finished for him, "Henceforth the 'Sword of Damocles' represents whatever danger hangs over someone's head and threatens their endeavors."

Peter caught on to where they were going with this. "Just like if something went wrong onboard this ship, which is going to be hanging above the gun." That very day, they named her *The Sword of Damocles*, calling her *Damocles* for short.

So here they were, a warm mid-July day, surface temperature around 80 with the water temperature around 75. They brought the *Damocles* to a full stop over a flat plateau with two hundred feet of water below her keel and dropped anchor. Of course, they still had their two naval escorts, one flanking her on either side.

They were just swinging the first of the two test loads over the side of the *Damocles* when Peter noticed a small boat crossing aft of their position and heading for the *Vella Gulf*. When he turned his head to follow it, staying well back of the lifting operations, he noticed another boat coming from the *Vella Gulf* heading directly for the *Damocles*. "Probably Commander Wallace wanting to watch again," Peter commented in a low tone.

"Sorry, Peter?" Jacob had been watching the unloading procedures from the aft rail, brushed the strands of hair that the salty breeze had blown into his face.

"Nothing. Just talking to myself."

Jacob turned to look in the direction Peter had been, placing both hands on the rail as he did so. He hadn't spent as much time as the others in this much open water. The approaching craft was about half way to the *Damocles*.

"You got a lunch appointment?" Jacob asked.

"No, we have work to do today." Peter responded.

Today was scheduled to be a busy day. First, they needed to get all their submersibles into the water. They were lucky; Mike Farrel in HR had found an experienced Exosuit/DeepWorker operator to join the team. Harry Trunnel had spent the last ten years, right out of high school, working the oil rigs off the Atlantic and Pacific coasts. When his company had chosen to deploy Nuytco submersible technology to support those rigs, Harry had been one of the ones they had sent to Nuytco Research Ltd for training. He really liked the Deepworker 2010 version of the DOV. When Farrell called Nuytco about who they would recommend as a DeepWorker operator, Harry's name was at the top of their list. Mike wasn't able to offer Trunnel any more money than he was currently making at Exxon, but once he heard about the goal of Nuclear Recyclers he wanted on board.

"Careful lowering that," they could hear Harry hollering at the crane operator.

They had two of the one-man Diver-Operated Vehicles (DOV) stored in the *Damocles'* center hold. Each hold was designed large enough to hold twenty of the nuclear waste transport canisters once normal operations got under way. And the *Damocles* had five such holds. Today was not a day to fill the *Damocles* to capacity. Harry would be operating the first DeepWorker to be unloaded, and according to the procedures he had written, he would be overseeing its lift into the Gulf. The second pilot would oversee her own.

The rail-mounted crane finished moving to hold number three position and lowered its hook. Harry, watching from the

47

catwalk overlooking the hold, gave hand signals to the crane operator; slowly spinning his hand with one finger pointing down, he told the crane operator to drop the hook slowly. Even with camera-mounted views of the hold, many of the crane operators expressed their thanks to Harry for personally supervising the operations.

As the men below reached the hook and pulled it just below the mounted loop on the second of the DOVs, Harry flattened his hand in the classic stop position. When he saw that the deck hands actually had enough cable to make the connection, he grabbed his right fist in his left hand, instructing the crane operator to lock things down momentarily.

It was the work of less than a minute to get the crane's hook secured in the DOV's loop and the hook locked for the lift. One of the men standing on the unit gave Harry a thumbs up. Harry shook his head and motioned for the men to get off. He was not going to let them ride it up. Every safety rule regarding lifts ever written said they'd have to take the stairs.

Once the last one had moved away from the submersible, Harry looked at the crane operator, pointed to him, and slowly spun his right hand again, this time with his finger pointed up. The crane operator moved a few levers and the DOV began to rise from the hold. It spun as it was lifted. Once it cleared the hold, Trunnel motioned to have it moved over the catwalk. He waited for the deck hands to get up there and take hold of the lines attached to the DeepWorker to keep it from spinning. Harry had not wanted them under it in the hold in case the cable gave way. The *Damocles* was double-hulled, but if the DOV fell on a man, there would be no chance for him.

With the spinning under control, they got the submersible over the side and lowered her into the water. Harry had to move to another position, but they got her down safely. Once the crane operator had locked down his controls, Harry and the deck hands climbed down the ladder on the side of the *Damocles* and onto a six-by-six-foot platform attached to her side for them to work. As soon as they had her unhooked and the cable pulled away from the work area, Harry opened the dome and climbed into the DOV. It felt like he was slipping into a comfortable chair, one that would allow him to view the beauty of the deep unfold before him. He loved sitting in these babies.

He pulled the dome shut, secured the latches and tested her controls. Everything worked perfectly; she had always been a good girl, and Harry always took care of her. He moved her away from the platform and around to the back of the *Damocles* where the Deep Caisson was in tow. He piloted her there by way of the *Damocles'* bow, taking time to enjoy the trip.

It took them another half-hour to unload and check out the other DeepWorker, but they left her at the platform. Judith Hurley would pilot her from there. She did not have Harry's experience with the Newts, but she had passed the Nuytco training course and logged one hundred hours in Nuclear Recyclers' newly acquired simulator. Harry would still be in charge of the underwater team today.

While all this activity was going on over the starboard side of the *Damocles*, the naval launch had arrived on the port side and Lieutenant Radcliff kept hollering for someone's attention. "Can any of you hear me?"

Finally, one of the deck hands rushing up to help move the second DeepWorker out into the Gulf waters noticed him. He brought both his hands up to his mouth to amplify his voice so it could reach the deck Peter was standing on. "Hey, Dr. von Scorio!" After Peter turned his head, he continued, "We got somebody in a boat over here."

Peter, being a deck above, had to move to where he could see over the port side of the *Damocles*. He saw the naval launch with a crewman at her controls and an officer, not Wallace, talking to the deck hand. *Why is that officer still standing in his boat?* he thought to himself. "I'm coming down. Find out what he wants. And invite him aboard."

"What's ya need?" asked the deck hand.

"Permission to come aboard," replied the Lieutenant. He had almost added a 'sir' at the end, but stopped himself in time. The

Captain had said respectfully ask and that was what he was going to do.

"Yeah, the bossman wants to talk at ya anyway. Listen, hop on over, I gots to get back to the haul lines." The crewman left before the officer even had a chance to thank him.

"Steady her against the side, Mr. Hartung," Radcliff said to his crewman. Picking up the line to secure the *Vella Gulf*'s launch to the *Damocles*, he stood on the gunwale of the launch and pulled himself up to the *Damocles'* deck. "A most undignified entrance for a United States Naval Officer," he said under his breath.

The lieutenant found a post to tie the launch to and called back to his crewman, "Mr. Hartung, the launch is secure. You may cut your engines."

"Yes, sir."

Peter came running up to where the navy man was. Unfortunately, he could see this slender man, who was slightly shorter than Peter, would have been impeccably dressed if not for the grease smears from where he had climbed over the deck rail. "I am so sorry to have kept you waiting," he said, slightly out of breath. *Why do all the naval officers have to be so damn thin and polished, anyway?* he thought.

"Dr. von Scorio?" the officer asked.

He had to grab the railing and give himself a moment to catch his breath. "I'm really sorry. But why didn't you just come on board?"

"Sir, we don't just **come aboard** when we're on the open seas. One must first obtain the owner's permission. The reason that I am here is to relay Captain Wallace's invitation for you and Mr. Dayton to join him for lunch."

Peter had to think about where they were for a minute and then caught what was being offered. "You mean aboard the *Vella Gulf*?"

"In the Captain's mess, to be exact. This invitation also extends to the Captain of this vessel, should he choose to accept."

"When? How? We don't have a launch to go from ship to

50

ship."

"I was to wait for your response and, if favorable, offer to bring you across myself. Captain Miller of the *Halsey* will be joining us also."

"Do you need to pick him up, too?" Peter shifted his gaze across the deck of the *Damocles* to look for any launches running from *the Halsey*.

"No, sir. He has a number of launches like this at his disposal. He should be heading over shortly."

"Do we need to dress up any?"

"You will be fine as you are. This is not a formal dinner. Captain Wallace wants to keep the lines of communication open between us."

"Well, it will be awhile before they're ready to begin setting up for the tests, and the crew will need their lunch breaks anyway. Yes, I accept."

"Your Captain and Mr. Dayton?"

"I'll just run up and ask them." Peter, thrilled with the idea of lunch in the Captain's quarters of a real naval vessel, took off at a run again to find Leo and Captain Harris.

Lieutenant Radcliff just stood there, shaking his head at the lack of self-respect in the man his captain had referred to as a genius. *The man could use a good dose of discipline*, Radcliff thought. He looked down at the grease on his uniform and knew he would have to change when they got back. There was no way he was going to touch it; that would only make it harder for Laundry to get it clean for him.

* * *

"Not one but two of your Deepworkers," commented Commander Roger Wallace as the two crewmen servicing the Captain's lunch removed their entree dishes and brought out the apple cobbler dessert for everyone. "No half measures for you people."

"We really don't want to take any chances. Everything we

do cuts new ground. There's no one out here to correct us if we start making a fatal mistake," Peter said after wiping his mouth with a linen napkin embroidered with the '*USS Vella Gulf*' logo.

"Don't get me wrong, Dr. von Scorio, I applaud that kind of attitude on the high seas. I just don't see it very often among private groups out here." Captain Wallace, as he was referred to while aboard the vessel he commanded, waited until everyone had been served, then forked a bit of the cobbler into his mouth to ensure the taste was up to his expectations of the cook. He nodded to the waiting servers, who then left, shutting the door behind them. After he swallowed, Captain Wallace continued. "No, I have seen too many companies not take enough safety measures. They mouth 'Safety First', then cut expenses trying to keep their stockholders happy. Too often this leads to tragedy. The oceans of this world are unforgiving when it comes to mistakes. I feel better knowing that you are looking out for yourselves."

Leo finished his portion in very few bites. "Hmm, that was good. You serve a very good lunch, Commander," he noticed the first officer beginning to correct him. "I mean Captain, but exactly why are you here?"

"As I mentioned to your partner," Captain Wallace laid his fork across his portion of the cobbler, choosing to talk now and save the food for a little later, "your project has been deemed important to the future of our nation. We're here to ensure its security."

"What the Captain is saying is that there will be some people who would love to see you fail. We're on the scene to make sure they don't try anything, or if they do, it doesn't succeed. When your project fails, it's going to be because the idea is flawed, not because some eco-terrorist has sabotaged it," replied Lieutenant Commander Mitchell.

"Now, Henry, they aren't going to fail," said Lt. Commander Anderson from across the table.

"You were in the same class as I was, Pete." Mitchell continued, but this time directing his words to his Annapolis classmate. "Why can't you accept Commodore MacIntyre's conclusions?"

"Because the earth doesn't have to be a world of shrinking resources. There's still room for expansion, if we do things smart."

Leo swung his head from one man to the other, trying to follow what they were talking about. "Shrinking resources?"

Peter broke in as he recognized the discussion from one of his undergraduate courses. "It's the Shrinking Resources Theory, if I'm correct." He looked over to see Anderson nodding an acknowledgement at him. "But I thought that'd been debunked by the time I got into graduate school, like its predecessor, the Limits-To-Growth hypothesis?"

Wallace rolled his eyes up to the ceiling, as he knew what was coming. Henry was a fine officer, but he did like to voice his opinions.

"No, it has not!" Mitchell became defensive. "Earth has a finite amount of resources for us to use. And when they are gone, they're gone. Each and every time we make use of them, we are shrinking the resources future generations will have available."

"But surely we're getting energy all the time from the sun," Leo commented.

"And every time we increase the available energy supply, someone finds some new way to use it. Requiring we find new sources of energy," was Mitchell's counter argument.

"We've been building space probes for a decade now to bring even more solar energy to human space. Maybe not on Earth, but it keeps our astronauts from using Earth's resources."

"Which they wouldn't need to use if they were not up there."

"They're up there to find new ways to exploit the resources available in the solar system. Find ways to bring those resources back to us." Leo, having never heard these arguments before, was giving the first officer the openings he needed.

"They will never be enough to replace everything that we have already abused. In fact, that very kind of talk has diverted our major decision makers from making the hard choices needed to keep this planet, the only planet we will ever have, livable. I believe your scheme is doing the same thing. We need to find ways to curb the amount of nuclear waste we generate, not justify the creation of more. If we were forced to store it, safely store it for the hundreds of thousands of years needed to make it safe, we'd quickly run out of room. There is a limit to a land-based storage system, and that would limit the amount of waste we could create. But here you come along and offer us a chance to remove that problem. Go ahead, nuclear waste generators, keep making your poison. We can get rid of it for you. It's just another false hope, one that keeps us from making the necessary changes to our life styles."

"Henry did his Master's thesis on the SRT," Captain Miller of the *Halsey* explained. "He redesigned the way the navy did business to cut its resource consumption, while still maintaining its core mission."

This got Peter curious. "What happened to it?"

"Like everything else coming out of the students of the Naval Academy," said the ship's doctor, Lt. Commander Marion Jones. "It got filed in the library, and if seen anymore, it will be as a paper weight. Unless it's the work of an Admiral, it's not important." She was the only woman present for the Captain's luncheon and had been quiet throughout the meal, but a bitterness came through in her last remark.

"And there it shall remain," Mitchell continued, "until the Navy sees the need to change. Whereupon they will have the blueprints they need to overhaul our way of doing things."

Lt. Commander Anderson looked over to the three civilian guests; Captain Harris had been able to turn his skipper duties over to his first mate. He didn't want to miss a luncheon on 'a real boat'. "The *Halsey* is equipped with a DSRV. I would very much like to view your tests first hand."

"DSRV?" Dayton asked.

"Leo, that's a Deep Sea Rescue Vehicle," Peter explained to his partner, then turned to Anderson. "I think we could arrange that. Just get with Harry Trunnel, he's organizing the underwater side of today's affair."

"Thank you very much," responded Anderson. "I've heard of Mr. Trunnel. You've got a good man there. Listen to him, he'll keep everyone safe."

"And what I really appreciate about the way he's doing it is that everyone is going to be working at atmospheric pressure. No need for decompression after you people finish your tests. Decompression is always tricky, too easy to get it wrong, and when it goes wrong, people get hurt. I was glad when all the coastal states started adopting the atmospheric working condition regulations for companies that conduct underwater operators off their shores," Dr. Jones said.

"Well, that's our plan." Peter placed his napkin over the small white porcelain plate with a US Navy emblem in the center and USS Vella Gulf in gold leaf around the edge. "Hopefully we can eventually work out a rotation of eight hour shifts in the Blockhouse."

"The blockhouse?" Dr. Jones asked.

"It's what we're calling our underwater control room. Since it, too, will be completely mobile, just think of it as a very large submersible with a bridge as complex as one of your nuclear submarines. It will have crew quarters and recreation space for two down shifts, in addition to the one actually working. At first, I thought about rotating the shifts out. But 1500 feet underwater, you won't really have any day or night, so why bother? Just let the people get used to the shift they are on and stay there."

Lt. Commander Mitchell leaned back in his seat, just slightly pushing himself away from the table. "And just how many of those eight-hour shifts will a man be doing?"

"Our Human Resources department is currently researching that problem," Leo put in as he turned his head from side to side looking for something. "By the way, is there a rest room around here someplace?"

"The head is right through that door," Captain Wallace turned his chair around and pointed to a hatch behind him.

"Thanks," Leo said as he rose from his seat and made his way over to it.

"But getting back to your thoughts, Dr. Jones," Peter continued as Leo clanged the door shut. "The use of normal atmospheric pressure on all our personnel will allow us to cycle them back to the surface at very frequent intervals."

"Afraid they'll go stir crazy down there?" commented Mitchell.

"Not at all," began Peter.

But before he could finish, Captain Harris explained, "They just want me to have to break in a whole new surface crew every week." At which point, all the Naval officers snickered, knowing what it was like dealing with new men.

*　*　*

Peter, Leo, and Captain Harris returned to the *Damocles* just as Harry Trunnel was placing the last of the magnetic rings into the water. The other four had been floated just out of reach so they couldn't be damaged if something happened during the lift.

"Harry," Peter called over to where he was supervising the lift. "You didn't work them through lunch, did you?"

Without even looking away from the ring hanging ten feet above the ocean and slowly descending, he answered, "No, we broke right after getting the second DeepWorker checked out. You guys sure took your time over there. We were beginning to think..." As the ring took up a buoyant position in the water, he held up his hand, then locked his hands together. "...they were going to hold you guys for ransom." As he saw his men remove the lifting strap that had been wrapped around the ring so that the crane would have something to put its hook into, Harry spun his hand very rapidly in an upward direction. He also keyed the radio in his vest's upper pocket. "Jim, as soon as you can, get the crane secured and get suited up."

"Right away, Mr. Trunnel," came back over the radio.

"So how soon will you be ready to lower the rings to the

bottom?" Peter looked over the side of the *Damocles*. Five rings bobbed with the rise and fall of the water, waiting to have their buoyancy tanks filled to the proper depth for today's tests. They weren't the full-sized electromagnets Nuclear Recylers were planning to use to fire waste cylinders into the Earth's core, but four-foot diameter test versions, to see how they would work against water pressure. To keep the rings from straying too far, David was piloting a Deep Caisson keeping them corralled.

"Just give me and Jim a chance to get into our Deepworkers, and we'll be ready." Harry was in one in no time. He had already stripped down to his wetsuit while he was moving the rings overboard.

"Radio me when you're ready, then." Peter walked back to Leo, and they climbed back up to the *Damocles'* bridge. Captain Harris was already there, as he always seemed to be.

Since they had yet to construct an underwater control room, the entire test would be controlled topside. Peter scanned the large console they had temporarily mounted here. Each of the rings had its own separate control panel; eventually they would all be electronically tied together. Right now, he wanted to be able to raise or lower them independently. Each ring had its own set of maneuvering thrusters, controlled from those panels. Once they were tethered together on the ocean bottom, Peter planned to link their controls into a sixth panel, so he had to begin testing their joint operational capacity. Today, they would be tethered with steel cables, but Peter was hoping to eventually use a magnetic tether to connect the rings together when the gun was finally completed. He had to remember that today was only a test, simply a learning experience. Designs would be changed based on what happened this afternoon.

"Hey, Peter," came Harry's voice, a bit louder than usual over the radio. "Wake up, man, did you okay a naval officer to oversee our test?"

"He just wanted to watch. I told him to check with you. You're in charge. That decision is up to you."

"Harry, I've got a back seat here in the Caisson," said Wong over the radio. "He would have a great view with me."

Peter looked out of the bridge's rear window and saw Trunnel sitting in his DeepWorker with the bubble hatch still up, talking with Anderson. The DSRV from the *Halsey* was parked on the *Damocles'* port side, away from all their activity. "I don't see how he could see anything from his submersible, anyway. What do you think, Harry?"

"Okay by me. Let's get this show on the road." Trunnel reached up and pulled his clear hatch closed, then locked it watertight. He waved at his crew controlling the Deepworker to cast him off. Then he immediately decreased his buoyancy to lower the sub's center of gravity to where his head was just above the surface. He maneuvered over to the floating rings and began his descent. He would be waiting on the bottom with the Deep-Worker for Peter to maneuver the rings down to him one at a time. Wong would be carrying the other supplies they would need in the Caisson.

You start losing color at a hundred feet, but there was still enough light to work with. Not a lot, but better than working from artificial ones. So Jim's double blink of lights was a clear signal that he was ready. About fifty feet away, right where he should be.

"*Damocles*, Newt One here. We're in position and ready for the first ring."

"Great, Harry. I'm sending number one down now." Back on the bridge of the *Damocles*, Peter flipped the switch that would allow computer control of the buoyancy bladder he had mounted around the outside of the ring. He punched in 95 feet, as they were hoping to hold the rings just slightly off the ocean floor. He looked up at the television screen showing live feed of what was happening off the starboard side. The ring that had been designated number one slowly began to sink. He also saw Deep Caisson close her hatch and begin her descent.

"I've got the ring on sonar, *Damocles*." There was a slight delay before Trunnel was back on the radio. "Now I have a visual. It's drifted a little bit; could you compensate fifteen forward?"

Harry watched as the ring began to move forward very slowly. "That's good, *Damocles*. Stop movement and allow it to settle where it is."

Standing in front of the console, Peter back-fired the ring's jet thrusters to stop its forward motion. He watched as the depth indicator counted down to 95 feet and stopped. "You should have access to the ring, Newt One," he radioed down.

"Roger that, *Damocles*. Deep Caisson has just shown up, and we are proceeding to anchor ring number one now. You may begin ring number two's descent."

It took them a total of forty-five minutes to get all the rings into position, anchored to the ocean floor, then tethered to each other. Peter sent the 'bullet' for today's test down on Harry's instruction. Today's shot was with a steel bullet made of very thin 18-gauge steel that was just under four foot in diameter and filled with water. Peter had simply to instruct the surface workers to open the holes in both ends of the can to allow it to fill with water and sink to the test site. No sense wasting expensive high tech stuff on a throw away slug.

"I have a visual on the bullet," David began.

But he was interrupted by their underwater foreman. "Newt One here. Deep Caisson, you will identify yourself before sending any messages. There are too many of us down here to try to remember voices."

"Yes, sir. I mean, Wong here, yes sir."

"Newt One here. I would rather you use your submersible's designation, Deep Caisson. If you don't mind." Both men were very enthusiastic about underwater work, but David did not have the professional experience Harry had. It showed, and that bothered Harry; he knew David was the boss's friend.

Commander Anderson leaned forward and placed one hand on David's shoulder. "Don't worry, Mr. Wong, you'll get the hang of it."

"Deep Caisson here, I'm going in for the grab."

"*Damocles* here. Dave, remember it's very fragile when compared to the strength we built into your main arms." He had enough strength to crush the bullet flat, and a flat bullet wasn't going to work. They had two more on board, but Peter had hoped for three successful tests. David had been working with those arms for a couple of months now, and the next few moments would tell how effective that time was spent.

"Deep Caisson here, I am guiding the bullet down to the bottom. There, it has landed. I am now gently closing my claws around it. There, oops."

"Dave, what do you mean 'oops'?" Panic tinged Peter's voice.

"Deep Caisson here," came an unexpected voice. "Lt. Commander Anderson reporting my observations. The left arm has dug into your barrel slightly. Maybe an inch, no more than two. There appears to be a three-inch depression at the point of puncture. Is that still within your tolerances?"

"Easily," Peter said with relief. It could have been worse. Peter had argued with Leo about the nature of the test bullets. These were too thin, too easy to collapse, and wouldn't have enough mass to give them useful numbers. But Leo had insisted that unless they could successfully fire the gun underwater, soon, two of their investors were going to back out. So here they were, rushing the test and not getting all the data Peter would have liked.

"Newt One here. Then let's get that thing over here. I have a visual on you, Deep Caisson. Can you guys see us?"

"Caisson here, I've got the arms locked down and am approaching ring number one."

Peter switched his monitor's camera feed from the *Damocles* camera to the one mounted on Deep Caisson. David had the bullet rotated so it could fit into the first ring and was slowly creeping up on it. It slid into the ring with inches to spare all around it.

Wong rested the far end of the barrel on the ring, "Caisson here, I have the projectile loaded into the gun. Are you ready to have me release the back end?"

"*Damocles* to Newt One and Two, how do we look?"

"Newt Two, looks good to go."

"Newt One, I agree with Jim. Whenever you're ready."

"*Damocles* to Deep Caisson, release your grip and move away on my mark. Three, two, one, mark!" Peter flipped the switch that activated the electromagnetic in the first ring. In his monitor, he saw David release his submersible's grip on the bullet and back away as fast as he could. The bullet sprang from the Caisson's arms and centered itself within the first ring, right where Wong had placed it.

"*Damocles* to all submersibles. Everything looks good up here. How's it looking down there?"

"Newt Two, looks good."

"Newt One here, you have a go from this end."

"Deep Caisson, looks fine to me. But we need to do something about that moment of acquisition. We almost got pulled into the ring with your bullet."

"*Damocles* here, good to know, David. Something for me to work on." Peter called up the computer program to control the on-off cycle for the electromagnetic rings. It ran through the diagnostics for the remaining rings and green lighted them in turn. Peter poised his finger over the start button. "*Damocles* control here, firing on my mark. Three, two, one, mark!" He reached down and pressed the bubble button to start the sequence.

Nobody was able to see the bullet move through the rings. The moment Peter depressed the switch, the firing lights on the rings formed a single bright line and the bullet was gone.

Peter turned to the sonar operator of the *Damocles*. He was no more than a kid; he had completed one tour of duty in the navy, decided he didn't like the discipline and got out. He broke his eyes away from the monitor and shifted them back to the sonar screen. "Mr. von Scorio, I have contact with the object moving due north, away from the gun. Its speed is falling off rapidly. It's down to five knots now, four, three, two, one, it's barely drifting now... and it's stopped. I have it about a mile away from the starting point."

A mile, in under two minutes, with only five rings. He hoped the sonar recording could give him the initial speed when they went over the numbers, but this was a good start. A very good start indeed.

Chapter Ten

Carlos—or Charles Newman, as this splinter group of self-styled militiamen knew him—lay perched on top of the hill over-looking the chemical plant. The thought that he might be checking out their security was a joke. At night, they employed one minimum-wage security guard and locked all their chain-link gates. Even the plant operators were only out about every hour to check the gauges listed on their worksheets. Opening those tanks of ammonia and lines of nitric acid would be no problem what-so-ever. The little community of Blair, Nebraska was about to be completely depopulated.

He set down his binoculars and turned to the other man with him. Harvey Matland was a forty-five-year-old *right-sized* factory worker. The Hamilton Valve Company plant where he had held a job for over twenty-five years moved its production to Colombia. Part of President Oswald's effort to replace drug jobs in that country with American jobs. Matland had been out of work for the last seven months, no longer even part of the unemployment statistics. He didn't see any prospects in the near future, either. *The Man* had taken his job and now *The Man* was gonna pay.

Carlos looked at his watch again; 11:15. This operation had been planned for 2200 hours. Angered by the delay, Carlos turned back to the elder Matland and hissed, "Where is that brother of yours?"

Thomas was only a year younger than Harvey and still had his job on one of the new casino boats floating on the Missouri River. Though not actually part of the militia, he had been contacted by Harvey via e-mail once. Carlos had put a stop to that right away and demanded snail mail or in-person only. So Thomas had made a trip up from Missouri to visit and have the plan explained to him.

Not really wanting to be a part of it, he agreed to watch his brother's back as well as some technical support. With absolutely no connection to any known terrorist group, Thomas was able to access the Right-To-Know information at the EPA. The worst-case scenario maps allowed them to pick their target. The problem Carlos had now was that in the trunk of Thomas' aging Dodge Neon was a third of the C-4 he had smuggled into the state. It was less a need for the explosives, than a worry that the little shit would get himself caught by the authorities. Thomas was less vigilant than his brother; Carlos would worry until he had them both in his sight.

Carlos looked at his watch again, 11:25. "With or without him, we begin at midnight," he said just loud enough for Harvey to hear.

*   *   *

That aging Dodge Neon and Thomas were currently by the side of I-680, which circled the adjoining town of Omaha. Thomas had bought his car new ten years ago and never bothered to replace its tires. Now he had blown the front passenger one. Thankfully, the traffic had been light and he was able to pull over to the outside shoulder just past the 72nd Street entrance. Fortunately, this section of interstate had some lighting over it, as it had never occurred to Thomas he might need an emergency kit.

He had just opened his trunk when he saw the flashing lights approach him from behind. He looked behind him and saw a van rather than a police cruiser. It was Motorist Assistance. He breathed a sigh of relief until he remembered what he had in his trunk. He slammed it shut just as the other man opened his door.

"Need some help there?" asked the volunteer as he got out of his van. He was decked out in an orange reflective vest to make him visible to approaching traffic. He walked off into the grass of the shoulder and approached the Neon's trunk.

"Just a flat tire, sir." Thomas had to get rid of him quickly. "I don't think it will be much of a problem." A lie; Thomas didn't even know where the stuff he needed was stored.

The older man—Thomas could now see this was a retiree volunteering to help others—went around to the front of the Neon and looked at the wounded tire. "No, we can get that one changed in no time. But you had better not go far afterwards. These other tires are looking pretty bare. When was the last time you had them checked?"

"Not for awhile." Thomas hoped he sounded less afraid than he felt. *How to get rid of him?*

"Well, you had better get some new ones here pretty quick. Pop the hood, will you?" Thomas couldn't believe it; he stayed in front of the car.

"The hood?"

"Yeah, I have to get your jack out."

It would never have occurred to Thomas to look under the hood for the car's jack. Wasn't it kept with the spare? "Sure, just a minute." And he started around to the driver's door.

"Stop," the old man firmly commanded. "Never come around the side of your vehicle bordering traffic if you can help it. Use the passenger door."

"Oh, sure, that makes sense." This guy kept spooking Thomas, then just explaining it away. Well, if he helped fix the tire, Thomas could catch up with Harvey that much quicker.

"There you go," as they heard the clank of the hood being released. The old man unlatched it and raised the hood out of his way. "I'll just get the tire." Best to do this with the old man out of the way. He walked back behind the Neon and keyed the trunk open. There was no tire here.

"Where the hell is the spare?" Even as he said it, Thomas knew that would bring the old man around and he would see what was hidden in the trunk.

Instead, the old man hollered, "Look under the mat."

"Oh, sure." Thomas pulled up the mat covering the bottom of his trunk. He quickly threw it over the orange-colored bricks of Semtek lying there. He looked into the wheel well where the tire had been stowed and couldn't believe how small it was. He grabbed it out and took it around to the old man.

"This thing gonna fit?" Thomas asked.

"Sure. You never seen a donut tire before? Again, don't go too far before getting these tires replaced. These things," he took the tire from Thomas and hefted it, "aren't designed for high speed or long distances. Just enough to get you somewhere where you can get your regular tire fixed. Say, fifty miles or so."

Then another set of flashing lights appeared behind the Motorist Assist van.

"That must be John," the old man said matter-of-factly, not even looking up from the squatting position he was in, trying to set up the jack. "He's patrolling this stretch of road. By the way, I'm Jeff Morrow," he offered Thomas his hand without getting up.

"Oh, I'm Tom Matland. Thanks for stopping," he said without thinking.

The state patrol stepped out of his cruiser and held his flashlight in the air. "Jeff, that you?"

"Who else would it be? Just a flat tire," he said as he took the tire wrench from Thomas and loosened each of the lug nuts.

The officer approached the Neon keeping his light high in the air. "Really wish you'd get someone to help you this late at night. It worries all of us when you're out here alone after dark." He shined his flashlight down on the tire Jeff was loosening.

He had a bit of trouble loosening a couple of them, but once he was done, he moved back to the jack and raised the side of the Neon. "You know I have to do something."

"But let the kid fix his own flat."

"I think it will go much faster if I do it. He didn't even know where the jack was."

"Yeah, officer," Thomas replied. "I've never had to do this before."

"Okay, but you keep an eye on my friend here." The officer was looking around the area and stopped to look into Thomas's still-open trunk. "What kind of bricks are these?"

He'd seen it! Thomas had to get out of there fast! The car wasn't going anywhere suspended in the air the way it was, so he ran. He ran down the bank and into the woods bordering this undeveloped stretch of interstate. He just had to get away from that car.

* * *

Nebraska State Patrol Officer John Simmons had been on the force ten years, mostly pulling over people for traffic infractions. He had stopped his share of illegal drug shipments and undocumented workers. It was just a bunch of orange bricks, why had the guy bolted? There was no way he was going to be able to catch him now, so Officer Simmons used his portable radio and called Martha to send him some backup, giving her a complete description of Matland.

Even if the trunk didn't now stand wide open for his inspection, it could be truthfully said that he had probable cause to search it. He pulled the trunk mat back into place and saw that those bricks were labeled "High Explosive Semtex-H". It felt like some kind of putty. Underneath, he found a Garfield student papers folder. He pulled it out; within, he found several computer-printed maps. He could make out the town of Blair, but the circles around it and around the surrounding area, those didn't make any sense. Where was that backup?

* * *

Well, that's it, Carlos thought, looking at his watch, which showed the time at 12:00. The operator who had just arrived on duty began to make his rounds of the chemical storage area. If he was true to form, the area would be clear in about ten minutes, giving them a fifty-minute window of opportunity.

"Let's move. Cut that fence while he's getting his readings," Carlos whispered commandingly. The two of them slid down the hill and up to the fence. Harvey pulled the heavy-duty wire cutters he had and snipped a four foot gash in the chain link fence.

They waited until the flashlight the operator carried entered the air-conditioned building where he would reside until 0100.

They worked their way through the gash. The storage tanks were just ten feet away, over a small three-foot-high earthen dike. They went to the first of the three bullet-shaped storage tanks. Silently—as they had practiced—they took out the Semtex and det-cords from the backpack Harvey was carrying. Then they laid them out on the northern end of each tank. Carlos held up the first strip and attempted to press it into place. It wouldn't stick. He pressed it in harder, but it still would not adhere to the tank's steel surface. He ran his hand over the tank and felt... water? There was water on the side of the tank? As hot as it was, still 80 degrees in the middle of the night, there was condensation flowing down the sides of these tanks?

It took Carlos but a moment to grasp what was happening. "These are refrigerated tanks. This surface is cold enough to precipitate the moisture right out of the air," he said more to himself then to Harvey. It was a very humid night, as were most summer nights in the vast plains of America.

"Per-what-tate?" asked Harvey in a louder voice.

"Keep your voice down," Carlos said as he moved closer to Harvey. "The explosive won't stick to the tank like it is supposed to because the tank is cold enough to precipitate the humidity right out of the air." He needed a new way to attach the explosives. He needed it quick. Tape, no tape won't work. It wouldn't stick for the same reason. There was no way he could find straps long enough to go around the tanks. *Magnets! These are steel tanks. Magnets will stick to them. They would just need enough to hold the Semtek against the side of the tanks.*

He turned to Harvey, "Go into town. Find a hardware store, break in and get all the magnetic stripping you can find. We're going to mount our charges with magnets."

"Okay, but what you gonna be doing?" Harvey seemed a little reluctant to leave.

"I'll set the charges on all the non-refrigerated storage tanks." He pointed down the containment area to the five tanks that were shaped more like storage bins than the big caplet ones they had started with.

* * *

Normally, John Simmons rode in his cruiser alone. In fact, he normally didn't leave the county with it. Right now, the FBI needed every vehicle they could get, as well as drivers who knew these roads.

When a cruiser finally got to where Thomas Matland had fled his flat tire, its officer was Jim Sherman, ex-army. He made the bricks as they were labeled; Semtek. But there had been no igniters in the trunk.

"That means he's got an accomplice somewhere," Jim noted. "Martha." He keyed his radio, and John slapped his hand over his to prevent feedback. "Come in, Martha."

"Go ahead, Sherm," came the reply over the radio.

"Martha, get ahold of Sheriff Wineman. Let him know we have a trunk full of explosives here. Better call the FBI, also. Have Captain Andrews get everybody he can over here on the double, we've got a bomber running loose."

"A bomber?" Martha sounded startled.

"Yes! Martha, please move; we're going to need the cavalry here fast."

* * *

Simmons radioed for a tow truck to bring the vehicle to the evidence lot. The Omaha office of the FBI mobilized a team and was going to meet them there. Despite the fact that his shift with Motorist Assist was over, Jeff convinced Officer Simmons to let him tag along to satisfy his curiosity. Just as he was pulling onto the interstate to follow the tow truck, the first of the local area news trucks appeared. He didn't want to be the one to talk with them, so he sped off to catch the tow truck. The KETV news van pulled off the interstate right behind the three cruisers that had arrived to help Officer Sherman in his search for the missing driver. Jeff breathed easier knowing he wasn't going to be stuck as media contact.

* * *

It was 0030 when Harvey left. Carlos worked on the other storage units for twenty-five minutes before he went to the backpacks and took a nine-millimeter browning and its accompanying silencer from his. He quietly walked over to the operator's shack, attaching the silencer to the pistol's barrel. A little after 1 AM, the operator opened the door to begin his rounds. Carlos pumped three bullets into his chest before the man even registered Carlos' presence.

Carlos grabbed the body under the armpits and drug it over the dike of the storage area. On the belt of the operator was a radio, much like the ones Carlos saw police carry these days. He removed it with its holster and attached it to his own belt. Just to make sure he wouldn't miss any calls, he went through the man's pockets to see who he was. Peter Johnson. Now he was going to have to pay attention to the radio.

* * *

The FBI commandeered the Douglas County Sheriff's office. They excluded everyone except for Officer Simmons and—after much discussion and realizing that he was the only other person to actually see the suspect—Jeff from their briefings.

"Okay, what have we got here, people?" Abrahams was a slender man who wore suits that were always neatly pressed except when he had already been in them for a full day's work. As senior agent, he was pulling together everything they knew.

"There were twenty-five bricks of Semtek-H. I've sent off a sample of the stuff to lab to check the tagits. We also found a binder full of Cameo emission release plots."

"Cameo plots?" Officer Simmons asked.

"Cameo is a program for plotting emission patterns of various types of chemical releases. Agent Jenkins is checking with the EPA database now to see where they are for. Rameriz' team had combed every inch of the Neon after they got it away from those county Mounties."

"We ran the plates and have the vehicle registered to a Thomas Matland, 2065 North 15th Street, Kansas City, Missouri." Agent Wu then looked over to Officer Simmons.

It took him a minute to realize they want his input. "That was the name that the man gave Mr. Morrow when they were working on his tire."

"Odd that he wouldn't use an alias," commented Abrahams. "Continue, gentlemen."

"Thomas Matland of that address is currently employed at the casino in the KC area as a security officer and has no prior record. We have a call in to his internet account to pull his e-mail records and a unit staked out at his address. At this point, all we can do is wait." Wu finished.

Abrahams had been listening to the reports, concentrating by keeping his back to his men, not looking at anything in particular. Now that they were done, he turned around and allowed his gaze to scan the entire office. "No, we can't. Gentlemen, we have to find his accomplice!"

"Accomplice, sir?" asked Agent Fellows, who was new to the Omaha office.

"Yes, accomplice, kid. Where are the igniters? Semtak is useless without them, so whatever they had planned, they would need both parts. And from the way you make him sound, I don't think they would have given Matland all their explosives."

"Chief, I got it!" The only missing FBI agent, Lindsay Jenkins, burst into the office. "The Cameo plots, they're for the complete release of the ammonia tanks at the Falco Fertilizer plant on highway 75 just south of Blair. Each of these plots," he spread the sheets of paper across the desk, "is for the complete failure of one of the ammonia storage vessels at the plant. With the number they have available, I had EPA run another projection based on a loss of all containment simultaneously. Sir, they have enough ammonia in them to blanket the entire town with a 100% casualty rate."

"Gentlemen and lady, saddle up." He then directed his words to the local enforcement representative, "Officer Simmons, can we count on your help?"

"Blair is Washington county and outside our normal jurisdiction..."

"We don't have time to coordinate with another branch," Abrahams commented under his breath. He turned to Rameriz before he could get out of the room. "Tell Wineman I need his men temporarily assigned to the FBI." And again to himself, "that should get us over the damned boundary issue." Then loudly, "Let's move it, people!"

* * *

By 0210, Harvey had not yet returned. But Carlos had completed work on the other storage tanks and the feed lines to the absorption towers of the nitric acid plant. In all that time, the radio had been quiet except for seven calls to various operators. Pete, Peter, or Johnson had not been amongst those. *Not a very popular person, were you, Mr. Peter F. Johnson?* Carlos thought.

He waited by the last tanks now, getting more impatient for his patsy's return. He was looking at his watch for the millionth time when he heard the fence rattle. He slunk towards the spot where the noise came from, their opening, and had his silenced pistol locked on whatever came over the dike.

It was Harvey, who froze when he saw the large black shape Charles was pointing at him. "Hey, man, it's only me," he whispered.

Carlos lowered his gun and swore at this man's incompetence. If he had not killed the storage area operator, this bumbler would surely have given them away. "Get down here and be quiet." As Harvey got closer, he asked, "Did you get the strips?"

"Yeah, I even found some really wide adhesive stuff."

"Idiot. That's why I sent you for magnets. Adhesive won't stick with all this water." The man was as much of a fool as his entire militia company. They played at being soldiers, but they would never have acted if Carlos had not come along. *Well, at least they gave him the cover he needed for this operation, as well as paying the bills.*

Carlos grabbed the sack from Matland and took the adhesive backed magnetic strips he had brought.

Surprise registered on Harvey's face as he saw the combat knife Charles pulled from out of his boot. Silently he watched as this mystery man cut the magnetic tape into short pieces and used them to hold the corded explosive against the side of the refrigerated tanks.

"Will you get over here and help me?" Carlos snapped. "This will go a lot quicker if you take these strips and work on the next tank." Carlos was getting louder as the night wore on.

They had the last tank finished by 0300 and were working their way back through the fence when the night sky exploded with colors. Red and blue lights, and they were coming down the road to the plant. Something or someone had alerted the authorities. And therefore Carlos was going to need to give them someone while he got away from this hell hole they called a state.

Carlos threw his backpack over the ten-foot-tall fence, grabbed Matland's and did the same. He then pushed the gash they had cut earlier wide enough to squirm through. When he got to the outside, he held it for Harvey. As his appointed patsy was struggling through the opening, Carlos let go of the links. Matland was trapped in the fence long enough for Carlos to pull out his pistol and crack him over the skull with it. Harvey's body sagged, held up only by the links of fencing he was caught in.

Carlos holstered his gun, grabbed both packs and headed up

the hill. He had to get one hundred yards to the west of the plant before he could trigger the explosives, since the dispersal plots they had obtained from the EPA (oh, how the internet was making his job easier) had shown exactly how the cloud would come out of the plant. He had to get to the safe spot he had picked out yesterday evening.

*   *   *

Carlos finally scrambled to his hiding place, safe from the clouds of ammonia and nitrous gases he was about to unleash and any prying eyes of the local constabulary.

The front gate had obviously been no hindrance to the army of flashing vehicles converging on the storage tanks. How did they know about the storage tanks? The younger Matland must have talked. For that, he would hunt the man down and kill him. It was still going to take him a couple of minutes to arm the radio detonator. He had to work fast. He had to resist watching the plant.

*   *   *

Sheriff Wineman rode with John Simmons. Good man, Simmons, it was his idea to get the radio frequency for the guardhouse at the chemical plant and clear the way for them as well as have the Washington County Sherriff waiting for them. The Falco guard had his own problems, though; one of their operators had been out of contact for almost three hours now and they didn't have the personnel to search for him until the day shift arrived. Not so surprisingly, the man was the ammonia storage tanks operator. Wineman let the FBI know over the cell phone number they had given him. The lead car increased its speed and the rest did likewise.

They blew through the open gates at the plant, only Simmons having the sense to stop and ask the guard how to get to the storage area. Then he took off in the lead.

They ran their vehicles right up to the dike surrounding the tanks, shoved them into park and jumped over the earthen wall designed to contain spills.

"Agent Abrahams, over here," cried Wu. But he didn't wait, he began tearing the orange bricks off the first tank.

Looking at the job the terrorists—and that is who Abrahams had to think did this—did, he changed Wu's tactics. "Don't go for the Semtek. Find the igniters. Pull them."

The agents fanned out, looking over each of the tanks. As each found a Primacord, they followed it back until they came to the main detonator control. A radio-controlled detonator box.

Then the dike exploded off to the north. Everyone was knocked to the ground. Several agents did not get back up right away. Those who did rushed to the meter cube of a box and frantically began pulling the wires from it. They thought they had been in time as the wires began to arc and the few bricks they had pulled out whole exploded away from the tanks they had been attached to.

Falco was a large fertilizer plant, and there were several stages to go through in the production of nitrogen-based applications. About a quarter mile away was the building where the ammonia was converted into nitrogen oxides to be later converted into nitric acid. A large number of explosions occurred in that area, rocking the ground again.

"Where is that operator they promised us?" Abrahams growled.

Rameriz jumped back over the dike and headed for the largest nearby building. Somebody had to be in there.

Simmons took a different approach. He keyed his retuned radio and got the guard again. "Sam, we need an operator. Where are they?"

Before the guard could reply, a new voice came over the radio. "What the hell happened out there?"

"Who is this?" Simmons barked into the radio.

"Alan Fried. Who's this?"

"Are you a certified operator?"

74

"Yes."

"Where are you now?"

"Ammonia control room."

"Listen, I'd love to play twenty questions with you, but we have a situation here. An FBI agent is at this moment heading for the large building due south of the storage area and I need you to meet him and help us check out that last series of explosions."

"I'll have somebody meet him, but I can't leave the board. Something is going on at the acid plant right now."

"How can you tell..." Then it occurred to Simmons. "Is there another channel for your radio system?"

"Yeah, we've got four of them. Ammonia, End Products, Emergency Response and Maintenance."

"Great," muttered Simmons to no one in particular. "Can you get a plant radio to the FBI agent?"

"Jake will have one when he finds him."

On the other side of the dike, Abrahams snapped, "Agent Fellows."

"Yes sir," the young man ran over to his superior.

"Take six of these locals, secure this area, make sure we've found all of the explosives and find me some evidence. I want to know who's responsible for this."

"Yes, sir," Fellows replied, then turned around and counted out the first six state patrol officers he could find. He assigned two of them to perimeter security and with the rest, began to sweep the area for any more explosives. Evidence could wait until they knew it would not be blown away.

"I want the rest of you men to saddle up," continued Abrahams. "We need to get to the other side of this place and see what happened. Where the Hades is Rameriz?" He climbed over the dike with the rest of the FBI agents and a couple of remaining troopers.

On the other side, he saw Rameriz and another man running back to their position. By the time they got back to their cars, he had returned.

A lot of squawking was coming over the radio of the plant

operator that Rameriz had in tow. Over the noise, Rameriz reported, "There seems to be some kind of problem over in their acid plant, sir. The operators in both control rooms are working to shut it down."

Atop the tallest building within the fenced area, a siren had been placed to give warning and alert people in the plant of emergencies. It could also be used to tell the plant emergency personnel where they were needed. It began to wail.

"Let's go, people." Abrahams opened the passenger door of his vehicle, but before he got in turned to Rameriz. "You and this operator get in back." Then under his breath added, "What a mess." Then raised his voice, "Let's move it!"

Moments ago, most of the open area of the plant had been deserted. With the triple blast of the siren, men began coming out of various buildings and heading for the main road. With its lights flashing, a rescue squad marked with Falco Chemical logos stopped briefly at various points along that road to collect them. It arrived at the explosions' site just as the FBI were converging on it.

Four men piled out of the back of the squad and after looking over the leaking reddish gas, abandoned the closest firehouse for a red shack not covered by the expanding cloud. Two ladies emerged from the passenger side door, immediately opened one of the vehicle's side compartments and began suiting up in long, silverish fire-fighting overcoats. The driver got out, saw the cars pulling up behind him and walked over to them.

"Who are you guys?" he asked agent Abrahams as he too was getting out of his vehicle.

"FBI!"

This took the short sandy-haired man by surprise. "Well," he began after a moment, "you're going to have to move back from here. That's N O X pouring out of those pipes, and it's not going to be healthy here until we can get it contained."

Abrahams looked at the expanding red tint the lights around the plant were taking on and decided, "How far back do you want us?"

"The other side of that building," he pointed to one due east of where they currently were. "They're getting the plant, er, acid converter shut down. We should have this under control in about fifteen minutes. And if we don't, Blair has emergency units on the way. I'll send for you." He handed the FBI man a radio, "If I need you to move. My name is Ralph Henderson."

The plant emergency personnel had already unrolled two sections of hose and were tying them into the fire hydrant. The two women already in bunker gear took the place of two of the men so that they could get into protective gear. When they got back, the four outfitted rescue personnel split up, two on each of the hoses. One man stayed with the hydrant while the remaining man positioned the loose hoses, keeping them from kinking and shutting off the water flow.

Henderson went back to his teams and directed one to set up a widely dispersed spray of water to act as a shield for the other team. NOX is easily absorbed by water, and while both teams were wearing SCBA air supplies, Ralph was not going to chance a chemical burn on any of his people. The second team sent out a continuous stream of low velocity water. Their goal was to pump a lot of water over the leaking pipes to dissolve the gas. Of course, that would make a lot of nitric acid to flow into the plant's drainage system, but the plant's spill response team was on the way to take care of that problem. A lot of personnel were being called out of sleep this night.

It took them another ten minutes once they had the acid converter shut down, but they swept all the corrosive gas into the containment area for treatment. Blair's first responders came rolling in at that time, as there had been no opportunity to call them off. Ralph felt proud of his men; it could have been worse. It was only after he talked with the FBI agents that he realized just how much worse it could have been.

*　*　*

With his binoculars, Carlos looked down on the men run-

77

ning like frantic bees about the plant. Unfortunately, they were organized bees and were undoing his plans. They had been able to disarm his main set of explosives on the ammonia tanks. It was only the extra ones that had actually gone off. The ones he had hoped would multiply the effects of the ammonia cloud by adding NOX to it. Since there was no storage units for NOX gas, he could only let loose the gas being produced at the moment. So it was easily brought under control.

Worse, they had found Matland, alive. That man was supposed to die in the ammonia cloud Carlos had released. He was to be caught by his own plan. Now the authorities had a witness, not the dead patsy Carlos had planned on. Someone who could identify Carlos even if they didn't have his real name. That meant that Matland was going to have to be silenced. Permanently!

Chapter Eleven

Peter switched the hotel room's television to CNN before tossing the remote onto the bed's pillow. It had been a tiring flight up here to Washington. Less because of the distance involved and more because of the nature of the trip. Peter dreaded what was coming on the morrow.

"There is absolutely no way you can guarantee that the cylinders won't leak on the way down," came one of the four talking heads on the show Peter had tuned into. What a twist of irony. Peter had always considered himself a liberal, and here the Nuclear Recyclers lobbyist was debating on the conservative side of the issue.

"There is no guarantee that the same canisters won't leak in their Nevada burial site. All the drop parameters have been worked out, and the impact from the drop will be tenfold less than the two-story test drop the canisters have to pass before they're allowed to be used," replied their man.

"And nobody can hijack the shipment in route?" asked the right-wing moderator.

The phone rang beside the bed. Peter walked over to it, grabbed the remote again, sat on the bed, muted the TV and picked up the phone.

"Peter," came Leo's voice. "Ready for a little dinner?"

He looked over at the bags the bellboy had simply deposited inside the door. Then he'd had the nerve to frown disapprovingly at the five-dollar tip Peter had given him. *If he had wanted a larger tip, why didn't he do something to actually earn it?* Peter thought. *I could have easily carried those two bags myself.* He sighed. Then remembered he still needed to get them unpacked, change out of his traveling clothes, and get his notes organized for the hearing tomorrow.

"I need a few minutes yet." Peter never understood how Leo was able to be ready as soon as they hit the ground. They had both arrived in the same taxi; Peter had actually gotten his room before Leo. While they didn't have adjoining rooms this time, they were on the same floor. Yet the man was ready to go before Peter could even settle in. Leo lived to be around people.

"Okay, I'll meet you downstairs in the 1331 Bar and Lounge. I want to see the reactions to the CNN debate." On their way in, Leo had noted that the JW Marriott Hotel's communal televisions were carrying the talking heads debate on CNN.

Peter took his folded suitcase and opened it up to hang on the room's clothes rack. He took out the two suits he had brought and arranged them so gravity could straighten the wrinkles that United had given them. He then placed his other suitcase on the bed and took out his three dress shirts and hung them up also. Damn, he had forgotten to pack a tie. He immediately took off the one he had been wearing and hung it up. If he didn't have time to acquire another, that one had better be straight; he'd use the room's iron, if he had to. And belt, what else had he forgotten? He unpacked the entire contents of his suitcase, cataloging everything to see what he would need to run out and buy tonight.

The only other things missing were his shaving supplies. They could pick up those while they were out for supper.

It had been warm when they arrived in Washington and since they weren't meeting anyone, Peter decided to leave his sports coat in the room. He grabbed the credit card style key that the Marriott gave guests to open their rooms and charge necessaries and headed down to meet Leo.

Half way down the hall, he remembered the TV, turned around and ran back to his room to shut it off. Easy to forget the thing since the sound was muted.

* * *

As Peter entered 1331, Leo stood up and waved him over. Leo was occupying a small table in the center of the lounge, sitting in a seat where he could watch the climax of debate, keep an eye on the entrance, and listen to conversations around him. Which, much to his disappointment, had nothing to do with the news program.

Peter walked over and sat in the chair next to Leo that had a Starbucks coffee cup in front of it. Sniffing through the rectangular opening, Peter could tell it was exactly as he liked it. Straight black coffee.

"Did they say anything we didn't expect?" Peter asked.

Setting down his own Latte, Leo responded, "No. I had expected more on the conservation end of the controversy, but Congressman Blair keep pounding Jenkins about the safety and security of the package, as he kept calling it."

"Any ideas about how I should handle him tomorrow?" Blair was the freshman member of the Joint Energy Committee Peter was scheduled to appear before on Tuesday, and, thanks to Leo's intervention, CNN and Fox News were planning to carry it live.

'Good publicity,' Leo had said when he had dropped it on Peter just last week. Damn it, he still had to finish the retrofit of the Alvin submersibles. 'People want to look the man behind all

80

this in the eyes and know he's real,' had been Leo's response when Peter had asked why Leo couldn't handle it.

"I think the best thing you can do is have a really good meal tonight. I made reservations at one of the top restaurants in town, aptly enough named Galileo's. The cab will be here in five minutes to take us. Good meal, good night's sleep, and you'll wow the entire country tomorrow with what we can do."

Peter sat back and took a small sip of his coffee. It must have been waiting here for him awhile since it was just below the temperature he usually liked.

"Peter?" came a voice from the entrance to the lounge, a familiar voice.

Peter turned to look. Walking in through the lounge's entrance was a tall redhead in a blue lady's pant suit whose squared-off shoulders were not due to padding.

Carol, it was Carol! Carol Bancroft had been his love interest while the two of them did their undergraduate work. "Carol?" he called back more in surprise than in greeting. Then he pushed his chair back and got up to meet her halfway. "It's been a long time." He stuck out his hand to shake hers, noticing that she was still gorgeous. She still had those deep blue eyes he always fell into when she was around. And she was still taller than he was. In fact, the only change he could notice was that she had accelerated her weight training, even more than when they were in school. She had always been a lady who could protect her date. Before he could get out, "What're you doing here?" She had slipped past his outstretched hand and wrapped him in a hug. More of a friendly hug than the ones she had greeted him with back at Cal Tech.

She looked down into his eyes and back up slightly. "I could say that I'm here to see you, but my nephew is a finalist in the national spelling bee."

Peter felt a little let down, "Really? Which one?"

"None, you dope. Don't you remember I've always talked about touring the capitol? I finally told my plant manager I was taking three weeks off this year to do it. I just spent yesterday and today exploring the FBI building. You'd like it, they've got lots of cool toys. Tomorrow I'm starting a week-long tour of the Smithsonian. I just got back and saw you walk in here." She looked over Peter's shoulder. "Who's your cute friend?"

Leo had just come up behind him. "My name is Leo Dayton. Carol, isn't it?" He was talking so fast she could only nod. "I helped found Nuclear Recyclers with Peter. And I must say, you don't look anything like the other friends of Peter I've met."

She looked over at Peter. "Other friends?"

"He's only met David," Peter said in his defense.

"Underwater Wong?" Carol asked. "No wonder he has a bad impression of your friends. Has Dave finally decided to grow a beard or does he still shave religiously once a week?"

"He wasn't that bad," Peter came to his friend's defense. "Besides..."

Carol put her hand over Peter's mouth. "I was only kidding." She dropped it when she felt his mouth relax.

Then a thought occurred to Peter. "Carol, Leo and I were just heading out to dinner. If you don't have any other plans, I, er, would like you to join us."

"Well, let's see. They have that Heckle and Jeckle marathon on the Cartoon Channel tonight. So let me think, cartoons or dinner? Cartoons, dinner?"

"Carol!"

"Okay, I guess I can squeeze you in," Carol finally admitted.

The taxi was waiting when they got to the front door. They climbed into the back for the fifteen-minute ride to Galileo's Restaurant of "Fine Italian Cuisine". When they got there, the *maitre d'* was not overly pleased with their last minute addition, but Leo smoothed things over with help from the company's petty cash account.

They discussed Peter and Leo's plans for the company over dinner, though Leo did most of the talking. It was only when the after-dinner espressos had been served that they got around to current topics.

"So what are you two in town for?" Carol finally inquired.

"This is a long way from New Orleans."

"Well, Peter gets to testify before the Joint Committee on Energy Policy tomorrow. So I thought I'd tag along for moral support and look up a few old friends," Leo filled her in.

"I still don't understand why I have to talk to them," Peter continued to protest.

"Same ol' Petey," Carol butt in. "Always wanting to play with your toys, but never wanting to share them with others. As I remember, you ducked out of a few seminars you were scheduled to give."

"Carol, that's not true."

"Oh, do tell." Leo leaned closer to this intriguing woman.

"Did he ever tell you about his undergraduate research project?"

"Carol," Peter tried to cut her off, even though he knew from experience that wasn't possible.

She looked at him for the briefest of seconds. "Didn't think so. Peter had arranged to work for that old stodgy Prof. Linden, his advisor, and measure the tidal forces on the bottom of the continental shelf. Worked it out that he and David would get to plant all the sensors and collect all the data." She momentarily turned to Peter. "You did give Dave credit on that paper, didn't you?"

"Not as an author, but I did get his name worked into it," Peter confirmed and sat back in his chair. There was no way he was going to stop Carol now.

"Everything was fine until they got the paper ready for submission to the review committee of AGU, whatever that was."

"The American Geophysical Union," Peter offered.

"Right, those guys. Anyway, that would have been fine except that Dr. Linden scheduled a seminar for Peter to give his findings to the entire physics department and invited a couple of his AGU friends to hear directly from his very promising student. Peter was throwing such a fit, I almost moved out then."

"I was not," Peter protested.

"That was why Linden threatened to pull your credits if you

didn't come through with the lecture?"

Peter just looked deep into his espresso.

"But that wasn't the worst of it. The seminar went so well that Linden scheduled Peter to give a talk on their paper at the summer meeting of the AGU. It made for a bad summer. We were graduating. I got a job in Ohio with Hellios Plastics and moved away. Then I'm afraid I just got too busy to stay in touch. When I did write you, they said you were in graduate school somewhere in the Midwest. How did the presentation go?"

"About as well as could be expected. We weren't offering any radical ideas. I just wish Dr. Linden had fielded more of the questions instead of passing them off to me."

"I know," Carol offered, "if you have to talk to the public you want to be told exactly what to say. You've got to loosen up and enjoy the spontaneity of life."

"I do, just not in public."

"That's why you always let me talk to the investors," Leo concluded. "I think you're right Carol, I've got to get this boy out more often."

Peter lifted his hand. "Waiter." He was going to need another espresso.

After another half hour of conversation, Leo finally got around to asking, "Carol, what did you finally get your degree in?"

"I finally settled on an MBA and did my thesis on work/stress management under severe working conditions. Nothing nearly as productive as Peter's. At least nobody wanted me to give a seminar on it."

"What kinds of conditions?" Leo pressed on.

"People who work in extreme environments; building skyscrapers, undersea oil workers, test pilots—private sector not military ones—that sort of thing. It's incredible what those people have to go through just to get the job done. They have some very special needs, and if a company doesn't get them met, they risk losing a highly specialized work force." She paused for a moment in thought and took another sip of her espresso. "So look what I'm doing now. Baby-sitting a bunch of mold injectors on an assembly line."

Leo looked over at Peter, caught his eye and said, "I think we can change that. How would you like to manage a group of workers who will have to perform flawlessly under the most extreme conditions man has worked under to date?"

"What?" Peter exploded. Though he was hoping Carol would grab the job offer.

Chapter Twelve

Peter poured himself another glass of water from the provided pitcher. Less because he was thirsty but more to give himself some control over the events for which he was now center stage.

"I ask you again, Mr. von Scorio. What guarantees can you give this committee that your **bullets** will not rupture at the excessive depth you'll be working?" The Democratic Representative from Massachusetts, Matthew Blair, continued pressing Peter on this issue.

"As I have said before, each and every cylinder has been and will continue to be drop-tested from a height of twenty feet onto a concrete pad before they ever have any waste material added to them. Both DOT and DOE have agreed they are suitable for protecting the nuclear waste stored within them." Peter drank half his freshly-filled glass of water. At this rate, his bladder would force him to leave before the committee would allow him to. He was thankful DOE had sent a representative over to pull him out of the fire Senator Marquart had set under him about the project's security.

"But those specifications were designed for land transportation, at normal pressures. You're planning to take those canisters down where the pressure will be a thousand times greater," pressed the Congressman. "Down to where submarines have been crushed to pulp."

Peter looked up and down the table of Senators and Congressmen arrayed in front of him. He noticed that they did not have to drink water from a communal pitcher. They each had their own bottle of specialty water.

Of all the members of Congress on this joint committee, only Senator Farnsworth of Connecticut hadn't asked him tough questions so far. In fact, he hadn't asked any questions.

"We're only taking them to a depth of 1500 feet. At that depth, the pressure is 700 pounds per square inch, that's only 48 times greater than the air pressure we are currently under. Easily within the design specifications of these cylinders." Peter automatically picked up his water glass again, but set it back down when he realized he wasn't really thirsty, just nervous.

"So where is your test data?"

The Energy Department's representative began to answer. "I refer you gentlemen to the DOE documents I provided at the beginning of this hearing. Number..."

"I asked for **his** test data, Mr. Fuller. Mr. von Scorio, what actual tests have been done with travel cylinders at those depths? Where's your proof that the DOT specs will be good enough to protect the public from a catastrophic release of highly radioactive nuclear material?"

"No one has actually dropped one of them that far down, sir. But we have fired one through a prototype gun at a depth of about one hundred feet. Which is about 60 PSI. Without even springing a leak."

"I sincerely hope it contained no nuclear materials in it."

"No, sir, it just contained water."

"Then how do you know it didn't actually break open somewhere?"

"In our second series of test firing, we used fresh water as a monitoring agent. A check of the salinity after the series of test firings showed absolutely no salt water infusion."

"But you didn't test it at your working depth," the Congressman pressed on. "At the crushing pressures of the Mid-

Atlantic Ridge, have you?"

"No, sir, we haven't. Our plans call for us to complete a full-scale working model of the waste gun before we actually do any deep water testing." The half pitcher of water he had already consumed was beginning to press on his bladder. As he eyed the bottles of water at the committee table, he noticed that Senator Marquart had left the hearing.

Congressman Blair pressed for his attention. "Then I ask you, how do you expect this committee to rubber stamp your project when you admit that you're guessing at your numbers?"

"Congressman, these are engineering estimates, not guesses."

"Estimates, guesses; I fail to see the difference. All I see is that you can't give us a guarantee. And until you can, and can furnish this committee with the documentation needed to back up that guarantee, I don't see you being able to proceed with this project. Mr. Chairman, I move that we vote no on the Nuclear Recyclers petition."

"Mr. Blair," Senator Farnsworth finally weighed in. "Your motion is again out of order. We are not through with all the witnesses set to testify before this committee, let alone this first one. Senator Lynch?"

"I have another series of questions I would like to put to the witness, if I may?" began the senior Senator from the state of Utah.

"Please proceed," acknowledged the chairman.

Senator Lynch, who had already declared not to seek another term, had begun to allow his gray hair to recede with normal male pattern baldness. He leaned forward to talk into his microphones. "Dr. von Scorio, and I believe your actual title is 'doctor', if I may correct my colleague?"

Peter watched as Blair leaned back in his chair and folded his arms in front of his chest. "Yes, it is, Senator."

"Dr. von Scorio, exactly why should this committee consider your company's proposal over the current storage facility in Yucca Mountain?"

With just a few words, Senator Lynch had changed the whole tone of the session. Peter noticed that the antagonism of the last questioner was missing. "Any storage facility, no matter how big it is, will eventually fill up. Landfills are closing all the time in this country. While they have the luxury of being returned to productive uses, it's going to take hundreds of thousands of years before the Yucca Mountain storage facility can be considered safe, let alone returned to any productive uses. With the current number of nuclear power facilities in this country alone, Yucca Mountain will be filled and sealed within two decades. Then we're back to square one. We'll have to find and build another storage facility. We will have to cordon off another piece of Earth from future use for those thousands of years.

"And that's just us.

"What about the rest of the world? President Langley promised them we would care for their spent fuel in return for full inspection privileges.

"I put it to you that as long as we rely on storage of the byproducts of nuclear science, we will be limiting its effective usefulness. We need to actually recycle this material back into the Earth where we extracted it from."

After a moments' silence, Senator Lynch added, "Thank you, Dr. von Scorio. I think you've made my point. Mr. Chairman, I have no further questions."

"Well, I have another," broke in Congressman Blair. "What happens to the Yucca Mountain Project if this **Waste Gun** goes into service?"

The company lawyer, Jason Riley, tapped Peter on the shoulder and placed his hands over Peter's microphones. "Be careful. He's probably going for the jobs' angle. You are not required to speculate for them," he advised into Peter's ear.

"We might as well get it out on the table now, though," Peter whispered back. Turning back to the microphones, he responded for the whole committee. "Even if we began our maximum recycling effort today, it would take us several years to empty what is currently stored in the storage facility. And we don't plan to start there, anyway. There are numerous nuclear facilities just waiting for our facility to come on line. The Department of Energy will have plenty of time to wind down Yucca. Workers would have plenty of time to find new jobs before the facility would be mothballed."

Peter noticed the committee chairman sit up a little straighter on that one. He had struck a nerve there.

"A multi-billion dollar program," shot back Blair, "and you expect us to simply mothball it so you upstarts can make a profit? Take money from the public trough?"

"Sorry, Peter," Riley leaned over and whispered in Peter's ear. "I forgot Blair is a spending hawk, not a jobs advocate."

But Blair was still going. "Decades of work by several congressional committees, not to mention the departments of Energy and Transportation. And you waltz in here and expect us to scrap all of it. Well, I, for one, honor the efforts and sacrifices our forefathers sweated over to better our nation. We can't just turn our backs on the wisdom they displayed. If they thought the Yucca Mountain Project was the solution to our nuclear waste problem, we should give it a chance. Mr. Chairman, I move that we reject this petition."

"Mr. Blair, I again remind you that there are many more witnesses to come before this committee before we can even begin our deliberations. But, due to the hour, I will entertain a motion to adjourn for lunch."

"I move," said someone from the left of the Senator.

"Is there a second?"

"Aye," came a voice from his right. It was all happening too fast; Peter didn't have time to see who was actually making the motions.

"Is there any opposition?" He waited for a few seconds, then banged his gavel on the table. "We are adjourned for lunch. Dr. von Scorio, you may resume your testimony at 2PM." Then the distinguished gentlemen rose from their seats and left via the backdoor of the hearing room.

Peter stood, but waited until the last of them had left before making his beeline to the men's room.

* * *

Jason and Peter had agreed to meet Leo for lunch in a small
bistro near the capitol building. Leo's morning had been spent in
the company of the more sympathetic members of capitol hill.
As he pushed open the restaurant's doors, they could hear him
whistling Mozart's Ode to Joy.

"One of us had an easy morning," said Riley as he raised his
hand to signal their waiter.

"Jason, good to see you." Leo looked over to the older attorney. He still had exactly the same number of gray hairs he did for
the last decade, still had the same leather briefcase he had carried
since college, but he seemed to have gained a few pounds despite
the tailoring of his gray suits to hide the fact. "Sorry, I missed
your plane this morning. Lots of people to see and places to
meet."

"That's people to meet... You did it again," Jason smiled at
the slip.

"Every time, my friend, every time." Leo looked over to Peter, who was deliberating over his beer. "Rough time with the
committee?"

"Nothing that we hadn't gone over." Peter answered without
looking up. "Though that Representative Blair is pushing harder
than you prepped me for."

"He's in a tough reelection bid. The polls rate his primary
opponent in a dead heat with him. He needs the exposure. Don't
let him get you down. Just watch Farnsworth, he's got a tight
control on that committee. Whichever way he goes, so will the
vote."

"That's just it," Peter finally took his eyes off his bubbling
cold beverage to look across at Dayton. "He hasn't asked a
thing."

"He's just letting the junior members vent their spleens,"
commented Riley. "Personally, I was surprised at the questioning

from Senator Lynch. It was almost as though he was feeding you that opening."

"So Blair could jump down my throat again."

"I don't think so. The Chairman keeps cutting him off every time he makes that silly motion."

"Not having been there, I still say wait to see what Farnsworth has to say." The waiter arrived, and they placed their orders.

* * *

When they returned from lunch, Peter found an envelope waiting for him on the witness table. He opened it immediately, as the congressional members had not all returned.

Dr. Von Scorio:
After the hearing is over, please meet Senator Farnsworth in his office at 4 P.M. If he is available, please bring Mr. Leo Dayton with you.
Lawrence Westfield
Aide to Maxwell Farnsworth, U.S. Senator

Peter passed the note to Riley. He read it and asked Peter, "Can you handle them alone for a few minutes? I'll have to go outside before I can turn my cell phone back on."

"Go ahead, they're not even back yet." Riley left the hearing room and was able to get back before the committee reconvened.

As the last to arrive, Senator Farnsworth took his seat, looked up and down the row of committee members, with their aides seated directly behind them. "I call this meeting of the Joint Committee on Energy Policy back to order." He banged his gavel on the table and continued. "I wish to remind the witness that he is still under oath. Not that we've had any reason to doubt your word so far in this hearing." He looked back and forth across his colleagues and as Congressman Blair made a motion towards his microphone, he jumped in ahead of the younger man.

"Exactly why are you here today?"

This was the opening Peter had been waiting for. Representative Blair had blocked his attempt to give an opening statement in the morning. "Thank you, Senator. Nuclear Recyclers Inc. would like to take a completely different approach to industrial-governmental interactions. It is our goal to carve out a niche for ourselves in an arena that has scared the public for three-quarters of a century. The nuclear arena; specifically, the disposal of extremely dangerous nuclear waste. If we attempt to carry out our plans without the public having full knowledge and confidence in our actions, we would be inviting a panic. Secrecy has been the watchword for too long.

"I am here today to invite, nay, demand governmental oversight of our actions. And that those actions become part of the public record. I want everything we do to be seen, to be photographed, to be published in every media that will have it. I want every American to see exactly what we are doing and why. So we come before you today, petitioning you to allow Nuclear Recyclers to go forward with our recycling project, but also petitioning you to appoint a watchdog from amongst yourselves to keep an eye on us. To question anything we might want to do, and report back to you and the American people."

Peter stopped talking. The second of pure silence that followed gave him more than enough time to regret getting as wound up in his appeal as he did.

But the silence only lasted that second, and afterwards, Senator Farnsworth continued, "I commend your cooperative spirit, Dr. von Scorio. But I have to wonder, why come to us? Surely you could get all the coverage and press you desire from the established news media?"

Peter took a deep breath and released the last of his pent up emotions. "We plan to also get the attention of the national news bureaus. But their news coverage is limited to the perceived interest of the public. It ebbs and wanes over time. You have an interest in safeguarding the nation, and as such, will be there from start to finish. You will be there when we are no longer newsworthy."

"There is that," the chairman commented. "Does anyone have any further questions of this witness before I release him?"

"I have a few more—" began Congressman Blair.

Senator Farnsworth leaned back to say a private word to one of his aides. The aide then went down to talk with the aide behind Blair and then to Blair himself. The Congressman then turned back to his microphone.

"I guess I have no further questions of this witness," he said, and sat back in his chair.

"Then I would like to thank Dr. von Scorio for his testimony and release him from his oath." With that, Farnsworth banged his gavel, making his dismissal official.

*   *   *

At exactly four that afternoon, Peter, Jason and Leo entered the office suite of Senator Farnsworth. Lawrence Westfield met them as they entered.

"I'm so pleased the three of you could make it on such short notice. The Senator is most anxious to talk with you. He's been a bit delayed. I'm afraid an important bill came up for a vote on the floor. He should be with you in just a moment. He wanted you to wait in his office." He led them into the very polished office of the Connecticut Senator. "Can I get you anything while we wait?"

"No, I think I've had enough to drink for one day," said Peter.

"Iced tea," replied Jason.

"Coffee, black," asked Leo.

"I'll be right back." The aide closed the door behind him as he left.

"Now why do you suppose ol' Farnsworth sent for us?" Jason asked. He shifted in his chair, the furthest from the door, to look at his clients.

"It sure wasn't a move I'd been expecting," Leo replied.

He'd taken the chair closest the door, leaving Peter sitting between them.

Peter was completely out of his element in this office. This was the largest space he'd ever been in for a single man's office, bigger even than the Dean's office at Iowa University. The desk alone was larger than the queen-sized bed Peter slept on at night. The red leather chair was almost as tall as Peter, were he standing next to it. Three different pictures were currently being projected on the wall behind him. The Senator could watch at least three separate channels from here; fifteen, if he had the latest picture-in-picture technology. Peter was noticing that one of the pictures was a live shot of the Senate floor and there were only a few Senators milling around on it.

Then the door opened, and Senator Farnsworth hurried in. "Sorry to have kept you waiting, gentlemen." He walked behind his desk, pressed a button and said, "Lawrence, send in one of your power drinks for me." Then he sat down in that large chair behind his desk.

A second later, his aide marched into the room carrying a tray. He handed the Senator a tall glass of a thick brown liquid, Jason a glass of iced tea, and Leo a large paper-wrapped cup of coffee.

"You're not having anything, Dr. von Scorio?" the Senator asked.

"Too much water at the hearing."

"I thought you were hitting it a little heavy," the Senator laughed. "You shouldn't let the others rattle you too much, they're looking to get a sound bite for the evening news. Especially Blair. As far as he's concerned, the more press attention he can garner, the better. I have no doubts that your petition will be adopted by the end of the week. Especially if you gentlemen would do a little favor for me."

Peter had never thought politicians were so blatant about asking for money. "Exactly what kind of favor?"

"It would look good—as well as getting the press away from our hearing for a while—if we sent you three on a tour of the

Yucca Mountain Facility. Show your concern for the plight of the surrounding residents as well as the workers who would eventually lose their cushy government jobs. And you could help me out by taking Mr. Blair with you."

The Senator held up his hand before Peter could say anything. "Having Blair along will guarantee your trip will pull the press away from our hearing." He looked over at Leo, "and that would allow the United States Government to fund the trip. I know how cash strapped your company is right now, Mr. Dayton, even if you don't have to make public filings. I think we need to remind the public exactly what your project would be saving us from. So what do you say?"

Peter looked from one of his companions to the other.

Jason's eyes lit up as he spoke. "You're offering them a forum to pitch their ideas directly to the public."

Senator Farnsworth just nodded.

"Leo, this is the opportunity you've been looking for. It might even get you the final venture capital you need to get through to startup."

Peter turned his head quickly over to Leo.

"We're coming up a little short, kid. But I think with the right PR, we can get over this hump and start earning enough revenue to keep going." He stood up and offered his hand to the Senator. "You've got yourself a trip, Senator."

Peter felt railroaded again. All he had wanted to do since getting to Washington was to get back to New Orleans, work on the remaining rings, and finish the plans for his blockhouse. Now it was going to be another week before he could get back to work.

Chapter Thirteen

Carlos handed the state patrol officer a cup of coffee as he sat down in one of the empty chairs of the third floor nurses station.

"Thanks, doc," the officer replied. He blew the steam forming above the dark liquid.

"Better wait until you taste it before you thank me." Carlos looked every bit the resident doctor making his night rounds, checking up on his departments' patients. Complete with a forged laminated ID clipped to the breast pocket of his official Lutheran Hospital lab coat. He had acquired the ID off an internet site. "I think it's been heating up all night. Real strong, real bitter."

"I know. The nurses come on at eleven, make a pot, then forget it's there. Well, at least it should keep me awake the rest of this shift." The officer took a tentative sip. "Man, that is strong." He went over to the water fountain and added a little fresh water to the brew. He took another sip and came back. "But at least it's got some punch to it. My wife keeps wanting me to switch to decaf. I ask you, how the hell you gonna stay awake on decaf?"

Carlos just smiled and pulled out a couple of patients' charts, hiding the fact that he really was only going to be studying the patient in room 310, Harvey Matland.

The officer left him alone long enough for him to finish the cup Carlos had given him. "Hey, doctor..." using the pause for Carlos to fill in his name.

"Longworth, Timothy Longworth."

"Yeah, was there any more coffee left in the pot?" The officer started to rise, became a bit wobbly as he got to his feet, and fell into Carlos' waiting arms.

"If you'd had any real will power, a mere Nembutal wouldn't distract you from protecting your charge."

He slid the officer to the floor, then under the desk. He had already tied up the night nurse and her assistant, leaving them in the janitor's closest. He had used the nurse's key to get into the medicine locker and acquire the double dose of Pentobarbital elixir or Nembutal to add to the officer's coffee. He could now go to work preparing the potassium chloride injection for his friend.

Carlos had shown up at the hospital early enough to have dinner in the cafeteria. Not only did this allow him enough time during regular visiting hours to case it out without drawing suspicion, but it allowed him to acquire the five packets of co-salt, a salt substitute he needed for its potassium chloride content. When visiting hours ended, he made his way to the doctors' lounge and waited until now. Nobody had questioned his right to be there even though they didn't know him. After all, he had a badge giving him that right.

Carlos opened a mixing vial of sterile water and added the contents of all five packets. He had calculated they would contain between 500 and 700 milligrams each. The resulting total should just about give him a saturated solution with the ten cc in the vial. Exactly what he was going to need. He took a syringe and sucked up all the liquid, leaving just a few crystals at the bottom of the vial. He then capped the needle and walked down the empty hallway.

Using the keys he had taken from the state patrol officer, he unlocked room 310. He then slipped swiftly and quietly in. Harvey was sleeping away with an IV dripping into his right arm just as his chart had indicated. Carlos removed the cap from the syringe, plunged the needle into the self-sealing valve of the IV's medicine chamber, and emptied its contents so they would be added to the 5% saline solution the nurses used to administer Harvey's pain medication. He watched as the two solutions merged, then he opened the clamp controlling the speed of the IV all the way up. He then shook Harvey awake.

"Har-vey. Oh, Har-vey," he whispered into his ear.

Matland woke up, still groggy from his last dose of pain medicine. "Charles? It is you!" Thinking that his partner had come to rescue him, added "You gotta get me out of here."

"Everything's been taken care off. First, I have to find your brother. He's gone into hiding. Do you know where?" Carlos' fingers thumbed the bed rail in time to the dripping of the IV. Neither man noticed.

97

"Great, then they didn't catch him. Get me out of here and we can meet him at the old church."

"What old church?"

"On North 30th Street. Just south of the community college down there. Just get me out, and I'll show you the way."

"I have read your chart. You are in no condition to travel. How do you know he is there?"

"When we were kids, we found a hidey-hole way to get inside. It's been our secret ever since. Besides, he was joking with me about it the other day."

"Good. Then I will go find him and we'll both get you out of here."

"Well, okay. Listen, on your way out, see if you can find a nurse, this IV's starting to burn."

Carlos moved the call switch outside of Matland's reach. "Sure. Have a pleasant sleep."

Carlos turned to walk to the door.

"Thanks," Harvey said as the drowsiness of his pain meds caught up with him again.

Carlos turned back and watched Matland's head fall limply to one side on his pillow, then turned back to the door and left.

On his way past the nurse's station, he grabbed a copy of the evening paper that had been sitting there. There was going to be no time for any of them to read it once they finally woke up.

* * *

He drove past the unmarked pig mobile twice before deciding that was what was sitting outside Harvey Matland's single story ranch home. He could hear the police helicopter circling overhead, searching the area. It wasn't shining any lights down to the ground, therefore Carlos assumed they were using an infrared camera to search for warm bodies. He was going to have to be careful.

He had to make sure little Tommy wasn't holed up in the house somewhere. Then he could check out that church Harvey

98

had talked about.

He pulled his car around the block and parked on the street behind the house. He shut his car off and waited until he could no longer hear the police chopper. Grabbing a reflective thermal blanket from his backseat in case they came back before he could get to cover, he walked through the backyard of the house behind Harvey's and jumped the fence separating them.

The police had either already searched the house or Tommy was careless about his locks. The backdoor didn't need any finesse to open. A quick, quiet search revealed that Tommy had never even returned here after their failed terror attack.

* * *

It was getting on five in the morning, and Carlos had gone up and down Thirtieth Street three times. All the way from one interstate entrance to the other. Nothing!

Then, on his fourth trip south, it was finally light enough for him to notice that Thirtieth Street itself did not end at the North Freeway entrance. It kept going south via what he had been mistaking for a side street.

Two blocks from the turnoff, he found the building he was looking for, an old church that was up for lease.

He pulled into the car wash next door and went to the back to look for the opening Harvey had told him about.

There it was, an old coal chute. Carlos pushed on the panel and swung it back. He could see a little light coming from the basement. He stuck his head in. The light was coming from a candle that had burned almost to the concrete floor. By the candle, someone was wrapped in another thermal blanket Carlos had acquired before this mission. He hoped it was Tommy.

He looked down at the bottom of the chute and saw nothing to ruin his landing. He stuck his feet in first and slid down the chute, getting remnants of coal dust on his clothing, hands and hair.

After a quick brush of the worst pockets of black dust, he

quietly walked over to the sleeping form. But apparently not quietly enough, because Tommy began to stir. "Harvey, it that you?" he said a little too loud for Carlos.

"No, it is I, Carlos. Keep your voice down."

Tommy looked up at him and was rather puzzled. "I thought your name was Charles?"

Carlos had been using too many alias on this job. "That's what I said, Charles," he whispered.

"No, I could have sworn you said Carlos." Tommy turned over to prop himself up on his elbow and proceeded to roll over on the candle, snuffing out its light. "OW!"

Carlos had managed to get close enough to clamp his hand over Tommy's mouth before he could make any other noise.

"You will not speak again until I tell you to," Carlos hissed into the young man's ear. He took a small pen light from his pocket and blinded Tommy. "What happened that you did not make our rendezvous?"

"Please get that out of my eyes." When Carlos didn't move it after repeated pleadings, Tommy just closed his eyes.

As Carlos heard the tale of what had happened to the young Matland, it was all he could to do to keep from pummeling the incompetent whelp into a bloody pulp. But he resisted, he had to know why the authorities came roaring into the plant. He kept inwardly cursing the damn blind bad luck of the situation.

When Tommy had finished, he moved his head to the side, getting his eyes out of the light, and looked around for his brother. "Hey, where's Harve?"

"Due to your incompetence, the police killed him," Carlos stated dryly. He reached behind his back. "How safe is this hideout? Does anyone else know about it?"

"Harvey's dead?" Tommy was so shocked that he looked back into the flashlight. He pushed it away when it hurt his eyes.

Carlos brought it back, only this time against the side of Tommy's head, with enough force to draw blood. "Does anyone else know about this place?"

"That hurt, man," Tommy slid back against the wall, sat up,

grabbed the side of his head. "You're crazy. Get out of here. Now!"

Carlos pulled a knife from behind his back and drove it into the center of his coconspirator's chest. "Very well." He slid the knife back out and wiped in on Tommy's shirt sleeve. He pulled down the young man's eyelids when his eyes lost focus. "I will leave you now. Try and stay undiscovered for a while."

* * *

Carlos pulled out the Omaha paper he had taken from the hospital while he waited for his breakfast. He had stopped at Denny's in Des Moines. He drove as long as his tank had allowed him before stopping.

The story on the second page caught his attention. Nuclear Recyclers Inc. was going to fire nuclear waste containers into a fiery rift under the Atlantic Ocean. Shoot radioactive bullets into Mother Earth, stab their foul contamination into the very heart of Gaia. This he could not allow! He left the paper on the table and walked out of the restaurant just as the waitress was bringing his apple pancakes.

Chapter Fourteen

Jonathan Peters turned the page of the paper he wasn't reading while he waited for his quarry to show up. This Peter von Scorio would turn out to be just another greedy capitalist; he would bet his very soul on it. Well, this time, CADRE would get to him first, before he could make the Earth worse.

Founded in the late nineties, the Citizen Activists Determined to Remediate the Environment, CADRE, had used the Internet to keep track of industrial pollution and keep the public aware of what was happening. Every major industry in the country had to disclose exactly what they had on site through an annual SARA filing with the EPA. It would state just what they could pollute the land with, and exactly how bad a spill could become; and that information was the public's right to know. CADRE just took that information and repackaged it into rallies as often as their budget could afford. It had effectively swelled their ranks to over a hundred thousand.

Sure, they had taken a hit over the last year with the Eco-Now bombing in Oregon, the Save America railcar attack and that aborted explosion in Nebraska. But Jonathan's wife, Marion, was currently down in Texas on a speaking trip, denouncing that state's efforts to hide the truth from its citizens. Eco-terrorism would not save the Earth, only people working together, with knowledge, could get the job done.

He turned the page again, the clock over the registration desk said it was 1:40. The flight carrying the Nuclear Recyclers had landed on time, at 1:10. Jonathan had had the desk clerk check for him. He glanced out the window and saw the black limousine pull up. He recognized Lawrence Westfield as he got out, having spent enough time in Senator Farnsworth's office. Senator Lynch and Congressman Blair followed him out of the limo; again, men Jonathan knew well. The next three were new, but from the pictures he had obtained of the hearing, he recognized two of them; Jason Riley, the company's attorney, and the man he had come here to corner, Peter von Scorio. He folded the paper neatly and stuffed it under his arm as they approached the front desk. He watched as the congressional aides obtained room keys and handed them to the two members of congress. The other four men had to go through registration.

Jonathan walked up behind them to register for his own room, making sure he was standing directly behind Dr. von Scorio. It was how he was able to find out that Dr. von Scorio was staying in room 525. He watched them meet back up with the lawmakers, as the clerk asked if he could help him.

* * *

With a room on the sixth floor, Jonathan had walked down the stairs to the fifth. The resort actually employed elevator operators, and he didn't want any of them to know he'd even been to the fifth floor. He knocked on the door and waited.

"Just a minute," came from inside. Waiting a few minutes, the door finally opened. Surprisingly, the room occupant was not using the safety catch to secure his room. He actually pulled the door completely open. "Can I help you?"

"Dr. von Scorio?" He was not as timid as the news photos had portrayed him, standing just a bit straighter than Jonathan had remembered from watching the news footage. And much more comfortable in a bright red polo shirt, than the blue pin-striped suit he had worn in the publicity shots.

"Yes," he stretched that word out waiting for Jonathan to respond.

"Dr. von Scorio, my name is Jonathan Peters, and I represent CADRE, a environmental group of concerned citizens. May I have a word with you?"

Looking at his watch, von Scorio responded, "I have to be back down in the lobby in about forty-five minutes. But I think I can spare you a few of those. Won't you come in and have a seat?" He motioned Jonathan towards the end of his two-room suite.

Jonathan walked into the small office, and took a seat in one of the three chairs surrounding the oval table in the center of the room. It was a bit lavish for his taste, and he was a little ashamed that the government was paying for Dr. von Scorio's use of it. But if this trip hadn't been a congressional junket, paid for with public money, CADRE would never have been able to track them here.

"What can I do for CADRE, Mr. Peters?" He held out his hand, even though Jonathan was already sitting.

Jonathan quickly stood and shook the offered hand, then re-seated himself. "It's your waste gun. We can't find out anything about it, other than what you said at the hearing last week. Frankly, it scares us."

"In what way?" Peter took a seat next to Jonathan rather than the one across the table.

The invasion of the personal zone he had established made the Cadre leader a little nervous. "First, in the transportation of the nuclear waste. Second, in your ability to safely fire this gun without rupturing the canisters and spreading that waste. And finally, if everything goes as you plan, will it cause disturbances in the Earth herself?"

"I'm a little surprised you aren't worried about us exploding the nuclear material." Peter shifted his chair so it was facing him. "But I must admit that last one is new."

"Then you haven't even considered the environmental impact if you succeed?"

"Actually we have. Leo—that's Leo Dayton, our CEO— hired two geo-chemists and posed that very question to them. They ran through the numbers for us and determined if we shot a canister into the same spot at intervals of at least ten minutes apart, the rates of magma flow, canister destruction, and waste dispersion would keep any of the potential waste from developing a critical mass. They assumed a worst case scenario of 100% weapons grade material in their calculations, since we would have no idea what was actually in any of the canisters we would be firing."

"But where are those numbers? And where are all the other details about your operation? CADRE is very web-oriented in our investigations, but also has print research capacity. We have been unable to find out anything about the nuts and bolts of your operation."

"You have to understand, Mr. Peters. Most of what we are working on is proprietary information. Until we actually have a monopoly on this technology, with the patents to enforce it, we would be vulnerable to other companies stealing our designs. This is a multi-billion dollar project, we simply can't afford to take that chance."

"But you have to give us, and the public, something. You

can't really believe you have all the answers? You can't really believe that your project couldn't benefit from an open public debate? At the very least, it will let everyone know what is about to happen!"

"And this is where your group comes in, I suppose?"

"No. I came here today to ask you to call the whole thing off."

"We've come too far for that to happen. We've already run several proving trials and..."

"That's what I mean. Why all the secrecy? Why not come out in the open? Every other company in this country has to file environmental impact statements, 'Right-To-Know' disaster plans, along with hazardous material storage and disposal statements. We can't find anything on Nuclear Recyclers Inc. Why is that?"

"Leo—Mr. Dayton—got us a waiver from the DOE until we had enough research into the project to see if it was feasible."

"Do you really want to hide behind a cloak of governmental secrecy? Is that how you plan to get the American public to support your project?"

Peter looked at his watch. It was almost three o'clock; he had to get down to the lobby soon. "You've given me a lot to think about." He stood up. "But I have to be going now. Is there somewhere I can reach you with the information you wanted?"

Jonathan stood up also, knowing that this interview was over. "Just post it on the web, we'll find it."

"No, we can't do that for proprietary reasons," Peter said as he took Mr. Peters' hand for a goodbye handshake. "But I would be willing to share the information with your group, if you were willing to sign a non-disclosure agreement. Even listen to your advice on how to best inform the public. After all, what we are doing is for their benefit."

Jonathan pulled a business card from a shirt pocket and handed it to Dr. von Scorio, then made his way to the suite's door. "I hope you mean that, Dr. von Scorio. We will be waiting for your call."

Chapter Fifteen

Peter understood, when he had gotten up the next morning, why Mr. Westfield had scheduled their trip for a nine o'clock start. With limousines at their disposal, most of the men would be sleeping off the previous night in the hour-long trip from Las Vegas to the Yucca Mountain Storage Facility. Peter, who had turned in early to think about what Mr. Peters had discussed with him yesterday, had nothing to do on this trip but look at the miles and miles of desert they drove through. He wished he'd at least thought to bring something to read.

Maybe a website would be a good idea, he thought. But that would mean yet another drain on the resources they'd need to complete the gun's construction. He hoped Leo would figure out some way to get the most PR out of this trip so his time here wouldn't be wasted. So far, the reporters that were following in the fleet of rental cars behind them had been more interested in Congressman Blair's reelection campaign.

They came to a stop in front of a chain-link fence gate. Peter, being in the second limousine, watched as a young army sentry checked the papers the congressman's driver had brought for him. He made a brief trip back to his air-conditioned sanctum. At least, Peter hoped the poor boy had air-conditioning in his guard hut; it was 90 degrees outside already. He made a phone call while a second guard walked all around the parked vehicles holding a detection dog on a leash. After a minute, the guard in the hut bent over to press something on his desk. The gate slid to the right, opening the way for the convoy of automobiles. He returned the paperwork to the first driver before any of them entered the compound.

Watching behind him, Peter noted that while each of the press cars had to stop at the gate, none of them were turned away.

Leo stretched as he woke up, forcing Peter to push away the arm he was pressing into his face. Jason shook himself into an almost-alert position, while Westfield simply opened his eyes. Of the three in the dual seats with Peter, Westfield now appeared the most awake. Working for the Senator the way he did, the aide had to have developed an incredible tolerance for late night congressional parties.

Westfield checked his watch and pressed the window control for the dark glass separating the driver from his charges. Peter could hear the mechanical drivers rolling the window down and out of Westfield's way.

"We still meeting the plant manager at the storage entrance, Bill? Or has Lynch and Blair changed our schedule again?"

"No, Mr. Westfield, we're still heading for the loading dock entrance into the mines."

"Thanks." Closing the window again, he pulled a cell phone from an inner pocket of his suit coat and called the other driver to confirm that there had been no further changes, then dialed the plant manager to let him know they would be there in a couple of minutes.

As they approached a massive hole in the side of the mountain, Peter could see an automated ramp going from an unloading dock into the hole. Three flatbed semi-trailer trucks were waiting; each had three of the huge travel canisters loaded on their flatbed. There was a small shack at the base of the loading ramp and a man in a business suit waving at them. *90 degrees outside*, thought Peter, *and the guy is in a business suit?* Turning his head he looked at the vehicles following them. *Oh, the press.*

The two limousines pulled up to the shack. "Wait here a second," Westfield said as he opened the side door and got out. He walked up to the plant manager and talked to him for a couple of minutes.

Then he walked over to the congressional limousine and helped Senator Lynch and Congressman Blair out. Leaving their aides to fend for themselves, he walked back to the limo Peter was in.

He opened the side door and motioned for everyone to exit. "Okay, gentlemen, it's time for our tour."

Harold McTaggish, the plant manager, was introduced to everyone and led them past the unloading dock. He radioed one of his operators to have a robotic forklift approach them at the head of the ramp and showed off the remote controlling characteristics built into the unit.

"Henry, grab a 55-gallon drum of Polysorb and run the forklift into pillar 55G." The lift drove over to the chemical storage area, found the indicated drum, rotated its prongs for a grab and picked it up. The forklift then turned towards one of the internal pillars and proceeded at high speed towards it. It stopped inches from the pillar. "Sensors in the forklift can detect an obstruction and bring the unit to a halt," he said, "until the operator has time to access what he did wrong and take corrective actions."

He radioed the operator again. "Henry, drive the forklift over the loading dock. Miss the ramp entirely." The machine sped off to the end of the loading dock at close to 20 miles per hour, then it slammed to a stop at the edge without going over. "Avoidance features again. If it's not safe, this vehicle won't follow your commands. We're looking for a Zero Accident Environment at this facility, gentlemen.

"And remotely. No human need ever come into contact with the travel canisters once they are loaded," he concluded. "Once we've unloaded the trucks, these remotes place the canisters onto the low-bed mine transports just inside here." He opened a door leading into the mountain, while the operator activated the large loading doors and his forklift proceeded in through them.

Inside was a large garage-like facility. Tools were racked for the repairs of the various robotic vehicles used, with the necessary space off to the side to make those repairs. Which was fortunate, since the press corps joining them was filling up that extra space.

"Sir," Peter could hear one of them call out, "could you run that forklift into the pillar again."

108

Leading away from the loading bay was a large tunnel heading deep into the mountain. It was lighted by a string of lights along the ceiling running down its length on either side. Peter could discern several branches from the main tunnel a good distance away. They were standing next to an empty tractor rig that had a bed for carrying the canisters barely an inch over the top of its set of twelve 8-inch tires. Even this low to the ground, the canisters would have only three inches of clearance as they went down the tunnel system. Peter saw one being loaded at the far end of the loading bay.

McTaggish again used the drum of floor-dry to demonstrate the loading procedure. "Each vehicle can hold five of the containers, and once loaded, the operator can remotely drive the canisters to where they will sit for the next 100,000 years. Let me show you the control room."

He lead them into a room with almost a hundred monitors mounted on the wall and a large work station in the center of the room. Two operators each had control of six feet of terminals at this 12-foot hub. Both of them were neatly dressed in a white dress shirt and tie.

They both had their hands out in front of them and wrapped in gloves, with data wiring coming from those gloves. From their actions, Peter could get an idea of the type of machinery they were operating.

"We have this room set up so two separate shifts can be working at the same time. This allows for a smooth transition from one shift to its replacements. Since we are working nine-hour shifts, we have two hours of overlap between the two shifts. No, we don't work 24/7. Just a sixteen-hour day, I don't want anyone falling asleep on the job due to low circadian rhythms. Should a situation require a peak loading of the facility, those overlap times would give us the capacity to complete the job. And another work station can be brought in if we need another pair of hands."

He walked up to the bank of monitors built into the wall. "This wall gives us the ability to rapidly scan any area of the complex to see what's happening. Everything you see here is also recorded on a twenty-four-hour recording. Should the unthinkable occur and we have an accidental spill, our disaster team is trained to respond either robotically or in HazMat gear."

"Very impressive, Mr. McTaggish," began Senator Lynch, "but exactly what happens when the facility is full?"

"We have the ability to drill more tunnels into the mountains north of the current complex and continue to absorb the nation's output of nuclear waste. But based on our initial size, we shouldn't need to do that within our lifetimes."

"But we're talking about having to store this stuff for 100,000 years," said Congressman Blair. "What is the prediction during that period?"

"Sir, there is no way any storage facility could keep absorbing nuclear material for that length of time. We've never run those calculations; the variables would be impossible to predict."

Peter, who had stopped behind an unloading forklift operator and had been watching canisters taken from the low beds and set next to other containers deep in some cavern, looked up at Blair's remarks and saw the congressman stare at him for a moment. He had that faraway look of someone deep in thought.

* * *

An hour later, they were walking away from the reviewing stands after watching the disaster drill staged for their benefit. Representative Blair pulled Peter aside as everyone else made their way to the podium built especially for the press conference the two members of Congress had planned.

"I just want you to know that I don't trust for-profit enterprises when our national security is on the line, Mr. von Scorio. But I can't avoid the fact that we're pushing this issue onto future generations, and it could have disastrous consequences to this planet, let alone America. So I'll go along with your proposal. I'll put congressional and regulatory watchdogs in your facility to keep an eye on you guys and watch everything you do.

And if it looks to me that you're cutting corners to maximize profits or compromising our national security, I'll nationalize your company and lock you away so deep you'll forget what daylight looks like. Am I clear?"

"Crystal clear, Congressman. We actually do want to keep the public reliably informed."

"I don't care what you want. Farnsworth sent me on this little junket to convince me of the folly of perpetual storage. Okay I'm convinced. You have an answer to this problem, I'm not sure that it's the right one. So I plan to keep a very close eye on you, not give you the PR bonanza you're looking for. Don't screw up!"

Representative Blair didn't wait for a reply. He quickly turned and marched over to the podium where Senator Lynch was already monopolizing the assembled media.

Chapter Sixteen

Neil drove his black, FBI-issued Ford Escape up the dirt West Virginia road. As he got close to the mine entrance, news vans from several different agencies began lining each side of the road. Twice he had to stop to allow the employee from the temporary Starbucks facility to dash across in front of him.

He maneuvered around so he could parallel park in front of the West Virginia State Patrol Officer guarding the barricade tape. After locking his vehicle, he walked around it and approached the Officer.

"FBI," he announced, holding his badge for the Officer to examine.

"I was told to expect you," he responded, "though I don't see how you can help." He lifted the tape so Neil could duck under it.

"Probably not with the rescue. How many are still trapped underground?"

"A total of fifteen miners were in the mine when it exploded." He turned and led Neil towards a large tent that had been erected to house the command personnel. "They radioed in that everyone was far enough in to be away from the blast when it happened, but we haven't gotten to any of them yet." As they got to the tent, they each grabbed one side of the entrance flap and walked in. "We had to stop our efforts when we discovered the unexploded bombs." Stopping in front of a blue-suited man wearing a "Police" vest and a green campaign hat who stood as tall as Neil's 6-foot frame, "Sir!"

"Thank you, Officer Conrad. I'll take Agent Corsair from here. Return to your post."

"Yes, sir." The officer turned 180 degrees and marched from the tent.

"Neil Corsair," Neil began before he was cut off.

"I know. Your office was thorough when we contacted them. Right down to your photo. I'm Lieutenant Mark Gibbons," the officer announced. "In addition to being the FBI and ATF liaison, I am also Incident Commander."

"You certainly have enough equipment set up here," Neil said as he noted the banks of communication gear, the large table with maps both rolled and ready for use, and the ATF mobile lab on the back of the tent. "Is that Harold Fellows back there?"

"ATF Agent Fellows is working on identifying the unexploded ordinance we found in the mine entrance." He began walking around the large center table.

"Then it is military?"

Gibbons just nodded as he passed the tent flap to Neil.

Sitting in front of a computer screen that showed a microscopic slice of explosive was a short, stocky man in a green polo shirt with an ATF vest over the top of it.

Neil dropped his hand on the man's left shoulder. "Found anything interesting, Harold?"

The man slightly jumped, swiveled his chair and said, "Agent Corsair." Then he jumped up and grabbed the FBI man's hand. "I'm glad you could make it."

"Your message said you found something?"

"I still need to run a full analysis back at the lab, but look at these taggants." He centered the computer image on one of the plastic strips and increased the magnification until the lettering on it could be read. "That's the same code as was on the Semtek we found at the rail explosion and the Chemical plant attack."

"Could this be the same guy?"

"That's what I'm thinking. And why I had Lieutenant Gibbons get in touch with you."

"Thanks." Neil turned back to the State Patrol Officer, "You have a crime scene here, Lieutenant. If you find any more of this Semtek, rush a sample to the FBI lab. If this guy is leaving some of his ordinance unexploded, it means he's getting sloppy. Maybe sloppy enough to leave a fingerprint."

Neil took two steps to the door before turning back to the Lieutenant. "And let those men know down there that everyone in the Bureau is pulling for them."

Chapter Seventeen

As he walked down the central aisle back to his seat at the main witness desk in the Senatorial Committee chamber, a few things came to Special Agent Alan Turner's attention. Since they had broken for lunch, news crew with their cameras and lights had been brought into the chamber. Also, the five chairs at their desk had been reduced to a single brown leather upholstered office chair with only his placard anointing it. Despite none of the Senators being in the room yet, the gallery was filled to capacity.

So that was the text messages everyone else got at lunch, they were dismissed by the committee, Alan thought as he stood for the Senators as they filed into the room and took their seats at their semicircular raised desk. *I thought we were supposed to keep the Watkins case under wraps?*

"Order, will everyone please come to order," Committee Chairman Wyoming Senator Richard Marquart began after all his fellow Senators were seated. "Please, everyone take your seats. I hereby reconvene this session of the Senate Homeland Security Oversight Committee. I'll remind the witness that he is still under oath."

After sitting down, Alan bent forward and spoke into the only microphone left on the desk. "I understand, Your Honor."

"Are you prepared to give testimony to this committee?"

"I am, Your Honor. On July 17th, members of the Milwaukee bureau launched the raid that apprehended one Lawrence Watkins and five others."

Senator Marquart cut him off, "Excuse me, Special Agent Turner. This committee is not interested in the details of an already completed investigation. You are here today to inform us of your progress with the Eco-terrorism cases that have plagued our great nation these last few months. What have you been doing about the eco-sabotage that is destroying our way of life?"

"We have a team looking into the incidents," Alan began as he stumbled through his notes. There had been three other completed investigations that the committee had asked him to speak about, with the simultaneous triple physical- and cyber-banking robberies that the Watkins case represented being the most spectacular. He had to set those aside to get down to the file Neil had given him just before he left the office.

"I'm glad you have a team looking into them. But I was hoping for a little more action from our nation's premiere law enforcement organization," the Senator baited him.

"Ah, here they are," Alan was glad that for once, Neil had filed his report in a file folder. He pushed all his other notes to his left. Then he opened the folder and spread out the papers, searching for the most recent analysis. "I have placed Special Agent Neil Corsair in overall charge of this investigation. He has several agents in the field investigating the incidents. Just this morning he returned from the West Virginia mine explosion."

"And what, pray tell, did he find out?"

"We suspect this to be another incident caused by the same terrorist from many of the earlier incidents. Semtek was involved in this occurrence, but we have to wait for Quantico to confirm that it was the same batch as was used before."

"So you're just waiting for this man to strike again?"

"Sir, his pattern of attacks has been fairly random up to now."

"There is a pattern here, Special Agent Turner, and it is your job to find it. Predict where he will strike next and be there to stop him. Is that too much for your country to ask of the FBI?"

"No, sir. I assure you we have every available resource trying to figure out who this man is and apprehend him." Alan was on the defensive now. *Why is this Senator attacking the FBI?*

"A fact, I understand, that had to be anonymously faxed to the Bureau. Otherwise, you wouldn't even have connected the dots. You wouldn't even have started a proper investigation. You would still be fumbling around in the dark. Are you relying on someone out there," the Senator swept his hand out to the audience, "to do your work for you?"

"Sir, Special Agent Corsair has been working this case since the incident in Oregon. There is no better man for this job."

"Isn't there?" The Senator leaned forward and spoke more forcefully into his microphone as he grabbed a sheet of paper from his desk. "This fax would say otherwise. Somewhere out there is a patriot doing the job the FBI is incapable of. How do you answer that, Special Agent Turner?"

"The Bureau does not condone vigilantes. When a private citizen provides us with a lead, we have always investigated it." *I don't remember that fax being released to the Oversight Committee,* Alan thought. *How did he get ahold of it?* "Right now, this terrorist has stayed behind the scenes, working through surrogates that couldn't give us any details to begin to prepare a proper profile. But we are continuing to collect evidence, and he will slip up. We will find out who he is and bring him to justice."

"I hope so, Special Agent Turner, I certainly hope so. For as you can see, America is watching your progress." Senator

Marquart pointed to each of the network cameras that were covering his hearing. "Should the Bureau be too antiquated to carry out investigations in today's world, we may have to look into another agency to take over that job."

Chapter Eighteen

Carlos followed Mike Farrel into the large production building, a building large enough to have hosted a World Cup soccer match in it, if the space wasn't being used to construct so many things, simultaneously.

A ring, over fifteen feet in diameter, was suspended from the ceiling and moving from one end of the building to the other by a large overhead crane. Two more were set up on the far end; each had two men welding clips and brackets for the electrical components to be later installed. On the end they came in, three more were mounted on mobile racks so their three-piece structure could be maneuvered around and welded together. On one side of the room's center were two different styles of submersibles. Carlos recognized the Alvin that was being modified, but he'd never seen the cigar-shaped one that was also there. On the opposite side, an even larger vessel was being constructed. It was round and single-storied, like some type of military bunker. He could see sparks coming from the openings where windows were likely to be installed, so something was being done to its interior.

"Mr. Roland," the HR manager said as he adjusted his hard hat for the nth time. "I know we spent a lot of time this morning going over safety manuals, but I think you can now see why we need those rules. Working in here can be quite dangerous unless we maintain situational awareness and watch out for our fellow workers."

"You do have a lot of construction going on here," Carlos said to keep him talking while he thought about the vulnerable points in this abomination's construction.

"Yes, and this is just the beginning of the adventure. Your underwater welding skills are impressive, as well as knowledge of submersible operations. I think you will find this job quite a challenge, once we actually get working underwater. Oh look, there's Dr. von Scorio. I need to introduce you to him."

They walked across the construction building to where a young man wearing old blue jeans, a Cal Tech tee-shirt, and a white hard hat—compared to Carlos's green one—stood holding a darkened screen in front of his eyes to watch the welders install a third console in the bunker.

The noise that greeted them at the facility's entry way was considerably quieter than inside this bunker they were now entering. Carlos was glad for the earplugs he'd been required to insert before they'd entered the building.

"Peter," Mr. Farrell shouted as he tapped the man on the shoulder. When the man turned, he spoke loud and slow to be heard over the machining tools turning out the precision components other workers were installing. "Peter, I'd like you to meet our newest employee. This is Charles Roland."

The man looked Carlos up and down, then offered his hand. "Pleased to meet you, Mr. Roland. While my name is Dr. Peter von Scorio, I encourage everyone working here to call me Peter. We need too many differing ideas to make this thing work to get hung up on rank around here. You come to us with an impressive resume, I hope we can keep you challenged until our water trials. 'Cause then I know we will." Turning to his production manager, Peter continued, "Have you introduced him to Carol yet, Mike?"

"No, I think she's in the dock yards today. But I saw you over here."

"Understood. I can take him over to her if you want. I need to see where they're at, anyway."

"Thanks, Peter, I've got another interview in half an hour. It's going to be quiet around here when we finally get everybody we need."

"For you, maybe. I'll see you about five." They watched as

Mr. Farrell walked back towards the entrance to the production facility.

"Shall we see if we can find your new boss, Mr. Roland? May I call you Charles?"

"Of course, Mr. von Scorio."

Chapter Nineteen

"Director Turner," Neil said as he closed the Director's door behind him.

"Sit down, Neil." Without getting up, he motioned to the two chairs in front of his desk. After Neil got comfortable, "I hope you have some progress for me on those eco-terrorism cases."

"They keep rolling in, sir. Just this morning we had another report of an aborted attempt to blow up the Garrison hydroelectric Dam in North Dakota."

"I was hoping for just a little more than a catalog of what is going on out there."

"I need to get the Semtek they recovered from this latest incident. Yeah, Semtek again! If its analysis is the same as the rest, we are looking at all but the earliest case being explosives from not only the same manufacturer, but the same batch. I suspect it all came from that Armory job last year. The one where a one-ton case of Semtek was stolen before it could be loaded into their warehouse.

"We've managed to pull fingerprints from a couple of crime scenes, in particular some of the unexploded ordinance." Neil passed a file folder across the light tan desk of his boss. "In each case, we have identified all of them except one set. And in each of those cases, that one set belongs to the same individual."

"I thought you had identified the groups involved in each incident. The separate groups, both physically and ideologically separate groups! One man was a member of each?"

"From the survivors we've been able to question, he was more than a mere member. Carlos Ramirez, Charles Newman, Carl Gaia; he goes by many names. He is always a new recruit and always comes in with a plan for the attack. The problem is that his prints are not in any of the American, European or Terrorist databases we have access to, nor do any of his descriptions match."

Director Turner sat back and thought for a moment. "Widen your search." He opened a side drawer on his desk, pulled out a flash drive, which he then handed over to Agent Corsair. "This will give you access to the Israeli Secret Police database. If he is a foreign-grown terrorist, they may have a record. You can use those files for twenty-four hours, then I want them returned."

"Thank you, sir."

As Neil started to rise from his chair, the Director added, "Twenty-four hours, Agent Corsair, and no copying those files."

Chapter Twenty

Finally, Carlos thought. *We will get to the good stuff.*

"Now that we have acquainted all of you with the basics of what we do here at Marine Workers, Inc., it's time to show you the various pieces of equipment your respective companies have sent you here to learn how to operate," said the athletic, middle-aged woman instructing the dozen submersible operators assembled in the training facility of Marine Workers, Inc.

With all the work of assembling components for Mr. von Scorio's Waste Gun being conducted in their land facilities, Ms. Bancroft had sent Carlos, along with David Wong, Mike O'Donnell, William Danzig, and Judith Hurley up to the Virginia headquarters of Marine Workers, the company building some of the submersibles they'd be using. They were in for a month of training.

"Our first stop will be the assembly building, to let you see how the vessels you will be piloting are put together." As she walked over to the classroom doors, they retracted to allow everyone through.

Being located just across the bay from Newport News, Marine Workers' assembly building was located so they could have direct access to the ocean for launches of their completed vessels. Carlos could smell the clean, sea-laden air as they crossed the parking lot from the main building to the construction facility. *This is how air should smell,* he thought. *And will again, once I cleanse man from his continued fouling of it.*

"Mostly we produce ROVs here at Marine Workers," she explained as she waved at the half dozen Remote Operated Vehicles in various stages of construction they walked past. "But that is not what you guys are interested in." As they moved away from the ROVs, she pointed ahead. "This is our Exosuit, and our DeepWorker."

Most of the group peeled off to get a closer look at the vessels. Carlos saw something in the far end of the facility and drifted over to it.

"That is our newly-developed Dolphin, a two-man fully self-sufficient submarine. No surface support is needed for its operation. It will be fifty foot in length with a wing extension of twenty feet and two separate decks. This will allow the two-man crew to maintain the craft for up to two months of continuous underwater operation. With contracts from the AEC and the Navy, we have managed to equip her with the smallest nuclear power plant ever deployed on Earth. This vehicle will be in a class all its own."

"What will be her top speed?" Carlos said just above a whisper.

"We're looking at a submersed speed of 25 knots. But we haven't completed one for sea trails yet. She will be fast, though.

"But you're not here for this vehicle." The instructor draped her arm over Carlos' shoulder. "Let me introduce you to the

DeepWorker, the vessel you're here to learn about." She turned and led him back to the other trainees.

With this, I can shut down those burrowing into You, Carlos said internally. *With this, I can put an end to humanities fouling of your oceans. It will be mine!*

* * *

After three more days of text book instruction, the class was introduced to the simulators; ten boxes mounted in a special room of the main building. Each one was switchable to simulate the operations of any of the vehicles sold by Marine Workers, Inc. During the day, the crew from Nuclear Recyclers focused their training on the DeepWorker model as well as the ExoSuit. At night, Carlos slipped out of the dorm located on the second story of the building and switched to a Dolphin simulator. As he watched them complete the construction of the submarine, he became comfortable enough to know he could steal it.

Chapter Twenty-One

Carol Bancroft, holding a steaming coffee cup, took her seat around the conference room table for the weekly senior staff meeting. Mike Farrell caught the door before it could finish swinging shut and entered.

"Mike brings the donuts next week," David Wong announced.

"Lay off, Dave," he growled. "I keep finding pieces of clay in several of the already completed rings. I just had to pull a couple of the guys off construction to begin a complete re-inspection. We're going to lose a week on the schedule because of it."

"Any idea where the clay came from?" Peter put down his

donut and asked.

"This last one," Mike explained, "isn't one of the ones we used in that earlier test. It hasn't even left the facility. And there's nothing in its components that could have leaked this type of material."

"Do we know exactly what this 'clay' is?" asked Carol.

"No, but with this last batch, we should have about a half pound we could send out."

"Ship it out to the Louisiana State University," Peter began.

"With a confidentiality contract," legal counsel, Jason Riley, jumped in with. "No point in creating any press coverage over this until we know what we are dealing with."

"Once we know what this stuff is and where it's coming from, we can take reasonable steps to deal with it," added Leo. "Right, Peter?"

"All we can do now is clean it out, Leo."

"If that's concluded," Leo added. "Let get this meeting started so we can get back to the fun stuff. Carol, any progress report on the UW operators you sent off for training?"

"Shelia keeps sending me glowing reports of their progress. One of them seems to be doing extra simulator training at night. That Charles Roland you hired the week before they went up to Virginia," She reported.

"That reminds me," Louis Reed, their HR director for all of a month. "I need to get the last several employment verifications sent in."

"Better take care of that today," Jason said. "We don't want to run afoul of simple governmental regulations like those."

* * *

The computer on Neil Corsair's desk dinged as a completed search request popped up on his monitor. The set of fingerprints he had submitted for identification had finally found a match, one that not even the Israeli database could identify. Now he had a name to go with those prints, a Charles Roland! Probably a

122

fake, but it was a lead, something to pursue, something to work on.

As he was getting up from his desk to report to Director Turner and put in a travel request to New Orleans, his phone rang. "FBI. Agent Corsair," he answered.

"Neil, this is Fellows at ATF. We have another match on that SEMTEK. Nuclear Recyclers, Inc., of Louisiana, just sent a sample to LSU. Since it was a controlled explosive, the confidentiality agreement they signed was invalid. It's the same stuff, Neil, right down to the taggants."

Neil thought for a second, tapped a few keys on his computer, and said, "There's a flight leaving Dulles in two hours. Can you arrange to meet me on it?"

Chapter Twenty-Two

"Talk about full circle," Harold commented to Agent Corsair at the car rental counter. "Our guy was just three hours away from where we started."

"But only if we hurry, Harold." Corsair grabbed the receipts from the counter clerk and dashed out of the small parking lot office. "He seems to have a sixth sense about getting caught. I don't want him slipping away this time."

Harold could feel his friend's sense of urgency and slipped through the door before it could finish closing. The FBI man chose the first SUV they came to, red—not the usual black color—so he sprinted around to the passenger side so he didn't get left behind. "It's one in the morning, surely he's asleep with the other trainees?"

"I want to believe that, but I only will once I see it." Agent Corsair engaged the car, backed out of the stall and left the parking garage at the posted speed limit, not one mile per hour less!

* * *

"Test trials for this magnificent machine are about to begin," Carlos said to no one else in the cabin of the Dolphin prototype. "Just a few hours ahead of the schedule."

Twelve hours earlier, the wall separating the fabrication side of the construction facility and the launch side of it had been wheeled aside. The Dolphin, sitting on her cradle, was winched from one side of the facility to the other. She was due to be launched at 10 the next morning.

The launch side was a two-level facility which was rapidly filling with water to allow the Dolphin to develop enough buoyancy to float out of its dry dock cradle and into the deep water lane for launching into Hampton Roads. Now mere minutes separated Carlos from his new campaign to hit Gaia's defilers where it hurt the most, their pocketbooks.

But it was an agonizing ten minutes before he heard the alarms crying all around the facility he was in. Lights sprang on as the Dolphin began to float off the cradle she had rested on these many months of construction. Banging noises came from the doors that his pursuers discovered they could not open against the pressure of the flooded launch facility.

As he engaged lateral thrusters, he heard the pumps reversing. His pursuers were trying to lower the water level and stop him. "Too late," he laughed in the sub's control room. "You are too late."

The Dolphin automatically lined itself up in the launch lane. Almost simultaneously, Carlos engaged his forward thrusters and triggered the SEMTEX charges he had previously placed on the sea doors. The ship was clearing those doors as the smoke and debris floated into the harbor.

As soon as he was free of the Marine Workers facility, he set his depth for twenty meters along a course for the open ocean.

"It is time to trick out my new ride," he announced as he pushed the Dolphin faster.

* * *

Neil heard and felt the explosion that shook the marine end of the building. It gave him an additional boost of strength as he pushed on the locking level of the hatch barring him from his quarry.

It gave!

As the hatch fell inward with his weight, a small amount of water trickled back into the construction side of the entryway. Neil followed the hatch through in time to see the submarine's lights go dark as it dove beneath the calm of Hampton Roads.

Chapter Twenty-Three

"How much longer are you planning on holding up our production?" Leo asked the FBI agent. Every day that the FBI spent combing the Nuclear Recyclers' facility for whatever Charles Roland had left behind was preceded by a meeting in the conference room of the Marriott Hotel adjacent to the construction facility. No unauthorized personal was allowed in the construction facility until the search was complete. And that included NR employees or officers.

"Sir, so far we have pulled approximately five pounds of plastic explosive and detonators out of the magnetic rings you've been building. We haven't even gotten to the ones you've got in storage or any of your other equipment." Agent Corsair leaned forward with his forearms framing the reports he was quoting. "We still don't know the extent of the sabotage Mr. Roland has done your company."

Jason Riley placed his hand on Leo's shoulder. "Now, Leo, they're just being thorough. And that's to our benefit."

Arnold Jenkins added, "Imagine the press we'd get if a catastrophic explosion happened during one of our undersea tests?

125

Or worse, during an actual cylinder disposal? No, let them be as thorough as they want!"

"This prolonged delay is making some of our investors nervous," Leo said, falling back into his chair, which rocked just twice before holding in a back-leaning position.

"Bring them in and let me talk to them," Arnold replied. "After all, reassuring people is what you are paying me for."

"You work with congressmen, Arnold," Leo corrected.

"Investors are people, too, Leo."

"Gentlemen, if we can get back to this briefing, I can get back to work clearing your facility," Agent Corsair injected. "I understand that the five completed rings had been out to sea during the course of Mr. Roland's employment and so can be taken off the search list. Unless *Damocles* was docked at any time during that period?"

Peter von Scorio leaned forward. "No, she has been out to sea, running tests of submersible handling for the last month. The group of pilots Mr. Roland was going to be a part of would have been put aboard after their training at Marine Workers."

"Why did I ever hire that guy?" Louis Reed moaned.

Carol broke in, "He seemed a good worker to all of us Lou. As eager as the rest of us to see this project work."

"But there are tests. We run batteries of tests to determine worker compatibility. How did I miss the signs?"

"Mr. Reed," the FBI man said. "After every terrorist incident, we see 'the signs that we missed'. Everyone does, every time. They are never clear until after the incident. Hindsight is wonderful, it shines like a beacon, but it can also be a debilitating thing. Learn from it, but don't let it make you second guess every future decision you make. Charles Roland is the bad guy here. Not you."

"If only I'd..."

"NO," Agent Corsair stopped his recriminations. "FBI profilers have gone over the same pre-employment data you had. They could find nothing in them to indicate he was the terrorist we've been looking for."

Leo added, "We need you, Lou. You have the sound judgment we need."

"So how much longer do you think this'll take, Agent Corsair?" Peter asked through folded fingers.

"Your rings are the most complex pieces of equipment with the most places for hiding Semtek," he began. "Once we have them cleared, it should be just a couple more days. Possibly another week, total."

"The guys should be getting back from training by then," Carol added.

"With the extra manpower, I can ramp up ring production and have enough for deep sea trials a couple of weeks after that," Mike Farrel, the production manager, said.

"Three weeks?" Leo brightened up at something he could use. "I can sell that to the investors."

"Then I think we have a plan," Peter concluded. "Thank you, Agent Corsair. Your efforts are greatly appreciated."

Chapter Twenty-Four

"Carlos, my friend." Abbas Said extended his hand as Carlos stepped off the launch that had taken him from the submarine he had parked in the secluded harbor the West African arms dealer kept for his clients. "What can I do for you today?"

At the northernmost point, which had a depth of 20 meters, was anchored Carlos' purloined submarine, which he had named the *Suelo Defensor*, The Defender of the Earth. Pointing towards it, Carlos explained, "I have recently acquired a new instrument to war against the western capitalists who rape Gaia. I need your help to prepare her for the struggles ahead."

Abbas looked out into the harbor at the craft. "You need some torpedoes, my friend. You're lucky, I have been trying to unload a couple of crates of Russian APR-3Es. With the wings

127

you have on your Dolphin, we can mount aerial release mechanisms that should function like torpedo tubes for you. Unfortunately, you will have to replace your loads once you have fired them off."

"The *Suelo Defensor*, she is no longer the Dolphin. The capitalist enablers of Marine Workers have lost their right to her."

"Of course, my friend, of course. Let's get her into my dry dock and see what we can do." Abbas raised his right hand and snapped his fingers, pointing to the *Suelo Defensor*. A couple of men lounging on the wooden dock jumped into the launch in which Carlos had just landed and sped out to the submarine.

The first man climbed aboard and tied off the launch. Then the other man climbed onto it and opened the forward viewing hatch while his friend entered the aft one. They powered up the craft and cruised her to the docking ramp where about a half dozen men waited. Since the *Suelo Defensor* had a draft of twenty feet, they had to secure her into the docking cradle about ten yards from shore, then winch her in until she fit on the dry dock stand Abbas had for working on ships.

"Come, my friend, it is going to take them about an hour to get her ready for inspection. Let us share a drink and talk about old times. I hear you have lead those capitalist pig-dogs on a merry chase of late?" He led his friend into one of the several pre-fab metal huts around the camp that still had 'U.S. Marine Corps' stenciled on its side. Inside was a complete Marine Corps bar.

* * *

The two men emerged from the bar a couple of hours and several drinks later to inspect Carlos' acquisition. While sea water still dripped from her underside, Abbas ducked under the craft's wings to look at what he had to work with.

"I think we can attach two mounting brackets on the undersides of each wing. That would give you four shots before you had to reload. That you will have to dock somewhere to do, as

128

you don't have enough space inside to mount actual launchers, let alone store any of the torpedoes."

"Four per run should do me quite nicely." Carlos smiled, thinking, *I can do a lot of damage with those loads.*

"Remember, though, the APR-3Es have a depth of only 800 meters. This craft is rated for a much lower depth. You'll have to take that into consideration when you plan your attacks."

"If I must, I must." Carlos began mentally adjusting his targets. *First I will hit the shallower rigs, then blast the support structure of the deeper one.*

Climbing into the cockpit of the submarine, Abbas poked around until he added, "But I think I have something that might make up for that deficiency."

Carlos climbed up and peered in.

"I have a remote control device that we could rig into your dive controls that would allow you to remotely submerge this guy with a car clicker."

"These are great things you can do for me. But I know you, Abbas. How much?"

"For a good friend and comrade like you, one million US."

"That is no small sum." Carlos had to think for a moment, *How much is Mr. Simmons good for?* "I will have to contact my American backer. I will need an internet connection."

* * *

Later the same day, in the offices of Senator Richard Marquart of Texas, Alan Simmons walked in and planted himself in one of the Senator's chairs until the members of the Defense Appropriations Committee left.

"How happy are you with Mr. Rodunate's work so far, Senator?" He sat back and asked after everyone else had left.

The Senator leaned forward on his desk, keeping his voice down against anyone invading this private meeting. "So far, he has stirred thing up quite nicely. His targets have appeared appropriately random but have allowed me to push through just the right legislation. Yes, I like his work quite well."

"He needs another one million dollars."

"Whatever for?" the Senator sat back into his large black leather office chair.

"Remember that theft of the Dolphin from Marine Workers in Virginia last month?"

The Senator nodded.

"That was him. Now he is trying to arm it so he can bring offshore oil production to a halt."

Drumming his fingers on his desk, the Senator delayed his response for a moment. "I'm not overly comfortable attacking oil rigs. But, if he will adhere to the rigs we would like taken out, he could more than be worth that one million dollars."

"He needs the money wired to his associate as soon as possible. Then another week to get the work done, two more to cross the Atlantic back into the gulf before he can begin his actions."

"Then send him a list of our competitor's rigs and money at the same time. Get him going. I'll work up a bill banning any new off-shore drillings permits until the danger he poises is passed. Before long, our associates will be the only ones producing oil from American waters."

Simmons pushed himself out of his chair as the Senator added, "Yes, send him what he needs right away."

Chapter Twenty-Five

The Elevator, an underwater personnel transfer vessel, clanged with the metal on metal contact it established with the Blockhouse. As soon as the lights came on, Frank Walsh, one of the original investors, was the first out of his restraints and heading for the floor hatch. The rest were not long behind. Leo, who was sitting up with the craft's pilot, was bringing up the rear. It hadn't been easy for Peter to persuade him to tag along, Leo didn't like being under so much water.

"Before we go down, or even open that hatch,"—Frank was already reaching for the lever to open it—"We need the Blockhouse to confirm a secure connection has been established. It wouldn't do to have a thousand feet of seawater pouring in."

Frank jerked his right hand back and grabbed it with his left behind his back, while he took a step away from the hatch. No one else offered to take his place as they milled around in the enclosed 5-by-10-foot cylinder waiting for Leo's okay.

"Blockhouse to Elevator," came over the ship's speakers. "Blockhouse to Elevator, you did a fine job, Bill. Clean seal, no leakage. Come on down, guys."

"Roger that," William Danzig replied to the announcement. "I'm looking forward to your VIP lunch spread." The pilot raised his hand and gave Leo an okay sign.

"Mr. Walsh, being the closest, would you do the honors?"

Before any of the six investors had been allowed on this trip, they all had been familiarized with the functioning of both The Elevator and the Blockhouse. Frank pulled the lever above the hatch to the right, jiggled it to confirm it was locked open, then grabbed the bar welded above it, pulled the hatch open until it too locked itself in the upright position. Then he engaged the magnetic bolt to keep the hatch from falling back and smacking anyone on their head. The Elevator was a stable craft, but it did not sit rock steady in the active waters of the Gulf of Mexico.

"What are you guys waiting for?" Harry Trunnel called up. He stood at the bottom of the ladder with his right hand on one of the rungs looking up at the waiting VIPs.

Frank took that as his cue to begin climbing down into the control center he'd help finance. The rest followed him with the pilot, William, bringing up the rear and securing the two hatches behind him.

At the base of the ladder, Dr. von Scorio, Harry Trunnel and Jacob Helman were waiting to greet the group of six owners of Nuclear Recyclers Inc. "Lady and Gentlemen, I'd like to welcome you to our underwater control facility; The Blockhouse."

Peter said, then before continuing, he put his hand on Harry's shoulder. "This is our Operations Manager, Harry Trunnel." Then after a minute of handshaking, "And this is our Electronic Specialist, Jacob Helman." After another minute of handshaking, "If you will follow me, we've set out a sandwich luncheon for you."

"I didn't come down here for a meal," said Patrick Radcliff. "Dad sent me down here to make sure you're going to be able to do what you promised him you could do."

Alan Hoffman interrupted the forty-year old younger man. "Well, I for one would like to see how they eat here under the sea. And try some of that coffee Bill was bragging about on the way down here. Lead on, Dr. von Scorio."

After lunch, Peter led the men from the vessel's galley, through the long-term crew quarters, stopped at the toilets (since Mr. Hoffman had had too much of that coffee), through the rec area and finally to the control room.

"Now, this is something I can understand," Frank Loranzo beamed as they entered the Control Room. "I have invested in enough power companies to know an ergonomic control room when I see one."

"Thank you, sir." Peter moved over to the first desk with monitors mounted on it. "From this station, we will be setting and monitoring the ring alignment. If you turn to page 33, we talk about how critical it is to have the rings aligned in precise order and exactly spaced. Even a minor arrangement error will result in the canister halting its flight in our barrel arrangement. If that happens, we would have to extract it and start the launch process all over again. This station is critical."

The next desk touched the Ring station but was mounted at a forty-five-degree angle to it. "This is our actual firing station. While firing could be accomplished by pressing a single button, we have tied several inspection controls into this operator's duties. Not all travel canisters will be filled to the same weight, water conditions will vary from time to time, and we don't want to impact any of the marine life that may venture into the area, so we will control the force applied to each load from this station."

"This third station," Peter moved to the last desk. "Will keep radio communications open during all operational hours. Mostly to the *Damocles*, but we can also be in immediate contact with the Coast Guard, our Louisiana headquarters. and the U.S. Navy vessels protecting us."

"One man is going to be in charge of everything?" Frank asked.

"Not at first, Mr. Walsh," Leo answered.

Jacob continued, "We can configure this arrangement for up to three people. We have it configured for single man operation for today's test. But for the actual sea trials next month, Carol Bancroft will be controlling the Rings, I will be the Radio Operator, and Mr. Trunnel will be pulling the trigger. I will have this center arranged in a line so each person will have plenty of room to do their jobs."

Peter dropped into the single operator's chair and announced, "I think it is now time to begin today's test. If everyone will have a seat, I will begin.

"We have twenty rings laying on the Gulf floor here, waiting for us to configure them into our Waste Gun." Peter flipped a few switches and illuminated the rings lying flat or stacked against each other.

"Activating the top thrusters, they pick themselves up into a vertical position for further alignment. By sequentially activating their magnetic grappling lines, we get them each into firing position, one at a time."

The ring furthest away did nothing. The next ring wiggled around until it was lined up the same as the first but about 18 inches away. Then the next ring completed the same procedure, followed by the next, until all twenty were lined up, pointing to the underwater trench that was several feet away from the first ring.

"Now that the gun is configured, it's time to load our canister. Today's test will actually use one of the DOE transportation cylinders, empty, of course." Keying the radio on the communication bench, he said, "David, you can bring our bullet into play now." The Deepworker unit with the canister in its claws moved into position behind the closest of the rings.

"The tricky part is getting our bullet into position without grabbing the entire submersible. But we have solved that problem by attaching an airbladder around the canister, setting it to neutral buoyancy and backing the Deepworker away. Once it is clear of the magnetic field, we key the ring to grab the canister and position it in the first ring, ready for firing." Peter used his left hand to adjust the power dial on the control board and his right hand to adjust the touch screen to move the cylinder into place.

"Gentlemen, Lady, if you are ready," he announced. Looking over the nodding heads, he turned back to the board, lifted the plexiglas cover off the firing button and pressed it. With no noise at all, the transportation canister leapt from one ring to the next, drug forward by changing magnetic fields until it flew out the furthermost ring and disappeared across the trench in front of it.

Almost immediately, the several people who were standing around watching Peter control the test firing, staggered and fell as the Bunker shook with the pressure wave that washed over it.

Peter and Leo jumped out of their seats and helped those investors, like young Radcliff, back to their feet. "That's why I asked you to sit in one of our magnetically locked chairs."

"Peter, it's Menendez." Leo pointed at the gash on the 50-ish business man's head. "Help me get him to the Elevator, so I can get him up to *the Damocles* for treatment." Leo supported the rising man by his right shoulder as Harry Trunnel began lifting him by his left.

"We've got everything we need to fix him up down here," Harry offered. "Just get him to the infirmary."

"No point in taking chances," Leo responded.

"Leo's right, Harry. Help him get Mr. Menendez to the Elevator. Make sure to send it back, Leo." *Any excuse*, Peter thought, *any excuse to get back topside*.

Chapter Twenty-Six

FOURTH OIL RIG IN THE GULF CEASES PRODUCTION

Neil Corsair didn't need to read the rest of the article to know what was going on. In the space of twenty-four hours, four off-shore oil platforms had lost their wellhead and had to shut down pumping operations. Since they all were along the same ridge in the Gulf off the coast of Mississippi, something had to be happening there. Since they had occurred in an easterly sequence, Neil knew that something was Charles Roland and his stolen submarine.

Flinging the Times to his desk, he called down to Travel. "This is Agent Corsair and I need a ticket to Gulfport-Biloxi International, then a helicopter waiting for me when I get there."

Still listening to his phone, he rose from his desk, threw some reports into his briefcase and grabbed his packed overnight bag from his lower left desk drawer. "I'm going to the oil rigs that just shut down. Yes, each of the ones that just shut down. And I'm leaving now. Just email me the ticket information before I get to Dulles."

He grabbed the closing elevator, a waiting taxi and was lifting off an hour after he had hung up on Travel.

*   *   *

"Hello, Agent Corsair." A tall, tanned man covering his short cropped hair with a round metal hardhat, handed Neil a white plastic, ball-cap style one before they emerged from the prop wash of the helicopter. "Safety regulations. Even shut down," he pulled a pair of safety glasses from his shirt pocket, "it's Safety First."

135

While Neil was putting on the plastic glasses handed him, the oil man spun him around and adjusted the inner band of the hard hat until it was a snug fit on the FBI man's head. "Now let's get out from under this thing," he said, matching his volume to the slowing of the helicopter's propellers, "and into my office where we can hear each other. The name's Henry Williams, and I'm the foreman of this facility."

"Neil Corsair," then realized how redundant that was. The man had greeted him by name.

"I'm glad to have you out here, sir." He opened and held the door for Neil to enter the office side of the facility. "It was a bit unusual, the way our rig just went down." He opened another door, this one leading into a room with two file cabinets, a desk and a refrigerator topped with a microwave oven. "Have a seat." He stopped over by his refrigerator. "Something to drink?"

"Water would be wonderful. It's been a fast trip from D.C."

Grabbing a bottle of water and a can of Diet Coke, he handed the former to the FBI Agent, then crossed around to his desk.

"We have a device on the wellhead, the Blowout Prevention System, or BOP. It slams the thing shut when something happens to the flow. Prevents leaks into the Gulf. Well, our radio communication with that device says it has done just that. All the wired sensors to it stopped feeding us data, like they were all severed." He held up his hand before Neil could interrupt. "We've had a false alarm or two since it was installed two years ago. Both were computer misinterpretations of the wireless signal. So we have a suite of wired sensors to collect enough data to allow us to make an informed decision to override the shutdown."

"And they have all stopped transmitting?" Neil asked.

"All at the same time. And sea water began coming up through the pipeline before we could shut off the pumps on our end. Something cut that line, Mr. Corsair, severing it from the wellhead. And not just us, I've been in touch with a couple of other rigs in the area. The same thing happened to them."

"What's the next step in your investigation?"

136

"We sent an ROV down about an hour ago. It should be reaching the wellhead in a few minutes. Would you care to join me in our control room to watch?" Mr. Williams pushed his chair away from his desk and rose.

"I would love to."

* * *

A variety of hard-hatted individuals stood behind the control-operator. She was seated in front of the monitor displaying the video from the ROVs camera. Settling silt was descending around the ROV, silt that it had not gotten deep enough to disrupt. Then the jagged top of the wellhead came into view.

"Something blew," said the control-operator.

"Do the logs show any pressure buildup before the incident?" Williams asked.

A white-hatted woman grabbed the log on the control side of the room. "Nothing! The pressure has been steady, within design specs for the last three months. Varying by only a single PSI the entire time."

"So external cause," Neil speculated out loud.

When everyone turned to look at him, he added. "Get lower. I need to see if there is any debris on the ocean floor."

Bringing the ROV lower revealed a line of debris stretching in a narrow cone almost straight north from the wellhead.

"Are the other rigs sending ROVs down to their wellheads, too?" Neil asked.

"It's pretty standard procedure," Williams explained.

"Contact each of them. I want as much of that debris as possible recovered. An internal explosion should spew debris everywhere; something hit that wellhead. And something in that debris will tell us what hit it. Pack it up and send everything to Quantico as soon as you get it. Mr. Williams, tell that copter to start warming up, I'm off to Louisiana." Neil turned and left the room quick time.

137

Chapter Twenty-Seven

Having worked late the night before getting the *Suelo Defensor* ready for this day's hunting, Carlos was enjoying a large coffee as he looked for the results of his previous days' activities. He'd seen a few newspaper reports of his first four, but no in-depth coverage. But on the morning news shows, he found no mention of anything amiss, nor any coverage on any of the 24-hour media outlets as he scanned through them.

"Wait", he told his hand and flipped back one channel.

"...a national tragedy," the man behind a large desk was saying to the two dozen reporters crowding into what looked like a large office.

"Live: Press Conference with Senator Richard Marquart regarding the disruption of Gulf Oil." Scrolled across the bottom of the screen.

Several hands were in the air before the Senator had even finished. The man to the right and just behind the Senator pointed at one of them. "Simmons," Carlos hissed through his teeth. "Alan Simmons," he repeated in his normal voice. "So, a U.S. Senator is your master. Next time, I will go straight to the American pork through him instead of through you."

"Routine maintenance is normal for any production facility. Do you know something different, Senator?" the reporter asked.

"Local authorities, the Coast Guard, even the FBI have issued statements. They claim these are natural occurrences. Eight facilities, within 48 hours all going offline in such a close geographical proximity to each other? I don't think so. This is an act of terrorism. A Terrorist group out in the Gulf of Mexico is preying on the isolation of American oil rigs, and we have to do something to protect those brave men and women providing America with the resources to make her great."

Hands shot up again and Simmons picked another.

"Senator, Jon Peters of CADRE, are you trying to inflame American passions for this bill you called us here to talk about? The very fact that all facilities are very close together could make their cause a cascading failure, not a series of attacks. From what we at CADRE have heard, the first four were completely contained through the industrial safeguards that were in place."

"I haven't heard of your news outlet, Mr. ..."

"Peters, sir. CADRE is an environmental watchdog group, and if we even suspected what you are claiming, we would be demanding that all off-shore activities be halted. Right now, our analysis is that these off-shore companies have been acting as responsible citizens, causing little to no damage to the environment."

The Senator looked over at his controller. Mr. Simmons called on another reporter.

"What are you planning to do about this terrorist activity?" the reporter asked.

"My American Oil Production Defense Act will halt construction of any new oil rigs..."

Carlos was out the door of his cabin and pulling the cord of his outboard motor before the Senator could finish. He hadn't even shut off the television he had been watching.

"All the rigs on that damned list must be equipped with those accursed shutdown valves," he said to himself as he cruised down the bayou towards the canopied location of his submarine. "No one will even see the damage they are causing unless I find targets without them. I must deviate from their list, I must find my own targets, I will make America pay for the life-blood they are draining from Gaia."

He pulled his boat up against the log mounted vertically as a pier for the two craft and made his way into the *Suelo Defensor*. He began the ship's power up sequence, then consulted the internet for a set of more suitable targets for today's activities.

The Gran Siena was one of the oldest rigs in the northern Gulf. After twenty years, she was still productive because she sat atop one of the largest oil fields in southern Alabama. Best of all, she had never been retrofitted with a Blowout Prevention System.

Cruising down 700 meters to the wellhead of the facility, Carlos brought his vessel to a stationary position while he lined up the first of his two remaining birds at the base of that wellhead. "No chances this time," he said to himself, "no half measures. I will take the whole thing out."

He flipped up the switch to arm his torpedo and pressed the button launching it towards its prey. Seconds later, a very satisfying explosion rocked his location. Rather than waiting for the debris to clear, Carlos turned his submarine upward towards the surface facilities of this oil rig.

Twenty minutes later, he was within 50 meters of the surface, passing the rigs' ballast column. With a single bird left, Carlos meant to have her fly directly into the heart of men raping his mother Earth. Heading bow first towards the surface, directly under the oil platform, Carlos armed his remaining torpedo and sent it soaring. It broke the surface of the Gulf and flew like a bird for about ten meters, plunging into the lower deck of the oil rig before igniting.

Carlos turned the *Suelo Defensor* away from the rig before the falling debris could jeopardize his ship. He surfaced two hundred meters west to observe the carnage he had wrought.

"Today, I gave you two off your list, Mr. Simmons. But I will be ignored no longer. The world will know what they have done and that an avenger is striking back in the name of Mother Earth".

Chapter Twenty-Eight

The crews of the *Halsey* and the *Vella Gulf,* having already seen the distant fireball, were out on the deck by the time the sounds of the explosion washed over their decks. They watched as a wave of water built, approaching each vessel's port side. Some of the sailors scrambled back into the security of their ship's hull. Others attached themselves wherever they could. Some just hung on.

But first, the *Vella Gulf's* left side dropped as the wave prepared to break over it. Followed a moment later by the *Halsey.* Klaxons sounded as both ships rocked under the watery assault. Men on the deck floundered as the Gulf tried its best to wash them overboard.

Tony Harmon was one of the unlucky ones. He didn't have a safety line to attach himself to anything as the wave approached, and had to grab hold of a vent too large for him to completely wrap his arms around. He held for a second before the force of the wave broke his hold on the metal structure and he rolled across the deck, propelled by the speeding Gulf water. He managed to find another sailor's leg to grab hold of as he passed under the far side ship's rail, only to have that grip broken when that sailor jerked to a stop.

Tony fell sideways into the Gulf of Mexico about three feet. His life jacket pulled him back to the surface only to have his head bang on the metal side of the Destroyer.

"Men over board!" cried several of the sailors as they saw their comrades bobbing on the calming sea. Ropes flew down from the deck of the *Halsey.* About four of the six floating sailors grabbed for the lines, but two of them made no effort to save themselves.

Deck Officer Lt. Mark Taylor tossed two circular life preservers into the water, grabbed hold of one of the slack lines and jumped over the railing. Using the rope as a guideline, he bounced a couple of times against the hull before he slipped into the Gulf waters near one of the unconscious sailors.

With practiced effort, he attached the line to the harness ring on the man's life jacket and waved for the men above to haul that fellow sailor up.

Looking around for the other man, Taylor couldn't find him. He looked up to the hands on deck to see them gesturing to his right.

The water was getting peaceful again and he got to Seaman Harmon in mere moments. By that time, Tony was starting to come around. Between their combined efforts, the two of them were being hauled over the ship's railing in only five minutes.

"Thank you, sir," Harmon panted as he pulled himself into a standing position on the now non-rocking deck. Weakly saluted the four-year-older officer as an afterthought.

"You don't get off my ship that easily," replied Lt. Taylor as he returned the salute. "Since you can walk now, get yourself down to sick bay. I have to check on those sailors who are really hurt. I'm just glad you made it, Seaman."

He ordered the other soggy Seamen to sick bay as well while he checked up on the remaining unconscious sailor. After a few instructions, a gurney was provided, the medic checked for neck injuries and sent him down for a proper examination. That was when Lt. Taylor was provided with a functional, dry radio.

"Bridge to Officer of the Deck," it was squawking as it was passed to him. "Officer of the Deck, please acknowledge."

"Officer of the Deck, Lt. Taylor here." He looked around at all the men circling him to find out what was going on.

The voice on the radio changed. "Mr. Taylor, this is Captain Miller. Prepare the deck for cruise speed, we're heading out to investigate that explosion. It came from the direction of the *Gran Siena* Oil Platform. Be prepared to rescue survivors."

"Aye, sir," he said into the radio, then handed it back to its owner. "Okay everyone, prepare to make way. Deploy rescue equipment. It's time to do some real work." The *U.S.S. Halsey* was already under way and turning left before he even finished his orders.

First the smoke became visible to Lt. Taylor as they approached the mangled oil rig. A steady flame danced on the ruins of the once magnificent platform. Where once a miniature city had sat atop the waves of the Gulf, now canted platforms and twisted steel rose above the water the *Halsey* was sailing in.

Burning oil surrounded the structure as Taylor leaned forward in the ship's bow, looking through his binoculars to try and find anyone alive in the wreckage. Eventually, they got close enough to see several oil workers swimming away from the flames that marked the *Gran Siena's* territory.

"Rig for ocean rescue," he barked to his men without even removing the binocular from his eyes. "Chief, prepare a boarding party, in case the Captain orders one."

"Aye, sir." He heard twice in rapid sequence.

He turned back to see what men he had available. "Everyone not involved in those rescue teams, get your eyes on that water. Some of those men may be unconscious and I don't want to leave any of them behind." Before he could turn back to his observations, he heard shouts of identification from his men regarding the floating oil workers.

* * *

Sergeant Henderson brought the rescue boat right up to the central spire of the burning oil platform. From the middle of the craft, Sergeant Richards called out, "The top ten rungs have been sprung from the structure. The ladder is not available."

"Corporal Danvers, Privates Matthew and Reynolds, prepare grappling lines," Henderson barked at his charges. "I want three stretching from the bottom platform in under five minutes."

As the three assembled their rifles to fire hooks and ladders up to a stable spot on the wreckage, Henderson kept making plans. "Richards, sling a grapple gun and see how far you can work that ladder.

"The rest of you get this thing moored to whatever looks secure. Take side arms and as much rescue gear as you can carry. We still don't have a count of how many are left up there."

As Marine Sergeant Richards pulled himself up to the third rung, three rifles barked below him. Three grappling hooks flew up over the railing of the lower oil rig platform. As quickly as the lines could be tested, rope ladders were attach to one end and hauled up to the pulley welded to the end of the grappling hook. As the ladders were fastened to the bobbling navy rescue vessel, marines began climbing up them.

Ten feet below the platform, Richards couldn't climb any further. He unslung his rifle, then drove a grapple hook through the open hatch at the top of the ladder into the main section of the platform. He swung out and pulled himself up the knotted rope onto the rig.

Fires were beginning to die out as the marines began climbing onto the platform, but the twisted metal that now made up the working space of the *Gran Siena* Oil Platform was still extremely hot. Contact with it was to be avoided.

Richards counted six men who had made it to the top and took command of them. "Danvers, Matthew, Reynolds; you three make your way upwards. Send anyone you find down here. Radio if they are too wounded to move."

He looked over to Corporal Reed. "Which means you three are going over to the barracks." He pointed off to the right and the ladder down and inside the rig. "Reed, you're in charge. Same instructions. Now move, we don't know how long this thing has."

As the next three marines emerged from over the railing, "Harris, set up a radio station on this deck. Keep in touch with Henderson. I need to know how many oil workers we are looking for. Davis, McDaniels, help him and keep this deck secure. I'll head for the control room and work my way down. I have to find the foreman of this thing."

He took off up the central ladder two steps to his one. He ran up three levels when he came to the end of the ladder and a hatch leading into a room with enough electronic equipment to make it the obvious control facility. Two men were face down on the floor with a slight trickle of blood oozing from gashes to their heads. One began pushing himself up by the force of his arms when his left one gave out and he fell back down. Richards rushed over to the other figure and checked his vitals before coming to the conscious man's aid.

"Take it easy. Let me do the work," Richards said as he took the man under his right, uninjured shoulder and lifted him into the chair he was also up-righting. "I need to find the Foreman. Do you have any idea where he might have been?"

Touching the blood on the side of his head, he gave the marine a questioning look.

"I suspect it looks worse than it is. Head wounds usually are. Do you know where you are?" Richards addressed the unspoken question.

"I'm Henry Lauden, and the Foreman you are looking for. Is Bekworth okay?" He motioned over to the other man, still laying on the floor.

"His vitals appeared nominal, but I don't want to move him until he regains consciousness or I have to. What happened?"

Lauden looked over the ruined controls of his oil platform and sighed. He turned back to the marine. "First something happened to the wellhead on the ocean floor, it just exploded. Several minutes later, while we were waiting for the oil to start spewing around us, something hit us from below the surface and exploded. Some kind of missile."

"Not good," the marine responded. "How many men were working on this rig today?"

"Twenty were on vacation, so we had about seventy men and women on board. The day shift was on duty, with about twenty-five off, probably in their bunks or the recreation area."

"Harris," Richards called into his individual radio. "Harris, do we have contact with Henderson and the *Halsey* yet?"

"Yes, sergeant," came his acknowledgement.

"How many men have been recovered so far?"

After a minutes' wait, "Fifty-one have been recovered from the water so far. Another ten have appeared at our checkpoint here, and Danvers says he has three who he needs to stabilize before he can move them."

"Sixty-six so far," Richards mentally added up but said aloud.

"That leaves three more," Lauden said. "Has anyone checked the infirmary? Doctor Olson had one man in this morning for a broken toe. Dropped a wench on his foot, then as he was massaging where the steel toe banged into it another wench hit it."

Richards scowled at the Foreman.

"First level off to the right of the drill assembly."

Richards radioed instructions to Danvers' team, who were working the upper structure. As the other man in the control room made a noise and started to rise, Lauden jumped from his chair, instantly grabbed his head, regretting the move, before moving to the rising man. Richards beat him there.

"Take it easy," he said as Lauden made it over to them. "You've had a nasty blow to your head." Richards had noted that the wound had stopped bleeding in his earlier examination.

"Jake, do you know what happened?" the Foreman asked.

"There was a ping on the sonar, Hank. Something was coming up fast. Then an additional ping started coming up faster. So fast I never had a chance to tell you about it before whammo. The lights went out."

"Let's get everyone over to the *Halsey*," Richards said. "The *Vella Gulf* can stabilize things enough to figure out what happened here."

Chapter Twenty-Nine

Peter used both hands to grab the edge of the desk as soon as his chair started to wobble. Otherwise, he too would have been on the floor with the rest of the people in the control room with him. The Blockhouse shook so hard that he ignored all the falling manuals to keep himself upright.

After things stopped shaking, he swiveled his chair around and leapt out of it. "Is everyone alright?" He went from one to another of the investors, helping them up and doing a quick check for injuries. Fortunately, no one had contacted with a metallic edge.

The eldest of the group, Franklin Rogers, asked as Peter helped him into a chair, "Does something like this happen often, this deep in the ocean?"

"Usually we are buffered from surface waves at this depth, Mr. Rogers," Peter answered. "I don't think this was a natural phenomenon. Something happened!"

Harry Trunnel hadn't waited for any help, but had gotten up and over to the radio. "*Damocles, Damocles*, do you read, *Damocles*? This is Blockhouse, please still be up there."

"*Damocles* here," came a response from the radio. "Give us a minute here. There's been some kind of explosion and we are still recovering from the ocean wave it threw at us." Then the radio went quiet for several minutes.

"Does anybody need anything while we wait?" Peter asked his charges.

"Are we in trouble if something went wrong up there?" The voice of Patrick Radcliff shook a bit as he asked the question. He was here at his father's request, and not because he wanted to be. Especially now.

"If *Damocles* should be out of action, the Elevator is again docked with the Blockhouse and could transfer us up to either of the waiting U.S. Navy vessels supporting our activities." Peter looked individually at each of the investors in turn as he explained. "If the worst should happen and all three support vessels have been put out of action, we would be able to get back to dock on our own. It would just take about a week to do so."

"Blockhouse," finally came over the radio. "This is *Damocles*. Blockhouse, please respond."

"Blockhouse here," answered Harry.

"Blockhouse, we think the *Gran Siena* Oil Platform, about a mile away, exploded. It caused the massive waves we've had to deal with. The *Vella Gulf* and the *Halsey* are steaming out to investigate. They asked us to pack up and return to base."

Peter leaned over and keyed the radio. "Is everyone alright up there?"

"We had to fish a couple of guys out of the water, but everything is go up here. How are you guys down there? If you can get the rig secured, we'll be ready to tow you back."

"Does Leo want us to transfer the investors up to the *Damocles*?" Peter asked. Then got a stern look from Harry and stepped back; this was the job of the Operational Manager, after all.

"Peter," the voice coming down to them changed to Leo's.

"Harry here, Leo."

"You got the radio away from him. Good for you, boy." Leo responded. "You have good people with you, Peter; let them do their jobs. Harry, what is your situation down there?"

He quickly scanned the monitors on all three benches before responding. "Everything is watertight down here. You laid in enough food to last a few weeks. I'd have to say we're pretty secure on this end."

"Then let's keep everyone where they are until we can assess everything for damage. No point taking any chances we don't have to. You guys think you can have the Blockhouse ready for travel in an hour?"

"You just have those tow cables ready. Blockhouse out," Harry agreed to the timeline.

He swiveled in his chair to face Peter. "I know this is going to be hard for you, but could you take our guests to the rec area and see to their comfort while we get ready to go back home?"

"I'd rather be doing something."

"You would be. Peter, you're the highest level company officer present, and these are VIPs. Their comfort and security are your most important task. We know what to do. Let us make you proud."

Harry swiveled back to the radio and called down to the DeepWorkers docked in their cradles. "David, Mike. You guys secure down there?" Feeling Peter hovering, he said over his shoulder, "Peter, take care of our guests."

Frank Walsh took Peter gently by his elbow and began leading him to the control room door. "Come on, Dr. von Scorio. I think a little food and information might keep the rest of us from panicking."

* * *

Alan Hoffman pulled the wrapped platter of ham sandwiches out of the refrigerator and set them on the large table in the center of the room. Banks of televisions and game consoles stood ignored as the group of investors sat down on the tall chairs that surrounded those sandwiches and picked them off one or two at a time.

"What's happening right now, Dr. von Scorio?" Frank Lorenzo asked before taking a bite.

"The DeepWorker operators will run through their checklists to ensure that the vessels are seaworthy, but the shake that we got wouldn't cause them problems, even if they were out working. We had them docked in their cradles for the test firing when the shockwave hit."

"So even less chance of damage, then?"

"They should have sustained no damage." He walked over to the banks of monitors mounted on the wall and flipped a couple of them on. "We should be able to get a picture from their

149

cameras once they put out to sea. Right now, it would just be the grey of the hull. Ah, there goes David."

The monitor showed grey steel receding, then on either side as it pulled back, until finally, it disappeared and the view swung around to open water. As it sped towards the first of the downed rings, the second vessel's camera came online and pulled away from its cradle.

"The first thing we have to do is secure the twenty rings we used for this test. David and Mike will be picking them up one at a time and sliding them onto the storage spike we have in the aft section of the Blockhouse. Once all of the rings have been stowed, they will add the locking ring to the end so none of them can slip off. With the rings secure, they will re-dock the DeepWorkers in their cradles, drain the water from their storage space, pop their hatch and proceed to the control room to personally report readiness to Mr. Trunnel.

"Once he is assured that all his personnel are safely aboard this vessel, he will retract our landing feet and ascend about fifty feet to allow cables from the *Damocles* to attach to our bow. Then we will be winched onto the bottom of the *Damocles* as she travels back to New Orleans and home.

"Once we have attached with the *Damocles*, you will be free to return to her and whatever Leo has planned for the three-hour trip back. Or stay here with me, as by then, we should get satellite reception and we can find out what happened out there."

With that, Peter opened the refrigerator again. "Anyone care for a beer?"

Chapter Thirty

"America; now that I have your attention,
you will listen to the edicts of Gaia.
"The days where you could rape Her of Her

resources are over.

"No longer will your deforestation of Her atmospheric cleansing system be allowed.

"No more will you create foul chemicals to be spewed on Her land, air, and sea.

"The treasures buried beneath Her surface are Hers and Hers alone. You will cease digging them from Her bosom for your unclean lifestyles.

"I am Her guardian, I am Her avenger, and I am watching."

Neil read the unsigned manifesto for the third time, gaining no further insight into its writer. Setting it aside, he grabbed up the envelope with the lab results from the first four oil rig explosions.

The metallurgical analysis of the debris was consistent with the types of materials that made up the oil pipeline. Further microscopic analysis found taggants mixed in with that debris. Taggants that matched those from the earlier samples of Semtek Neil had recovered from the Nuclear Recyclers plant, the Nebraska ammonia plant, the Indiana train derailment, the West Virginia mine disaster, and other attacks he was now attributing to this Charles Roland. Reconstruction of the pieces revealed an explosive detonation in the southern side of the pipe line.

In a flash of inspiration, Neil grabbed his phone and speed-dialed Marine Workers Inc. As soon as he was past the automatic operator, "This is Neil Corsair from the FBI, get me an engineer working on your Dolphin line."

"Sir, let me connect you to our employee list."

"Your chief engineer. NOW!" *I have no patience for automated responses,* Corsair thought, *especially when they come from non-automated people.*

The phone clicked twice, then, "Dr. Boykins here. How can I help you?"

"Neil Corsair, FBI, in charge of the environmental terrorist cases. I need to know if the Dolphin prototype that was stolen from your facility last month was equipped with torpedo tubes?"

"Torpedo tubes?" After a short pause, "Mr. Corsair, the Dolphin is a civilian submersible. You know as well as I do that Federal Laws prohibits civilian sea vessels from having any such armaments."

"Yes, yes, but did it?"

"No, sir, it most definitely did not!"

"Any type of manipulator arms?"

"Again, no, it was designed for rapid exploration of deep sea terrains for long periods of time. An underwater research facility. Nothing more."

Neil thumped his middle finger on his desk. "I need to figure out a way it could have placed a bomb while submerged."

The line became very quiet.

"Dr. Boykins, are you still there?" Neil asked after the second minute of silence.

"Yes." Another shorter pause. "How heavy would the bomb have to be?"

"Only a few ounces. But it would have to be attached securely to the object it was targeting."

"The Dolphin was equipped with an ROV for the recovery of samples for analysis. It was stored inside the Dolphin to allow the change-out of recovery modules. Then later retrieval of the collection of samples. One of those modules did have a manipulator arm which could handle up to a five-pound load."

"So our suspect could have attached his explosive to the arm to place it on the rig? Were there more than one ROV or could he retrieve the one he had for repeated use?"

"I'm afraid the latter is extremely likely. It was designed to leave the Dolphin, collect a sample and return it to the ship."

"That doesn't explain how he attacked the surface facility at *Gran Siena*." Neil was starting to get a picture of Roland's activities, but the massive platform explosion couldn't have been done by a planted device.

"I can't help you there, Inspector. Unless he had the Dolphin retrofitted?" the engineer speculated.

Yes, Neil thought. "Thank you, Dr. Boykins. You've been a great help." Neil hung up the phone, pulled his computer monitor closer and pulled up the FBI database on black market arms dealers. 'Now, who's in Roland's cruising range?'

After weeding through the list, Neil came up with three dealers within a week's travel of the submarine Roland had stolen. 'Time to talk to Director Turner again.'

After quickly checking with Turner's secretary, Neil knocked on the Director's office door and let himself in.

"Agent Corsair, Millie tells me you have a lead on these oil disasters?"

Neil seated himself in his usual seat in front of the Director's desk. "I need some help from the CIA. I'm thinking the person who stole the submarine from Marine Workers last month may have outfitted it with some kind of weapon, possibly torpedoes."

Turner squinted one eye at Corsair's revelation and asked, "And how could the CIA help us?"

Neil slid his list of arms dealers across Turner's desk for the director to read. "These three black market arms dealers are close enough to the Gulf for Charles Roland to have taken his submarine there, had them outfitted and returned to the Gulf to begin his attacks. I was hoping the CIA either had some intelligence on his activities or contacts that could find out what Roland has available to him."

Turner didn't take the time to go through his secretary but dialed the number himself. "This is FBI Assistant Director Turner. I need to talk to Analyst Thompkins please."

He switched the phone to speaker and replaced the receiver as the CIA man acknowledged his call. "Central Analysis, Thompkins here."

"Peter, I need some information. Which of these three arms dealers has the capacity to outfit a submarine with missiles or torpedoes: Nelson Osabee, Abbas Said, or Abioye Jefferson?"

"Both Jefferson and Said," said the CIA analyst.

"Both of them! Okay, do you have any indication of recent activity of that nature, or a submarine making contact with

153

them?"

"I need a time frame to check. And the type of submarine?"

Turner looked over to Neil to answer. "Our man stole a Dolphin prototype from Marine Workers, Inc. And I'm guessing he would have had it done sometime between late June and July 7th. That would give him enough travel time to get to the Ivory Coast and back to the Gulf in time to carry out his attacks on the oil rigs."

"Let me pull some satellite feeds and I will get back to you." The line's static indicated his disconnection.

A knock sounded on the Director's door. "Yes," Turner called out.

The day secretary for the Special Agents stuck his head in the door. "Sir, I have a fax for Agent Corsair."

"Let me see," Turner replied.

Mille Swanson walked across the room and handed two sheets of paper of the Director. She then went back, left the office and closed the door.

"Neil, you had better have a look at this." Turner handed the sheets across the desk.

The computer-printed note read:

> "Carlos Rondonate. The man you are looking for is Carlos Rondonate. He used his recently stolen one million dollars to outfit the *Suelo Defensor* with old Soviet-era torpedoes."

Neil looked up from the fax, "The *Suelo Defensor*?"

Turner leaned back in his chair. "Apparently someone knows more about this than you do."

"If it's who I think it is, he's got access to Federal Government vehicles."

Chapter Thirty-One

Peter had not expected to be flying in a Coast Guard helicopter with Dr. Boykins of Marine Workers and FBI Agent Neil Corsair to the *USS Halsey* to help track down a rogue submarine commanded by an eco-terrorist who was a former employee. Nope, he hadn't expected any of this.

At least they were at the point where Mike Farrel only had to construct the final twenty rings for the Waste Gun before actual sea trials of the completed assembly could be carried out. At least he wasn't needed right now.

"Everyone still strapped in?" came the voice of the pilot. Peter looked out the left window and saw the *Halsey* approaching, her helicopter landing pad growing ever larger.

"With all your work at the bottom of the Gulf, you are the most expert individual we have about it." Agent Corsair had said in the pre-flight briefing. "You also have met this Carlos Rondonate, or Charles Roland.

"Dr. Boykins, there is no one better qualified to advise us on the performance specifications of the Dolphin submarine."

At least someone in the Coast Guard knew enough to pack a cooler of sodas and sandwiches for this four-hour ride. Between the five people on the flight, they were mostly gone. "Captain Miller had better have a lunch ready for us when we get there," Dr. Boykins mused.

"Sir?" asked the helicopter pilot over the headset.

"Breakfast was a long time ago, son." Dr. Boykins responded, "I think we all need something to eat right about now."

* * *

An alarm pinged Carlos out of the fugue of thoughts he had

drifted into. *Moving into Atlantic waters will produce oil trage-dies of greater impact,* he'd been thinking. To no one present, he said, "That sounds like a sonar contact."

He was out of his bunk on the lower deck and up the ladder to the control room in quick order. Dropping into the pilot seat under the clear canopy that gave him a 360-degree view of the ocean surrounding him, he pulled up the vessel's sonar suite into the canopy display for his inspection.

"That is a very large object ahead of us," he said to himself. "A **very** large vessel." His hands danced over the keyboard af-fixed to the right side of the pilot's console. While not a dedicat-ed keyboard, it had been hooked into the sonar suite when Carlos had brought that system up.

"Ship Identification system," he muttered as he called up that subsystem.

"Scan and Identify," he selected, then sat back in his seat and waited for the computer to determine exactly what was ahead of him. 'No point in getting any closer until I know what she is.' Carlos turned to the forward console, brought his subma-rine to a full stop and waited for the sonar system to tell him what he was facing. "I am not ready for a direct confrontation with the Navy. Yet!"

In under a minute, the sonar suite pinged a result. Carlos looked up at the display, "A tanker. In fact, one of those double-hulled Super Tankers. Something the rapists think is perfectly safe. Something I can use to spread my message all over the coast line of these Florida Keys."

He brought the *Suelo Defensor* up enough for the canopy to break the surface and allow him to see his target. Still a mile away, she was out of his line of sight. At least until he brought himself within 500 feet of the tanker. Then her stern showed it-self.

"Not the best of shots." He dropped the submarine 25 feet below the surface and sailed around the tanker until he was fac-ing the tanker's starboard side.

He brought the sub back to the surface again and inspected

the tanker from 100 yards away. "Now that's what I like, a clear broadside shot."

He lined the *Suelo Defensor* perpendicular to the tanker and used his side maneuvering jets to hold his position relative to it. He chose the outside torpedo on the right wing of his sub. He set the control on the torpedo to a surface run, arming itself as it left the tube. "Five, four, three, two, goodbye, you rapists," he depressed the switch.

The torpedo spat from the wing-mounted tube, leapt to the ocean's surface and sped forward guided by the sonar ping from its electronic guidance system. Its 100-yard race lasted mere seconds before it ended its life in an explosion against the outer hull of the tanker.

The explosion opened a large hole in the side of the tanker. Carlos saw it begin to take in water and list towards him. "No oil," he screamed his frustration. "Where is the oil?"

Carlos scrambled to program another torpedo, lifted the cover off the other wing's outer tube, and slammed home the launch switch. Another missile sprang from the *Suelo Defensor* and slammed into the crippled tanker.

It hit just astern from the first one. It opened another hole and cracked the ship's hull enough to merge the two into a gash almost a quarter of the tanker's length. The ship listed even faster than before; moments from now, she would be underwater.

"Still NO oil," Carlos raged. "An empty tanker. Gaia, why do you taunt me by giving me an empty tanker?"

He calmed himself in his seat, sitting there while his first kill dropped below the waves with dozens of lifeboats drifting from where it had gone down. Then he set the controls to dive to 100 feet and hold.

"It was a good plan; I just have to find the right target." Carlos changed the canopy display screen to the ship's computer, called up the shipping lanes for commercial oil tankers and their schedules. He chose an incoming tanker heading into the gulf waters of the United States not far from where he currently was, then he set his course.

"Sir," called out the radio operator on the *Halsey*. "I have an incoming message from the Coast Guard."

"Put it on speakers, Mr. Madison," the Captain instructed.

"Key West Coast Guard to *USS Halsey*."

"*Halsey* here, Captain Miller speaking."

"Sir, I know you are looking for unusual activity. We have just received a distress signal from the *Haverton*. Two massive explosions rocked her starboard hull and she sank in record time."

"Don't you have the necessary rescue equipment?"

"Sir, we have already rescued the crew. But she was an oil tanker and one of the crew believes he saw missiles speeding towards her before the explosions. It sounds like she was torpedoed, sir."

Captain Miller looked over at his FBI guest. Neil nodded his agreement.

"Send us her position, officer. I think you may have found our quarry." He handed the transmitter back to Lieutenant Madison and added, "Get those coordinates to navigation immediately and tell them to proceed at best possible speed."

Chapter Thirty-Two

"As dawn is breaking over the Louisiana coastline this Tuesday morning, so is the oil from the *Senora Vega*," the local newsman reported. Wearing rubber hip boots, he was standing ankle deep in a thick, black, gooey liquid as the receding tide left a film of oil on the white sands of the Gulf beach.

"Last night, the *Senora Vega*, a double-hulled supertanker, considered one of the safest oil transport systems in the world, sank during a routine run in waters deep enough to handle her draft. The oil spilling from her since the incident, has now begun washing up on our beaches. Coast Guard officials have reported that the entire crew has been rescued early this morning. As of this time, oil is still being seen surfacing from where the vessel is now laying on the bottom of the Gulf.

"Captain Montgomery said in a press announcement an hour ago, that the *Senora Vega* did not strike anything, but rather, two massive explosions rocked her port side. Those explosions opened two giant holes in her massive double-hull, through which she began taking on water as fast as her cargo of crude oil could spill out into the Gulf waters. Within an hour, she sank beneath the waves.

"The crew of twenty-five were able to get to their lifeboats in time to avoid being pulled down as the ship plummeted to the depths. There has been no explanation at this time as to the cause of the explosions. But we are now looking at the second worst oil spill disaster to hit the coast of Louisiana since oil production began in these waters.

"For KLOU, this is Neville Montaine. Back to you, Henry."

* * *

Carlos snapped off the receiver with rage. "Second worst. **Second** worst!" It was fortunate that he had already docked in his covered hanger before turning on the afternoon news about his late night triumph. He was too mad at that broadcast to have safely brought the *Suelo Defensor* into dock.

"Second worst? I will have to do something about that. Maybe a couple more tankers, after I reload those torpedo mounts. Yes, maybe a couple more tankers. Or I could destroy another oil production line, this time without setting its platform on fire. The *Gran Siena* was capped too quickly. **Second best.** I must redeem my honor. I will not be **second** best to anyone."

* * *

Captain Miller and the crew of the *Halsey* had a very different reaction to the news broadcast. A broadcast that had been relayed to them through Navy channels.

"We're in the wrong area."

"Captain?" questioned Lieutenant Marshall, currently the Officer of the Deck.

"The bastard has moved. We're looking for him in the wrong place."

Peter looked down at the map stretched across the navigation table as the Bridge Navigations Officer stuck a pin in it where the news report had come from. "That's only a hundred miles from our construction facilities."

"Then you know that section of coast?" Lieutenant Marshall placed his hands on the edge of the table, taking a more active interest in the news they had just received.

"Not as much as I would like. I haven't had any reason to go out there, with the construction of the Waste Gun to supervise. I think David Wong, our chief Deep Caisson pilot, might, though."

"Mr. Marshall," said Captain Miller. He folded his arms in front of his chest and walked over to stare out the starboard windows across to where Key West lay some 30 miles away. "We have no reason to assume that our quarry has stayed in that area any more than he had stayed here."

Dr. Boykins stood beside the table, looking at the map from north to south, stroking his untrimmed beard. "Captain Miller, about how much does your standard torpedo weigh?"

As the Captain turned around to look at the man who had designed the Dolphin they were pursuing, Lieutenant Marshall answered, "Just over half a ton."

"Based on the time interval between the two attacks, the Dolphin has been able to maintain her normal cruising speed. Therefore, this Rondonate guy hasn't overloaded her with torpedoes. He could have added a little over 2 tons of weight to her and still maintained that cruising speed. That would equate to about four torpedoes, which I would have mounted under her wings. And if he had to cruise with the wings extended, her normal cruising speed would also be her max. And the Dolphin has no room to store any for reloading."

Captain Miller crossed back over to the navigation table and ran his finger along the shortest route the submarine could have safely taken underwater.

Then he added, "Two birds to take down each tanker could mean he was headed back to his operational base for reloading when he found a target of opportunity in the *Senora Vega*."

He stood up and went to the bridge's bow window, "Mr. Marshall, bring the *Halsey* around and set a course for the last known position of the *Senora Vega*, best possible speed. Then contact Naval Operations and let them know what we speculate and see if they can get some more ships out here to hunt this guy down." With hands clasped behind his back, staring out into the waters of the Straits of Florida, he added, "Dr. von Scorio, it looks like we may be needing your Mr. Wong after all. Mr. Roper, once you have completed our SitRep to operations, could you help him make that call?"

Chapter Thirty-Three

"I am a prisoner of my own success," Carlos cursed, spinning his chair away from the news reports he'd been monitoring.

The day before, he had re-armed and re-provisioned the *Suleo Defensor* to put back to sea early in the morning. But when he went outside to begin launching her, the oil from the *Senora Vega* had drifted in to his little harbor close enough to where he couldn't dive below it before his instruments would become fouled and inoperable.

By noon, he was pacing in his buried Quonset hut compound like a panther on the prowl. A frustrated prowl, for there was no prey to be had. Cleanup efforts were going to take at least a month before they even got to his area. Once they began cleanup the *Suelo Defensor* would be too easy to find, he had to have her secured and hidden by then.

He spent the rest of the day removing the aircraft launching racks from the wings of his submarine so those wings could be retracted. Then he used the remote that Abbas had installed to sink her to the bottom of the bayou. He removed the poles from the camouflage tarp and dropped it over the pilot and observer bubbles that still stuck out of the water. He finished the disguise by sticking reeds into the weave of the tarp to make it look like the rest of the grassland that surrounded it.

The next morning, he began formulating a new campaign. "There are plenty of poison-creating facilities in this area. If I can eliminate them and the human filth that maintains them, Gaia can wash her lands clean again."

Four hours later, Carlos was boarding a Greyhound bus with a backpack full of wadded newspaper for a trip north. It would take him a day to make the trip to Kansas City, where he would steal a car for the drive to the farmhouse where he had stored his remaining cache of Semtek. Then another bus trip back from St. Louis.

* * *

After two weeks at sea, Peter was glad to get back to the security of his work on the Waste Gun. Nothing was more frustrating than to be part of a team where you had no idea about what you're doing. And nothing was more secure than to work on a project you designed and knew every little bolt of. *It's good to be home*, Peter thought as he inspected production to see what he could jump in and work on.

Most of the rings had been completed and loaded in their storage rack on the back of the Blockhouse. His fabricators only

162

had two more to construct. The two Alvins, DeepCaissons, and the several recording ROVs, having finished their sea trials, had been loaded in the storage bays under the Blockhouse. *Damocles* was equally ready to go.

Peter stared off the bow of the *Damocles* watching the tide bring another load of oil from the *Senora Vega* and sighed. "Everything is ready and here we wait. Stuck in harbor by an ongoing oil spill."

"Maybe there is something we can do about it." Carol Bancroft walked up behind him and placed both her hands on the ship's railing.

"Like what?" Peter asked, continuing to stare at the black goo.

She turned to face him, leaning on the rail with her right elbow. Watching as Louis Reed climbed onto the deck. "We could finish those last two rings in as many days with just a single crew."

As Lou approached, he realized that Carol had brought their idea up to the 'boss'. "Everyone is just sitting around drawing pay. The guys I hired for you two don't like sitting around doing nothing any more than you do. Let's put them to work. Let's help out with the cleanup."

"Won't that look self-serving?"

"Of course it's self-serving," Carol added. "But the people doing the cleanup could use help, self-serving or not. And if you're really worried about public opinion, we just keep helping. Pick a section of coast twice as large as we need in order to launch, and challenge other facilities to join in the effort."

Peter's face brightened at the thought of actually doing something. "Great idea," he said as he turned and walked back to their production warehouse. "Meet me in the conference room, I need to find Leo and Mike."

As the five of them assembled around the northern end of the oval conference table, Peter began, "Carol, tell them what you and Lou came up with."

"As you know, we are essentially trapped here in port, waiting for the oil blocking us from the Gulf—and thereby the Atlantic—to be cleaned up. And with most of the work for our final trials already completed, most of our workers have nothing to do."

Lou continued, "Now we don't want to lay them off, since they have extremely specialized skills we need for this endeavor. It would take a long time to find and train people up to this crew's competence. But to have them sitting around, not using their talents, is extremely demoralizing. They need something productive, not just sweeping the floor, to do."

Carol again took over. "Lou and I talked about volunteering to help the cleanup crews along our section of coastline, as both a goodwill, neighborly thing, as well as to help us get out and start the trials."

"Mike, we only have two rings to go?" Peter asked.

"Actually Peter, we have both those rings mostly completed."

"Then you could pull one of the crews off and add to our available pool of volunteers," Leo added, sitting up as he realized this was a possible PR bonanza.

"Actually, I could leave Jonesy to finish both of them and give you the seven other men. That, plus the dozen others waiting for assignments, would give you a crew of almost twenty," Mike speculated.

"The crew of the *Damocles* could bring her to around thirty-five," added Captain Harris as he entered the room. "Thought you could keep me out of this little cabal? We're itching as much as you guys to get out of here and prove this little concept of yours, Dr. von Scorio. Count us in as well."

Sometimes having an open air conference room is a good idea, Peter thought.

164

Chapter Thirty-Four

Peter made the front page of the Picayune, Neil thought as he set down the still neatly-folded morning paper. It rested atop the stack of magazines left to entertain visitors while they sat in the stuffed chairs of the Ascension County Sheriff's office waiting room.

One of the deputy officers walked in the door as Sheriff Steven J. Adams, as his name plaque read, hung up the phone he had been on since Neil had entered.

Neil got up from the chair he had occupied the past quarter hour and both the deputy and Neil approached the Sheriff's desk.

Neil stood off to the left side as the deputy addressed his boss. "Steve, the fire guys have the fire at the Delcon Gas Refinery under enough control to allow us access for investigation."

"Then it looks like I got here just in time," Neil added.

Wearing a tan uniform that looked like he had spent the night in it, the Sheriff looked up and down his visitor. "And you are?" he asked.

"Neil Corsair, FBI." He took his badge from the inside pocket of his blue suit coat and presented it to the Sheriff. After a moment, he replaced it and extended his hand. "Your refinery explosion fits the M.O. of someone we've been tracking for several months now. I'd like my team to join you, so we can verify if it was him."

Sheriff Adams visibly relaxed and shook the offered hand. "We don't have a lot of resources in this here parish, Mr. FBI. So any help you could give would be muchly appreciated. As long as you let us take care of our own," he replied.

"I don't want to get in your way, but the man we're after has been hitting facilities all over the country. He is currently wanted for several Federal crimes."

The Sheriff was up from his chair and grabbing his hat before he pushed through his office gate. "In that case, we had better get going. Sam, have there been any casualties reported?"

"None yet, but at least two dozen are still missing."

Fifteen minutes later, both the Sheriff's cruiser and the black Explorer Neil had rented drove through the security gates of the Delcon Refinery, where a second SUV joined the convoy. The smoke that still rose from the shattered distillation towers was dissipating while fires continued to be attacked by firefighters on a few of the storage units. Several of the other refinery structures had also been destroyed, but none of those were still burning.

They drove up to the fire department field command vehicle, where the incident commander walked up to the patrol car as the Sheriff stepped out. "Glad you could join us, Steve. We should just about have it safe enough to begin your search." Looking over at the vehicles following the patrol car, "Who ya got with ya?"

"FBI, they think they know the guy who done this."

Neil got out of his car as the deputy came around to join the Sheriff. "Neil Corsair, FBI." He held out his hand for the firefighter. "And these are Special Agents Fellows, Brown and St. Martin."

"This is a lot of damage for one man to have caused," the firefighter stated.

"He's been using military-grade explosives. And if this was him, we will be able to identify him from the residue of those explosives. I just need to find something to send back to Quantico."

"We got the fire around the distillation towers contained enough for you to do a quick inspection. They seem to have been the epicenter of the explosions. So that might be a good place to start."

"I will defer to your safety experience, Chief..." Neil asked.

"Humphrey Augustus, my friends and colleagues call me Hump," he responded. "Pick up helmets and bunker coats from that unit," he pointed to one of the ladder trucks between them

166

and the tower, "before we proceed."

Pieces of the tower lay strewn about an asphalt slab adjacent to the production facility. Many of the pieces had been crushed and mangled by landing on the pavement. No individual piece was longer that six feet. Each of them had jagged edges, bent inwards, on each end. Neil was glad for the bunker gear; he could feel the intense heat they were still giving off.

The Incident Commander said, "No one's touched anything. That's how they came down." He pointed up to where the towers had once been standing. "Frankly, we haven't had time to move anything, still fighting this fire like we are. Besides, as you can feel, it's still too hot to safely move anything."

"Have you seen many explosions, Hump?" Neil asked the fire chief as he squatted down to inspect the jagged inward metal sections.

"We got lots of chemical facilities down here, Mr..."

"Neil, please."

"Lots of minor stuff happens. Much of it is taken care of by whatever plant it is Emergency Brigade. We get called in, nonetheless, mainly to assess that they've done things right. They're a good lot and mostly keep things well in hand. But, yes, I have seen my share of explosions over the years."

Neil pointed at the jagged segments he had been studying. "Then, would you say this was caused by an explosion?"

"Looks that way to me," Hump replied.

"Does anything about it strike you as odd?" Neil stood up to address the emergency responders.

"Now that you mention it," said Sheriff Adams, "shouldn't those metal edges be pointin' out?"

"If this were an internal explosion," the fireman answered. "That's what you're getting at, ain't it, Neil?"

"Yes, this was an external explosion. An attack on this facility." He squatted closer to the metal fragments strewn about them. As he swept his hand over the top of the debris without touching any of it, "I need pieces of this stuff collected and sent to Quantico," he handed Adams a card with the lab's address on it, "as soon as they have cooled enough to handle. Sheriff, treat this as evidence, but get me as many of these edges as you can find."

Martin walked back to Neil and addressed everyone, "I'm guessing this man climbed up the tower." He pointed back to several pieces of a ladder cage that was still attached to some of the fragments. "Setting explosive charges, from the looks of the debris, about every six feet, based on the lengths of the remaining ladder. If he's still using what he had before, he set all the charges to blow simultaneously. Most likely from a line-of-sight vantage point."

Neil looked over to the puzzled Sheriff. "It's been his M.O. His profile says he likes to watch."

They walked back to the command center to map out a plan to search for the missing employees when Sheriff Adams' radio announced in a hurried voice, "Steve, you there, Steve?"

Before he could answer, the Fire Chief's radio squawked also.

"What's up, Jessie?" the Sheriff lifted his radio slightly out of his pocket as the fire chief moved away from him to avoid a radio feedback frenzy.

"Steve, there's been another explosion. It's the Warberg Chemical Plant."

"That's twelve miles up I-10," he said to the FBI men. He keyed the radio again. "Any reported casualties?"

"I don't have anything yet. Just the first call in."

"I'm on my way." He let the radio drop into his chest pocket, began moving to his patrol car and said to Neil, "Saddle up, Mr. FBI. Looks like I'm needin' you on this one also."

"Martin, stay here. Fellows, Brown, let's get moving."

Since Martin had been driving the second Explorer, they all piled into Corsair's.

They pulled into the Walberg facility just behind the Baton Rouge first responders. The plant security gate was raised to allow everyone immediate access. The BR Fire Chief, Sheriff Adams, and Neil pulled up to the plant Emergency Brigade vehicle and got out to talk to the plant incident commander.

A short stocky man in full firefighting gear approached the trio. "You guys got here fast. Where's Hump?"

"Fighting another petroleum fire at Delcon," responded the Baton Rouge chief. "We're covering for him. What do you need?"

"We've got most of the fires under control. They were mostly hydrogen fires. Burned out with the initial blast, once we got the valves closed. Our ammonia storage tanks have been breached; we need every hose we can get to keep those fumes from spreading. Otherwise, it could be a disaster, the wind has them spreading down towards Delcon."

"This is an ammonia facility?" Neil realized.

"Yeah," replied the plant commander. "We've got about two dozen bullet storage tanks full of the stuff. And you are?"

"And they weren't blown also?"

"No, just minor punctures when the Ammonia Production Building blew. Steve, who are these guys?"

"They're from the FBI, Mike," Adams responded.

"But he set charges on the storage tanks in Nebraska. Why not here?" Neil thought aloud. Then turning to Sheriff Adams, "He's waiting to cause a secondary explosion! When are the winds predicted to shift?"

"Why does that matter?" Adams began.

"Around 3 PM, in about thirty minutes," Mike answered.

Neil ran up the nearest set of stairs he could find and spotted a slight rise that overlooked the fertilizer plant. Then he hollered down, "He's waiting for that wind shift. Sheriff Adams, get as many men as you can to comb those tanks, look for Semtek."

"Sem-what?" Adams hollered back at the descending FBI agent.

Neil ran back to the command center without breaking into a gasp. "Semtek, plastic explosive. Look for anything that appears like putty, feels like putty, or has wires connected to it. He'll have placed it on the bottom of the tanks. We have to hurry; he may blow them prematurely when he sees us coming."

169

"Sees us?" Adams asked.

"I think he around here somewhere, watching and waiting to radio detonate his bombs." Neil turned to the plant officer, "Neil Corsair, FBI. Is there any access to those tanks that can't be seen from the hills to the northwest?"

"We've got containment berms surrounding the lot of them, but you have to go up and over those berms to get to the tanks." He thought for a moment, then suggested, "If you don't mind getting wet, we could provide a water curtain to obscure anyone going over."

"I'll defer to your experience. How quick can you rig those curtains up?"

The Fire Chief broke in, "We can have two in place in five minutes. Mike, can you get another two ready?

"We're already there. We just have to adjust our spray pattern."

"Anyone going in should get into bunker gear, that will protect you some from the water," the Fire Chief explained.

"How many men can you spare, Mr. ..." Neil looked at the plant officer again.

"Mike, Mike Douglas. I have a dozen on the brigade, eight will be needed to handle the hoses."

"Get who you can into that berm. We have to find all the explosives before Carlos can pull the trigger. Sheriff, figure he has rigged each of the tanks to blow, probably from underneath, multiple times. If you can find the detonators, get them away from the Semtek. Just pull them out and get them on the other side of the berm. Do NOT keep them, they'll cause a small explosion when he triggers them. This guy doesn't use booby traps, just shear force. I'm afraid we don't have time to wait for a bomb disposal squad. Let's get moving!" Neil rapidly made his way over to the nearest fire truck and got himself dressed up.

There were twenty storage tanks on the inside of the containment berm when everyone going over it arrived. Neil took the first tank, assigned Fellows to the middle one and St. Martin the furthest. Emergency Brigade volunteers took the ones in be-

170

tween. Baton Rouge fire fighters took over the hose-handling details and set each hose for its widest possible dispersion. As ammonia was slightly water soluble, this would knock down any of the escaping fumes, and be the natural reaction of the plant to the pin-hole leaks. It would also blind any observer more than ten feet away from seeing the men going into the berm.

Four hoses pointed high into the air, spewed a watery mist over the confinement area as ten men ran up the three sets of wooden stairs leading into it. They quickly dispersed to their assignment tanks after reaching the bottom of the internal stairs.

Neil found the first explosive, directly under the back of the rightmost tank. Rontonate had rolled the Semtex into what would pass for a pipe under a casual inspection. Neil had been probing its underside with his fingers and when the pipe deformed itself, he got down to examine it. He found two more while he was laying on the ground and pulled their detonators out. He found another three on the far side of the tank.

He threw the detonators over the berm, away from any water spray that might have knocked them back. Then he proceeded onto the next tank, where the brigade member had already found the first three. Neil yanked out the others.

Within twenty minutes, six explosive charges had been removed from each of the seven tanks. The FBI agents had collected all of the secured Semtex and emerged over the berm just as the wind began to change direction.

They felt the change, held their breaths, and waited.

Nothing happened!

Nothing for ten minutes, upon which time, they moved the Semtek to where they had parked their SUV, and secured it to send to Quantico.

As they closed the hatch on their vehicle, a series of popping sounds could be heard around the earthen berm they had just left.

"Charley waited to make sure of the wind," Fellows said as he opened the passenger door to get into the SUV.

Neil turned to the Baton Rouge fire chief. "Are all your men okay?"

"They were when we left," he responded. As he realized what the sound was they had just heard. "Everyone check in, now!"

Chapter Thirty-Five

Carlos moved the oil containment boom back another dozen feet. Security at the cleanup camps was a joke to Carlos. In and out, with enough equipment to clean up his little anchorage. At least enough to get the *Suelo Defensor* back out to sea. One more hour and he would move the booms the final distance he needed to get under his oily message.

He entered the small shack adjacent to the short pier he would have moored his submarine to, if it hadn't been submerged. At least up to her sensor tower; this portion of the bayou was not deep enough to submerge her any further. That tower had to avoid the oil spill before he could return to the Gulf and his mission. As he walked over to grab another cup of Jamaican coffee, he pulled his dagger out of the wall, making sure that the news article from yesterday was still attached. He took another few steps, turned and hurled his rage back at the wall. The knife and impaled article were driven into the wall about two inches.

"Nothing," he screamed and swept his hand against his half-filled coffee cup. It shattered against his refrigerator as its contents splashed a trail across the room.

"All for nothing. That damned FBI man again, Cor-Sair. Again he found my voices and silenced them before they could speak to those in-no-cent people attacking Gaia."

He took another ceramic coffee mug from his cupboard and poured himself another cup of coffee. "No, I must find a new attack. Something he will not be expecting. A message that cannot be silenced. Something big!"

He took a small sip of the extra hot brew, set his cup on the counter and dug yesterday's newspaper, the one he had cut the chemical plant stories from, out of the trash. "There it is," he exclaimed as he saw the article on Nuclear Recyclers. "There is just the voice I need. There is the message to send. Nuclear waste up and down the Atlantic coastline might get them to rethink their lifestyles. Yes, Gaia shall sing loudly."

Chapter Thirty-Six

Two Bureau cars and three police vehicles drove down the unattended back road deep into the Mississippi coastline. Water lapped up to both sides of the built up bank where sparse bits of gravel had been driven into the dirt. Neil didn't notice any of their surroundings, he was focused on getting to the cabin that satellite surveillance had pinpointed next to a metallic object large enough to be the missing Dolphin.

Special Agent Fellows did notice how precarious their situation was. "Martin, slow down a bit," he said from the back seat. "It wouldn't take much to knock this road down."

Special Agent Brown, who had been watching the grandeur of the Mississippi bayou as they drove past, elbowed his fellow FBI agent in the ribs. "Stop worrying, Harry. This here road has to have been here for decades and will still be here after we're gone. I, for one, am enjoying this non-concrete jungle."

"Will you two knock it off," Neil turned around and scolded his two men. "We're here to do a job. Martin, how far?"

The driver glanced over at the Bureau car's GPS mapping system. "Should be over that berm ahead."

They drove up the small embankment and saw the small two-room shack that bordered up to a pier into the middle of the stream flowing out to the Gulf. A series of oil containment booms was holding back the encroaching oil spill from the *Gran Sienna*.

At the end of the road, next to the wooden shack, was a pickup truck with Louisiana plates. Punching a few buttons on his Pad told Neil that this was the truck that had been reported stolen just before the two chemical plant attacks. Neil was opening his door as the black Explorer pulled to a stop.

He was halfway down the pier before any of the other FBI men or Biloxi police officers could leave their vehicles.

"Damn," he said as he jumped down onto his chest and examined the water under the end of the pier. "It's gone. He got his submarine away before we could get here."

Martin Hughes, who had taken an extra minute to shut down their car, came up behind Neil and extended his hand to help him back up. "The guys are in position. The raid's ready for your word."

"Now!" Neil shouted loud enough to be heard back the 100 feet this dock extended. Then he turned back to his profiler. "Let's see what this guy left behind."

When the two Biloxi police officers swung the steel battering ram at the door, it splintered open. Its hinges barely moved with bits of old wood still hanging from them. The door knob was also still in place. But everything between those connection points was gone.

The other three police officers ran into the room, centering their service pistols in each of the remaining directions.

"Room secured," one of them announced. Inside, two tables were side by side in the center of the room, one a regular table with the other made from a door. A small kitchen was off to the north side, a desk and computer system set up against the south wall, and a doorway to the bedroom, sans door.

Larry, Paul, and Harry followed the police into the building. "Secure that side room," Neil heard Harry instruct the officers.

"Room secured," Neil heard the officer report as he and Martin entered. Martin made a beeline for the tables to begin sifting through the papers spread out on them. Neil made his way to the computer equipment, which Larry was already attempting to access. Paul and Harry were searching every cabinet and box, there were still several pounds of Semtex to locate.

"Security password on the files," Larry reported. Neil smacked his fist into his hand.

"Try G a i a," Martin called over without lifting his head from the papers he was examining. After a minute, he grabbed the waste basket off to the table's side and dumped its contents onto the tables.

"Nothing," Larry called back.

Martin stopped his examination and stood up for a second. "Try D e f e n s o r."

Neil watched as the computer screen came to life. "He's in!"

Larry went through one folder after another, looking for anything not game related. After a minute, the printer to the left side of the computer began printing.

As Neil pulled the sheet out of the printer, Martin was over to examine it also. It was a fax, dated a week ago:

"Why are you hitting non-listed oil rigs? The
Gran Sienna was one of ours. Stick to the list.
Otherwise, your funding will be cut off."

"Now, isn't that curious?" Neil began. "This fax was sent from the Ramada in D.C."

Chapter Thirty-Seven

When they were about a hundred feet from contact with the rising volcanic ridge about five days sailing time from the Miami harbor they'd left, William Danzig and Judith Hurley stepped into their individual DeepWorker units and closed the bubble dome that allowed them to see the deep ocean they were working in. They sat back on their benches and ran through the checklist to verify all systems were functional. A single mistake was fatal at a depth of 1200 feet. Once satisfied, they both slid their bench forward and extended their arms into the arms of their unit.

"Ready," Bill said over his voice-activated radio link.

Jude clicked her pinchers twice and said, "Let's get this show on the road."

"Flooding now." Mike Farrel, who was in charge of Operations for this test run, slid his finger along the touchscreen to open the valve and allow the Atlantic Ocean to fill the DeepWorker storage room. Once the room was flooded, the bottom swung open and the two divers floated to the ocean floor, having established a slight negative buoyancy while the room flooded.

As they drifted down, they engaged their external lighting systems and watched the bottom approach.

"Jude, off to your right," Bill radioed his partner.

"I see it, Bill. Right where they said it would be." Sticking straight up, as though it had landed like a javelin, were five four-yard long rods, wrapped with a plastic tie, waiting to be individually driven into the ridge to anchor the Blockhouse.

Bill rotated his pincers and pulled the packet out of the crevice it had landed in and held it up to Judith. She set her right pincher to cutting mode, a razor sharp blade extended through the middle of the upper half, and she pinched the tie wrap apart. She reached out with her left pincher and took the first anchor she would be driving half way into the ridge.

Bill set the rest of them down and took his first one. Finding the laser-marked point on the ridge, he drove his first one in exactly where the Blockhouse marked.

"That's the last one," Bill radioed the Blockhouse a quarter hour later. "We're ready for the cables."

"Roger, DeepWorker," Mike acknowledged. "I'm sending them to you now." The Blockhouse was a 1200 square foot underwater habitat that looked like three very large tubes had been set side-by-side and connected by three twenty-foot wide spokes running between them. It descended closer to its working divers. Bill and Jude had entered the ocean from the DeepWorker storage bays on the right side . Now five cables, one for each spoke, were released from the habitat and slowly drifted down for the DeepWorkers to collect. They each grabbed a cable and attached it to one of the pylons they had driven by a locking carbineer. Once screwed shut, a quick burst from the suit's welder made the connection permanent.

It took less time to tie down the habitat then it had to drive the pylons. "Blockhouse secured," Jude radioed.

"Tensioning the control room," Mike radioed down. The Blockhouse began shedding ballast until she had a slight positive buoyancy and very gently pulled against her anchors.

* * *

Running through the checklist they had established for securing the Blockhouse, Mike finally said, "Peter, everything looks secure to me."

"There was a little play on #3 anchor line, but I tightened it down." Peter von Scorio rolled his chair back a bit and looked over to Mike. "I think we can start setting up the Gun."

"DeepWorker One, DeepWorker Two, are you ready to implant the anchor points for the rings?"

"Roger, Mike," said Judith in DeepWorker Two.

"Send 'em out," said Bill in DeepWorker One. "Let's get started."

"Jacob," Mike said into the radio, "have you got the pylons for the rings loaded for deployment?"

"Squawk, Overqualified One to Controller, pylons are loaded on the skid ready for emersion, Squawk," came from another section of the Blockhouse, echoing a bit as it rounded the corridors.

Peter looked in the direction the voice had come from and smirked. Jacob Helman had installed all the equipment in the control room, knew it better than anyone else in Nuclear Recyclers, and would eventually be the control room operator before new recruits were hired. But as Production Manager, Mike had assigned himself as Controller for this proving test of the system. Jake had not been happy about that decision.

Mike keyed the radio to the hub Jake was working in. "Then send them out."

Peter mentally went through the procedures that Jake would be doing to transfer the pylons from inside the habitat out to the DeepWorker divers. The fifty steel rods, just like the ones already driven into the ocean floor, would have been loaded onto a plastic sled, would be placed in the water lock and secured in its lowering cradle. Once the door was sealed, water from the ballast tanks would be pumped into the room until it was flooded. Then Jake would crank—they had opted for manual controls for safety reasons when accessing the outside—the floor of the room back. Another manual control would allow him to crank the sled down one hundred feet to the ocean floor, where the two DeepWorkers were waiting to unhook the sled. Once the cables were retracted, the water in the room would be transferred back to the ballast tanks, thereby not affecting the buoyancy of the habitat.

"Squawk, lowering the sled now, Squawk," Jake shouted down the corridor.

"Use the damned radio," Mike shouted back.

Knowing he had better head things off, Peter got up from his plastic and nylon chair. "I'll have a talk with him."

The water lock was located in the aft, right hub of the habitat when you were facing forward in the control room. They had designated it #2 when numbered in a clockwise rotation. Only about ten feet down the twenty-foot-wide corridor was the entrance to the lock, where Jake was giving the crank one last turn.

"Squawk, touchdown, squa-," Jake shouted to the control room as he rose from his stoop. He stopped shouting when he turned and saw Peter standing nearby. "Oh, hi, Peter, I didn't hear you approach."

"You wouldn't. You were focused on your job." He placed his hand on Jake's shoulder. "I know you were supposed to be the one calling the shots today. I know what that means to you. She's your baby. But Mike is as concerned about this project as much as you are. Neither of you want anything to go wrong. Let him have the big seat today. Just play along, no distractions. You'll get your chance. Just think of it as a test of your design. If Mike can operate it, anyone can."

Over the speaker came, "We have the sled, raise the cables."

"Squawk, do you copy, Mr. Helman? Squawk," came from the control room.

As Jake opened his mouth, Peter pointed to the intercom button on the wall. "Jake, use the radio."

Jake closed his mouth, pressed the button and said, "Bringing the cables in now." Then hunched back over and began cranking up the cables he had just lowered.

"Thanks, Jake. I'll see you in the control room when you're done." Peter turned and walked away to let his Electronics Specialist finish.

As Peter sank back into his chair in front of the control boards, Mike asked, "Talk some sense into the boy?"

"Mike, he had been looking forward to this."

"I needed to make sure everything goes right. Besides, R.H.I.P."

"But management is about knowing when to trust your people. You should have trusted Jake to handle this while you took on the whole operation. Have you radioed *Damocles* to have the Deep Caissons sent down?"

"No," he said just above a whisper.

"You're focusing too much on the minutia. Call Captain Harris and get them rolling. They need to be here to carry the rings over to their anchor points when Jude and Bill are ready."

* * *

About ninety minutes later, David Wong in Deep Caisson One positioned himself directly behind the Blockhouse. After he had removed the locking cap, freeing the rings for removal, he extended the largest pair of his manipulator arms towards the first ring mounted on the starboard stem. He slid his claws into the anchor loops built into the bottom of the ring and lifted it up, off the stem. Locking his manipulator controls, he backed away from the habitat and headed for the first of the anchor points.

Bill and Jude were waiting there, each holding a steel cable to attach to the bottom of the oncoming ring. David moved his Deep Caisson, positioning the ring directly above the pylons and waited as the two DeepWorkers thread their lines through the loops and wielded them together. When Jude finally backed away, Bill having finished a minute earlier, David released his claws and moved away from the ring. It then floated up as far as its tethers would allow and hung under the ocean, waiting for its 24 brothers and sisters to join it.

Jude and Bill moved over to the next set of cables as Mike O'Donnell in Deep Caisson Two approached with the second ring. David moved back to the habitat to collect the third ring.

Chapter Thirty-Eight

The natural ocean breeze couldn't compete with that created by the Coast Guard vessel cutting through the waves at twenty knots. Once Neil turned off the deck and headed up the stairs to the ship's control room, even that breeze died away and the surrounding waters blanketed him in a very comfortable 88-degree air temperature.

Neil stepped onto the bridge of the USCGC Hamilton and pulled the hatch closed behind him. Immediately the temperature he felt dropped by ten degrees, the room was air-conditioned to keep outside conditions from affecting ship's operations.

"Welcome to the bridge, Special Agent Corsair," said Captain Margaret Williams. She sat back in a mounted center chair and watched the ocean break before the US Coast Guard Cutter's bow, not even looking at the man who had just walked through her door. The central console had about six stations mounted into it; two seaman were standing before it, monitoring the ship's progress, with a very large security officer between the console and the forward windows. "Now can you tell me exactly what we're looking for?"

He walked up to the temporary sonar station they had installed on the port side of the console and looked over the empty readings before turning to answer her. "A modified Marine Workers' Dolphin submersible."

"Very sea-worthy craft. How'd she get into trouble and why is it the concern of the FBI?" Putting a hand on each of her knees, Captain Williams looked into the FBI agent's face.

"She was stolen." Neil turned around and leaned against his sonar station. Being a temporary installation, a sonar pod was not mounted to the hull of the *Hamilton*. A wire ran from the sonar equipment, out the port side window, over the side of the ship and down to the sonar pod dangling below the cutter.

"We believe a Carlos Rondonate, he's been using many aliases, stole it from Marine Workers before they had a chance to launch her. With the recent string of oil rig attacks, we also believe he has equipped her with black market torpedoes. This isn't going to be an easy search; our target does not wish to be found."

"And you picked my ship, why? We didn't even have the sonar equipment for the job, you had to bring your own." She pointed to the green screen behind the FBI man.

"Availability. You were in the right place at the right time. We believe Carlos just put back out to sea yesterday. Probably to hit more oil rigs. We're assuming the *Gran Siena* disaster was his doing." He stood up and walked around the command and control console to get a better look through the forward windows. Lieutenant Danvers, he noted on the security officers uniform, stood aside for him to pass.

"That's a pretty bad spill." Captain Williams got down from her chair and joined him at the forward windows. "I shouldn't be glad you got us away from cleaning it up, but I am."

A pinging began from the installed unit. Neil almost ran around the control bench. Captain Williams just called over it,

"Helmsman, what's our present location?"

"29 degrees, 38.601 minutes north; 83 degrees, 54.795 minutes west, ma'am," he responded.

"Are we over an artificial reef?" she continued.

"Yes ma'am. It's that replica ship they sank a few years back."

"You're probably going to get a lot of false alarms on that thing, Mr. Corsair. They've been rebuilding the reef system around the Gulf with old ships for years."

Neil looked at the pinging result he was getting on his unit, reached into his coat and pulled his cell phone out of his pocket. "Martin, get up to the bridge. We need your best guess on where to look for Carlos."

*　*　*

"If we assume that all the oil rig shutdowns this month were the work of Carlos." Martin was seated in the second chair next to Captain Williams' desk in her cabin. Since it was mounted against the wall, she had turned her chair to face the two FBI men.

"And that the *Gran Siena* is an escalation of his attack pattern."

"Why do we assume that, Agent Hughes?" Captain Williams asked, tapping her pen on her desk with her left hand.

"When we raided Carlos' hideout, we found a fax that isolated the *Gran Siena* attack from all the others. It was not authorized by whoever is funding him."

"As Special Agent Corsair said. Additionally, the earlier attacks on the rigs simply shut them down, they had to discontinue drilling, but there was minimal oil spillage. That's not this man's style. He normally goes in for massive destruction and extreme collateral damage. He doesn't just blow things up; he focuses his explosions to cause a release that will effect the localities he is working in. An ammonia release here, oil discharge there, he's even used shaped charges to drive raw lumber into processing facilities. No, the *Gran Siena* disaster is more his MO than the earlier attacks."

"From what we know of the original equipment installed in the Dolphin," Neil took over, "he probably used that equipment to disable them. Things escalated with the tanker attacks, we believe he torpedoed them."

"And once he got a taste of that destruction, he turned his armaments on oil platforms. Ones his masters did not want him to, in order to send them a message. If we're going to look for a potential target, we need to look for something that will create more collateral damage than the *Gran Siena* oil spill."

"I can think of a few deep water rigs out here," Captain Williams speculated. She reached for one of the binders in the shelf above her desk.

"I don't think he will be going after another oil platform," Martin began.

"Why not?" Neil turned his chair to face his profiler.

"He doesn't repeat himself. If we look at the pattern of his attacks, he is always going after a different type of target. It's like once he plans something out, succeed or fail, he has to move onto another challenge. His attack on the second ammonia plant was more a target of opportunity. He had already hit the gasoline facility and probably discovered it was just up the road a bit. It's more like he needed to kill time for some reason. No, I think he will be looking for another target. Something bigger than the oil spill, something really spectacular."

"Damn, Dr. von Scorio's Waste Gun goes into trials later this week!"

"Nuclear waste all along the Atlantic coastline? That would fit."

"Captain, how fast can you get me to the *USS Vella Gulf*? She should be around 30 degrees north by 45 degrees west, if I remember where Peter told me they would set up."

She pulled out a chart and unrolled it to verify the location Neil had just given her. "About a week from here." She put up her hand to forestall Neil's objections. "But I could put you in

183

our copter and send you to Pensacola and they could get you out to the mid-Atlantic in under a day."

Neil looked over to Martin. "How soon can we leave?"

"All three of you?"

"No, I'm leaving Special Agent Brown with you in case Special Agent Hughes is wrong. We have to find Rondonate!"

Chapter Thirty-Nine

It had been a long day for Special Agent Paul St. Martin. One more year, he'd be able to retire from the Bureau and stop all this leg work. "Why couldn't they put all these guys in one office complex," he said as he walked down the hall to the office of Cadworth and Simmons.

Normally, he did the team's reference work. Like cross-referencing the oil platforms that had been hit to see exactly what they had in common. It had only narrowed the list of people who could have sent the faxes out to a dozen firms. The clerk at the Ramada hadn't been able to eliminate any of them, so Paul had to actually go out and interview each one. His feet screamed as he stood on them and opened the door to the last firm he planned to visit today.

"Can I help you?" said the receptionist as she sat back into her chair. The clock on the wall read a couple of minutes to five, quitting time.

He took his badge from his jacket upper pocket. "FBI Special Agent St. Martin." Putting it back in that pocket, he continued, "I need to speak to your bosses."

"Mr. Cadworth is out at the moment, but I believe Mr. Simmons may be available." She pressed a button on her phone and spoke at it. "Mr. Simmons, a man from the FBI is here to see you."

"Is it pressing? I have an appointment on the Hill at six,"

came back through the phone.

As his feet screamed again, Paul reached across the desk and pressed the blue button the reception had used earlier. "Yes, it is." He released the button and addressed the receptionist. "Which door?"

He walked over to the one she pointed at and entered without knocking.

Inside, the office was almost the size of the common space Paul's desk was a part of, back at the Bureau. A middle-aged man in a blue pinstriped suit with a matching blue collar on his white shirt that was held shut by a bright red tie sat behind a desk that looked small for the room. Off to the right of the door, the majority of the room was taken up by two overstuffed couches and several chairs grouped in a separate circle. Like the desk was an afterthought. Instead of racks of law books lining the far wall, a bar was stocked to the ceiling with every kind of alcohol Paul could imagine.

"To what do I owe this visit from the Bureau?" Simmons rose from his chair and made his way around his desk. He offered his right hand to Paul.

After shaking hands, Paul drew out his badge again to show to the lobbyist. "Special Agent St. Martin. Do you mind if I record our session? I find it improves my reports' accuracy."

"Certainly. How can I be of service?"

"We have reason to believe one of the terrorist suspects we are looking for has a Congressional contact. And as much as my feet hate the prospect, I am trying to interview people who have contact with them."

"Your feet? How thoughtless of me. Please have a seat, Agent Martin." He gestured towards one of the overstuffed couches that Paul knew he would never get back out of, this late in the day.

He chose one of the hard-backed chairs instead. Then set his recorder on the six-foot-long, rectangular, coffee table between the two couches.

Simmons chose to sit on the couch that was closest to the

chair Paul had chosen. "So how can I help the Bureau?"

"The military Semtex that the eco-terrorist has been using had been stored in a facility known to very few in the DOD. But I believe it had been divulged in closed door Senatorial hearings. I think you can understand why we would start with the people having contact with them before actually walking in and accusing a member of that body.

"So have you noticed any changes in behavior or mood swings in any of the Senators you routinely deal with?"

"No, not that I can think. Wait a minute." He leaned forward and looked Paul directly in the eyes. "Senator Dodson seems to have taken an interest in this terrorist's actions. He's asked me more than once to try and find out what you guys had discovered."

"And what did you tell him?"

"Why, nothing, of course. I can't get involved in an ongoing investigation. That would be against the law."

Paul began to rise from his chair. "Thank you for your time, Mr. Simmons. You've given me something to work on."

"Where's my hospitality? Do you want something to drink?"

"No, sir. I have to get back to the Bureau and speed along our investigation." Fully upright, Paul offered his hand to Simmons, then made his way to the door.

He'd already shown their photos to an uncertain Franco, who had narrowed his search down to the five people he had interviewed today. Hopefully, one of these voice recordings would generate a positive ID on the 'fax-man!'

Chapter Forty

The transport capsule banged against the water lock. A second later, the green light announcing a water tight seal lit up on the control console. Jacob, who was in control of the board, switched the outer door to open mode, knowing the inner door would hold if there was a malfunction in the indicator light. No water trickled into the chamber. He released the lock on the inner door and cycled it open for Peter to step across for his ride to the surface.

It had taken them about two weeks to tether and align the fifty rings that made up the Waste Gun. They had been running the last of their checklist items when they had received the message from Leo on the *Damocles* that Peter was needed. The tethered transport capsule was being sent down to bring him up. Two weeks earlier, Peter would have objected, but after seeing his crew working—and feeling useless in the process—he was ready to leave them alone from now until the first firing. He should get a couple more articles read on his half hour trip. E-readers were wonderful for magazine storage.

The capsule was large enough to comfortably bring the eight-man crew of the Blockhouse to the surface in case of an emergency. He had it all to himself this trip. Before taking a seat and strapping in, he signaled that everything was sealed to the surface crew who would winch the module up. Then he went over to the coffee machine and brewed a cup for the trip.

As he was sealing the lid on his cup, he could feel the slack being removed from the cable. He took his seat as he began his trip to the surface.

* * *

Through the portholes, Peter could see the capsule break the surface. Instead of docking next to the *Damocles*, they appeared to be hauling him directly onto the deck.

As he opened the door and walked out, Leo was waiting for him. "Sorry to pull you away from the fun, Peter. We've been called over to the *Vella Gulf*, by that FBI guy we met a few weeks ago."

"Any idea why?" Peter handed the door off to one of the deck hands, who would service it for the next time it was needed.

"None whatsoever." Leo turned to walk with Peter to the Starboard side of the *Damocles* and down the ladder to the naval launch waiting for them. "I did get a good view of the transport helicopter they got here in."

As the two men took their seats, the Ensign in charge of the launch ordered, "Let's get underway, Mr. Arnold."

"Any idea what's going on, Ensign?" Peter tried asking, but as the engines of the launch fired up, he couldn't even hear the end of his question.

* * *

"It's good of you two to make it," Commander Wallace greeted them as they came up the docking stairs. "Captain Miller and the gentlemen from the FBI are waiting in my briefing room. Shall we join them?" Turning, he took the two men by their shoulders and shepherded them through the open hatch into his ship and down the corridor into his briefing room.

"Peter," Neil rose from his chair as they walked through the door, extending his hand. "I wish we could meet under better circumstances."

Peter and Leo took seats across the table from the three FBI men and next to Captain Miller. Commander Wallace took his seat at the head of the table, the one furthest from the door.

"What seems to be the problem, Neil?"

"We believe a major eco-terrorist plans on attacking your Waste Gun."

"We're 1500 feet underwater," Leo said. "How's he even going to get to us?"

"We believe he has a modified Marine Worker's submarine equipped with Soviet-era torpedoes. He knows your procedures. Carlos Rondonate worked for you about six months ago under the name of Charles Roland." Neil slid a file across the table for Peter and Leo to review.

"I always wondered what happened to that guy," Leo said, looking at the picture of Carlos Rondonate from the FBI file.

"I don't know what we can do, Neil," Peter said. "We don't have any defense procedures, other than these two US Navy vessels."

"Never fear, Mr. von Scorio," Captain Miller injected. "The *Halsey* is equipped for submarine warfare. We'll deal with this Rondonate guy."

"I wish it were that simple," Special Agent Hughes added. "Carlos Rondonate has been eluding law enforcement officers throughout the mainland. Using the submarine he stole from Marine Workers, he's hit over a dozen oil platforms last month. He just hit a couple more chemical plants before heading back into the Gulf. We don't know how he is going to do this, but his profile suggests you would be his next ideal target."

"Just one of your transport canisters opened up would spew nuclear waste all along the Atlantic coast line," Neil added.

"Just the type of press this guy likes," Hughes finished.

Chapter Forty-One

"I do not like the profile of the ship heading my way," Carlos said as he climbed back into the *Suelo Defensor* and sealed the observation bubble.

He dropped into the pilot's seat, activated the military grade radio that Said had installed for him and set it to scan for the ship's frequency. While monitoring the radio, he checked the output of his nuclear reactor, then he filled the ballast tanks and dove as fast as she would go, down to the bottom of this manmade reef.

"If they did not see me, two hundred fifty feet of water should cover my tracks," he mused as the ship began to appear on his sonar screen. "She looked too small to be a naval vessel, and only they would have the necessary detection equipment if I can get down fast enough."

"*USCGC Hamilton* to base, *USCGC Hamilton* to base, over." He switched out of scan mode as the voice echoed through his tiny cabin.

"Coast Guard Liaison Office here, *Hamilton*. You haven't been out there long enough to get into trouble. But how can we help? Over."

"We've spotted a suspicious ship in the vicinity and are about to investigate. It appears to have dropped below the waves. I'm sure glad that FBI guy had that sonar unit installed. We'll call you back when we have something more. Over and out."

Just his luck. Carlos watched on his sonar screen as the *Hamilton* turned and cruised straight for his position. At first it passed directly overhead, then about a mile away, it turned around and headed back to the center point on his screen, where it became stationary.

Carlos looked over to his Automatic Identification System computer. "No, it is switched off. They cannot be using a signal from the *Defensor* to track me. But maybe they are broadcasting," he set the unit to receive only and switched it on.

"The *USCGC Hamilton*," printed itself across its screen.

"But she should not have sonar. Radar, yes, but not sonar. Yet there she is, circling directly above me." He got out of his chair and paced the short space in this part of the ship, two steps in any direction. "Wait, they said something about an FBI man bringing a sonar unit with him. This could be a long wait." He piloted his submarine as close as he could to the US aircraft carrier that had been sunk nearby, to help build this reef. "If they are using sonar, maybe this will mask you, my old friend." He stroked the side of the hull.

Eight hours and two MREs later, the *Hamilton* was still circling overhead. "I cannot wait forever," he said as he disposed of his fork into his meal's bag and closed it for disposal. He would eat his more sustainable meals once his mission was over, but now there was no way to prepare proper food in the *Suelo Defensor* and he must use these resource hogs to keep himself going.

190

He dropped the bag into his trash container and mounted the pilot's chair again. "I must relieve myself of these pests."

He engaged the drive engines, steered the *Suelo Defensor* into a vertical assent directly below his adversary, and purged his ballast water. Once he had a direct line on the *Hamilton*, he pinged it with his far left torpedo and launched it at the coast guard cutter. "I will only need one for their Waste Gun."

It had a straight shot, it was radar locked, it did not miss the *Hamilton*. It took out the back end of the cutter, tearing a large hole in her stern, and destroyed both of her propeller shafts, insuring she would not be able to follow Carlos any longer.

"Mayday, Mayday. This is the *USCGC Hamilton*, we have been struck and are sinking. Our position is thirty degrees, two point 6 minutes north by eighty-seven degrees, point 4 minutes west. We are taking on water and sinking fast. Everyone is being evacuated to lifeboats, but we need rescue. Repeating; Mayday, Mayday. This is..."

Carlos pulled out of his ascent, shut off the radio and surfaced beyond gun range of the vessel into the darkness of the Caribbean night.

After throwing back the canopy, Carlos could feel the cool breeze of the Caribbean wind. As his eyes adjusted to the darkness of night, he could see the lights of his adversary wink out as the ship slipped further under the water,; could hear the shouts of the men as they abandoned their sinking home.

He waited about an hour for the last of the lights to disappear before he reentered back into the pilot's station. "It is time we were moving. I have a mission to perform for you, Gaia." He dropped beneath the waves, where his stolen Dolphin made her best speed, engaged his propellers and resumed his course for the mid-Atlantic.

* * *

A day later, as he was weaving his way through the Florida Keys, Carlos realized that he was not going to make the Waste

Gun site before they were ready to begin firing. The land-based radio stations he had been monitoring gave few—if any—details about it. Coverage was even less sparse for it than it was for the private space program happening a couple hundred miles up the coast. Even the *Halsey* and the *Vella Gulf* were keeping silent about the event. He had hoped he could get there in time to torpedo one of the nuclear waste containers before his little surprise destroyed the gun.

Chapter Forty-Two

Peter fell to the floor. Thankfully, he had attached the lid to his coffee cup, or a lot more than a slight trickle would be spreading across the Blockhouse's control room decking. As the facility swung back and forth on its mooring lines, he tried getting his feet back under him.

Both Harry Trunnel and Jacob Helman had been sitting in front of the control board, Harry had maintained his balance by grabbing the edge of the desk with both hands as soon as the Blockhouse began shaking. Jacob wasn't as quick; his chair rolled to the back of the control room into the computer servers, then headed back to the control bench on the return swing. This time, he was ready, and grabbed the desk and pulled himself back into his station.

"What's going on up there?" came over the intercom. "I leave you guys for five minutes, and you try to blow the place up?" Down in the kitchen, Mike Farrel had been grabbing a snack before the power-up sequence that was today's test.

Peter finally got to his feet, stumbled over to the center's wall and hung on while he made his way back to the control boards. While the swinging was calming down, it was still worse than any storm-wracked deck he had ever walked across. After he had cut the distance to the central control desk down to three feet, as the Blockhouse reached the end of one swing and was about to return, he took a large step towards it then pushed away from the wall and fell into the back of the bench. He held on for a full return swing to make sure he had his balance.

"What just happened? That wasn't some kind of earthquake, was it?"

"Jake, give me a two-second burst on the aft stabilizer. Let's see if we can stop this swinging." Harry had been trying to arrest the habitat's momentum, now that the event wave had passed.

"Roger that. Burst commencing." A quick roar came from behind them just outside the Blockhouse, then quickly ceased. And with the quiet came a session of motion. Peter let go of the console and didn't fall over again.

"That felt like an explosion," Mike said as he walked up the spiral staircase from the galley into Control.

"I'm not getting a signal from the Gun." Harry spun his chair towards Peter. "There's no telemetry at all coming from the Gun."

"Jake, signal *Damocles* that we have a problem," Peter began. He pulled a chair out of the storage locker and sat in front of the Gun's control computer and began a reboot of the system. "Call Carol, get her up here. Then contact everyone outside and have them confirm their condition. Harry, get the ROVs back online. We need to see what happened out there. Mike, I need you to do a visual inspection of the Blockhouse."

"I'm on it, Peter." He turned and ran down the right spoke.

"I've got Leo on the line," Jake said as he handed the microphone to Peter, then he activated the intercom to their sleeping quarters. "Carol, Mike. We need you up here, ASAP."

"Peter, what's all the panic down there?" Leo said over the radio.

At that moment, Captain Miller of the *Halsey* broke in. "We have detected an explosion in your vicinity. Dr. von Scorio, can you confirm the safety of all your personnel?"

Peter looked over at Jacob, waiting for an answer.

He pointed at the diver monitors on his board. There had been three divers in the water finishing preparations for the test,

193

so two of the virtual boxes were unlit, two showed green, and the last red. "Everyone has reported in except Judith. I can't raise her Caisson."

Peter forced himself to not grab the headphones off the head of his electronics expert and call for her himself. The best thing for him to do was get a search going. "Harry, do you have any of those ROVs available?"

Harry rose from his chair slightly and gave the left side of the console a sharp rap with his open palm. Five of the monitor screens that had been nothing but static came to life, the other five were still blank. Each showed a different angle of the ocean floor where the Gun had been moored. "I thought it was just a loose connection."

ROV 1 showed the loading end of the Gun, the six rings it was focused on were wobbling but intact, with silt from the ocean floor falling back down. ROV 2 showed the same thing on the next 6 rings. ROV 3 showed three of the rings doing the same thing, but the next ones showed some type of damage as the cloud of silt, which had been higher than for the rest of the rings, cleared away from them. Each showed progressively more damage, with the one on the end only existing as a semicircle of its former ring. ROVs 4 through 8 were still offline, with 9 and 10 showing the same thing as the first two.

"My God, what happened to the Gun?" Harry said as the monitors resolved their images. "Jake, I lost feed on five of the ROVs."

"Harry, switch with me." Jacob rolled his chair over to Harry's board and looked at the readouts. "They're gone, ROVs 4 and 5 are completely gone. We aren't even getting a ping back from their position. I'm getting an acknowledgement of my signal pings to the others, but only that. Something must have damaged their transmitting capacity. What the hell exploded?"

"Get back on the link upstairs, Harry. Jake, see if you can get the ROVs you have working looking for Deep Caisson Two. We have to find Judith."

"Water-tight up here, Peter," Mike said as he raced to the

stairs leading to the lower level. "On my way below."

"When you're done, get suited up," Peter called back to him as he disappeared down the banister of those stairs. "Take a DeepWorker and look for Judith."

"Roger that," echoed from below.

Peter pressed the intercom button to the sleeping quarters. "O'Donnell, I need you suited up. How fast can you get your DeepWorker out there?"

"Peter, we have a problem," came his response over the intercom speaker. "Carol rolled out of her bunk and must have hit her head. I'm not finding any external injuries, but I can't wake her. Can you send someone down?"

Not Carol! Peter pressed the button, "I'm on my way."

He ran three long strides to the staircase, grabbed a railing in each hand and slid down the rails, barely touching each step as he fell past them. He ran forward through the common area that housed their kitchen/recreational area and into the crew cabin where two cots were mounted on each of the walls.

Mike O'Donnell was kneeling on the floor, pulling a blanket over Carol's supine body. He stood up as Peter entered the hub. "She's breathing with no obvious bleeding injuries. She's reacted to me poking her feet, so I doubt there is any spinal injury. I just can't wake her up."

Peter looked over to the First Aid kit next to Carol's head and knew Mike had done everything they could down here. "I'd love to get her back into one of the bunks, but she might have a partial injury we could exasperate. Let's not move her." *Damn, it had to be Carol! She needs me and right now, I can't stay here.* "Stay here with her. I need to go outside. We can't locate Judith or her Caisson."

"When did you get your DeepWorker certification?" Mike asked, knowing full well his boss wasn't qualified to operate one.

"I didn't! But I did test one out when we were negotiating our contract with Marine Workers." Peter stood up to leave.

"Grab all the pillows and blankets you can find." Mike grabbed the pillows from the cot Carol had fallen from and the one below it. "We'll immobilize Carol, and I'll go out." He shoved them against her body as tight as he could. Peter grabbed the ones from the adjacent bunks and did likewise on her other side. "From the sounds of things, you're needed in the control room, anyway."

Carol stirred a couple of times but did not wake up while they were securing her. Once Peter was satisfied, O'Donnell went aft to the water lock hub to suit up with Farrell. Peter knelt beside Carol a moment longer, then said in a low voice, "I'll get a doctor down here."

She fluttered her eyes open and smiled up at Peter. "Why am I wrapped up? On the floor?" She started to push herself up.

He put a hand on her chest to hold her down. "You fell. You've been unconscious since the explosion, but we don't know the extent of your injuries. Please, Carol, stay down. I'll arrange for a doctor to come here and look you over before we risk moving you."

She relaxed back to the floor, then tried to get up again. "Explosion?"

He held her down. "Something happened to the rings. We don't know what yet. The Blockhouse is secure; everyone is accounted for except Judith. We're making every effort to find her. If you'll promise me to stay still, I can get back to the search."

"Can you grab me a bottle of water before you go?"

He stroked her face. "Sure."

* * *

Peter had rolled his chair back to stare at the large monitors overhead showing the images of the four divers and five ROVs searching the ocean bottom, instead of the smaller screens mounted into the control station. Occasional bits of debris from the destroyed rings littered the area, but nothing that was positively from Judith's Caisson had yet been identified.

After about an hour into the search, a large piece of ring came into view of ROV 2. Jake programmed the remaining

ROVs to converge on the spot. "Farrell, O'Donnell, Wong; patch in the feed from ROV 2. Then converge on that spot."

As David, being the closest to the designated spot, turned his Caisson; the wreckage of the other DeepCaisson came into view. It was pinned on the ocean floor by the upper half of one of the Gun's magnetic rings.

ROV 3 came into David's search lights. Jake maneuvered it to where the crew component of the Caisson would be, but found that whole compartment missing.

Jake turned towards Peter. "She's not there!"

"We'll have to keep looking," Peter said as the radio to the *Damocles* interrupted.

"*Damocles* to Blockhouse. Peter, we've found Judith. Your escape system worked. Her crew compartment popped up here a few moments ago. Peter, Judith is alive and well."

"Thanks, Leo. We needed some good news right about now."

Peter looked over to Harry, "Blockhouse to everyone, Judith has been found. She's aboard the *Damocles*, she's safe."

Chapter Forty-Three

Agents Corsair and Fellows were waiting on the barge that had been brought in to receive the pieces of the exploded gun they'd recovered. Standing port side, they watched as the large wire basket broke the surface of the Atlantic, was pulled upward until it was a few feet above the barges' safety rail, then swung over to the deck area where it was to be set down. They kept well back as the officer in charge signaled his men and they gently lowered the basket onto the deck for inspection.

This had been the load Neil had been waiting for. The divers had identified this debris to have been from the ring at the epicenter of the explosion. As soon as the crewmen had disconnected the basket and raised the crane away to prepare for the next load, Harold snapped on his latex gloves to begin the search. With Carlos still on the loose, the FBI team was assuming any incident was a deliberate attack, even if the last word they had had on his whereabouts put him in the Gulf, not the Mid-Atlantic.

Then again, explosions were his MO.

Using a non-magnetic, extendable pointer, Agent Fellows probed several of the ring pieces. After a few minutes' examination, he set down the current fragment he was tipping up, reached into his suit coat pocket and pulled out a zip-lock evidence bag. After making a quick note on the bag, he picked up the fragment, gave it a sniff and a close visual inspection before turning to Neil.

"Neil, we need to bag this one. I think we might have some residue."

"It didn't wash off in the ocean?" Neil took the bag Fellows was dangling from his fingers and held it open for him to insert his find.

"It must have been forced deep into the pores. We need to find more pieces of this ring, if we can. But I think Quantico can confirm a deliberate explosion."

"Meaning Carlos Rontunate."

"Well, the taggants will tell."

Chapter Forty-Four

"I worried that I would not be here for the test shots," Carlos slammed the small refrigerator shut. "But they are still building the damned thing."

He dropped his Danish, plate and all, on the writing platform attached to his scanning console. Going back to the kitchen, he attached today's coffee pouch to the hot water dispenser and filled it. Shaking the pouch as he returned to the sub's science station, he dropped back into the chair he had been occupying for the last three days and continued his staring at the screen. Waiting for the activity around the gun's building site to cease.

Four days ago, he had crawled across the bottom of the Atlantic until he found a ledge high enough for him to keep an eye on Nuclear Recyclers' activities, yet hide him from the prying eyes of US Naval sonar from above. Thanks to the precise buoyancy control built into the *Suelo Defensor*, he was able to stay a foot above the floor and, using minimal jets, keep from stirring up the sediment on the bottom.

"I thought they had radioed two weeks ago they were ready to begin?" He took another pull on his coffee pouch. "And who am I talking to?" *This wait is driving me loco*, he internalized.

"Give that cable a test," squawked the radio he had monitoring the Blockhouse's frequencies.

The ring that was being welded into place moved slightly upward but stopped less than an inch from where it had floated earlier.

"Cable attachment confirmed, Bill. Now let's get everybody back into the Blockhouse. In case Charley left another surprise for us."

Charley? Oh, I was using Charles when I worked for them. That is why they are delayed. My little present did have a bite.

"Ten-four, Peter. Heading back now." Someone began moving away from the assembly and back towards the control submersible.

The cameras on the Remotely Operated Vehicles Carlos had deployed when he got here showed what looked like three large retired US Navy submarines laying side by side, connected by spokes running between them. The back ends of two of them had been sheared off, and a large cube-shaped structure had been attached. It was where all the worker subs were heading now.

Carlos watched the last one as it dove below that section of the Blockhouse. "The first couple of tests will be with empty canisters. There will be no point in wasting my three remaining torpedoes on them. Alas, more waiting." He took the last pull on his coffee pouch before executing a perfect toss into the recycling bin at the entrance to this compartment.

"David, have you got eyes on the first cylinder?" Carlos heard coming over his radio intercept.

I must have missed one. I thought they had all returned to their cozy Bunkhouse. He located the lone Caisson by radar and sent one of his ROVs over to see what was going on.

The submersible had its two large claw arms extended as it approached the travel canister sitting on the bottom of the ocean. Opening the claws to their maximum width allowed them to clear the sides of the bullet-shaped container by just over an inch. Once around the midpoint of the cylinder, the fingers of the claws began to extend forward, circling the canister until their two tips met and locked together.

With the two claws locked, one about a third of the way down and the other about two-thirds, the operator—*David Wong, if their radio transmissions are to be believed. I never liked that guy. He tried too hard to be friendly*—began lifting the load off the ocean floor and to the loading end of the ring assembly.

Instead of twisting the arms to line the canister up for insertion, the operator rotated his whole craft until the container was horizontal with the ocean floor. He drove his load to within a foot of the assembly. Once he was settled into place, Wong made a couple of twisting adjustments to get his load lined up with the first ring. He released the claws and side-maneuvered his Caisson away from the canister.

The canister didn't move, though. *Von Scorio said that the Gun would have the bullet locked in position at this point by the same magnetics that would launch it into Mother Earth.*

After the Caisson cleared the back of the canister, it turned and headed to the ocean floor.

"In position," came over the radio. A moment later, the bullet disappeared from the position it had been holding and a flash appeared in the river of lava that was the Mid-Atlantic ridge.

"Great shot," a different voice said through Carlos' overhead speaker.

Another voice piped in, "Right on the mark, Peter. The *Vella*

Gulf confirms a precise hit. We've already sent down the next test cylinder, it should reach your position in a couple of minutes."

"Thanks, Leo. We've got the second one on sonar now. It should land well clear of David's position.

"David, you getting all that? The second cylinder should be landing about ten meters north and three meters west of your position."

"Almost on top of the first one, if I hadn't moved it. I'm lifting off to intercept now."

"David, you let that canister fall. The Caisson can't take the stress of catching it."

"You take all the fun out of life sometimes, Petey."

Carlos watched the cylinder hit the ocean floor almost flat on, spreading up about three feet of sift that began its slow descent back down. The Caisson went through the same maneuvers as before and the bullet flashed into the volcano ridge with the same results.

Radio traffic went dead after Von Scorio acknowledged the second results and sent his numbers up to the *Damocles* and the escorting Naval vessels.

"Dr. Von Scorio, this is Jacob Randolph."

Carlos leaned forward. 'What did the United States Secretary of Energy want?'

"Son, I've been talking with Mr. Dayton and the Captains monitoring your results, and we all concur that it's time to take the kid gloves off. We're going to be sending you a fully-loaded cylinder. Get your recording instruments ready. We need to know that none of its contents come back."

"Yes sir, Mr. Secretary. We'll be ready. David, did you catch that? Expect a lot more wait on the next load."

"Roger that. It'll be good to finally make it real."

Carlos straighten up in his chair fast enough to have gone backwards if it hadn't been bolted to the deck. *Too early. I am not ready.* He jockeyed one of the ROVs to 50 meters above the previous landing site, another he sent to 20 meters. He targeted his torpedo on the descent path he had seen earlier about 20 meters above the ocean floor. He wanted to hit it before it got to the rings, then blow the rings, and finally, finish the Nuclear Recylers themselves with his last torpedo.

Leo Dayton's voice boomed out of the speaker. "It's on its way, guys. Good luck."

After an excruciating ten minutes, the nuclear waste travel cylinder crossed in front of his 50 meter ROV. Carlos finished the prep of the torpedo he had mounted on the far side of his right diving wing. As it came into view of his deeper ROV, he acquired a target lock and fired.

The torpedo crossed the distance to the cylinder in under a minute. It exploded against the side of the cylinder and ruptured into small fragments. The debris fell away from the impact site and much faster than the original container.

"It was empty," Carlos shouted. "Empty! Wait, that means this is a trap."

He jumped out of the science station and down to the vehicle controls. Quickly reactivating the engines, he sped directly forward, then did a ninety-degree turn to port, followed a few seconds later to starboard. He then put the *Suelo Defensor* under the tenth ring of the structure and grounded her, powering down everything he could.

Minutes later, the depression that he had been hiding in for the last few days exploded. The Navy had flushed him from his safe spot. They knew he was here.

Chapter Forty-Five

"Blockhouse, this is *Damocles*, do you read? Blockhouse, this is *Damocles*, is everyone all right?"

Peter picked himself up from the floor and took the single step to the communications console. He reached down to help

Harry back to his seat. Jacob had already picked himself up and was pushing his chair back to the computer console. As Harry got his feet steadied, Peter slapped him on his shoulder and grabbed the mic connecting them to the surface.

"Blockhouse, this is..."

"Blockhouse here. Leo, what happened?"

"Is everyone okay?"

He looked over at Harry, who was checking on those not in the control room. Harry, upon hearing Leo's request, gave Peter a thumbs up.

"We're fine down here. What happened?"

"Special Agent Corsair of the FBI is coming down to join you guys. Charley Roland's in the area. Agent Corsair thought he might be, so he set a trap to flush him. We sent the last of the test travel canisters down, announcing it was a real one. He took the bait. The *USS Halsey* verified his location from his torpedo launch and dropped depth charges."

Four of the five Deep Sea Operators walked into the room. "Harry, signal David to get in here." Judith Hurley carried two coffee cups. When Peter got close enough, she handed him one. "Thanks," as he accepted it. But he couldn't stop himself from staring at the wet stain on the front of her jumpsuit.

"And it was plenty hot when you guys dumped it all over me."

"Did you get him?" Peter couldn't spare the time to bring the newcomers up to speed, but was back on the radio to the surface. He waved everyone over to Harry and did a quick talking motion with his hand. They all huddled around Harry for an explanation.

"Captain Wallace here. We're not showing him on our sensors, nor are we showing any debris. We have no idea if we got him or not."

One of the Dolphin channels opened up. "Carlos is slippery like that. I've been following him around the country for the last year. Every time we think we have him, he's managed to get away. Dr. Von Scorio, I should be to your Blockhouse in about," there was a short pause before he returned, "ten minutes. I'll be coordinating the search from there. Corsair, out."

"Okay everyone, we can't just stand around until he gets here. Grab a station and run a complete systems check. Those explosions probably knocked things around a bit."

Everyone took a position in front of one of the banks of computer monitors arranged in a circle around the center of the room. Locking wheels on each of the chairs allowed two people to run normal operations, sliding between monitors, once production disposal was established. The six of them, while Peter remained standing, covered all the stations independently.

"I've got a wobble in a couple of the rings," Harry announced. "I'm compensating for it now. They must have attracted some of the debris, weighs a bit heavy."

"Reverse the magnets, see if that dislodges things."

Harry opened a few apps and touched the computer monitor to engage them. He waited a minute for the results. It allowed Peter time to move behind and peek over his right shoulder.

Harry turned to look up at his boss. "Didn't work."

"Just compensate with maneuvering thrusters until we can get out there and fix things."

"Sonar's working," Judith said. "I've got Sarah on the way down."

"You're assuming it's her bringing our guest."

Judith pointed at her non-touch screen monitor. "That's her recognition code."

Peter swung his head around to Jacob.

"I had some spare time after we got things installed, so I wrote an app to ID our submersibles."

"Leo's not paying you guys enough. Thanks for covering my goofs."

"The Blockhouse is showing no leaking, we're still at a stable 1020 millibars of pressure," Bill reported. "We've got a mess in some of the compartments, unsecured things got knocked around, but nothing a little janitorial work can't fix." Peter watched as the images on his quarterly-divided screen flicked between the different rooms of the Blockhouse.

He reached over Bill's shoulder and touched the image from the DeepWorker hanger and froze the image. "Looks like David's back," Bill said as the water level in the chamber began to lower.

Peter turned to Mike. "Flood the Dolphin Bay and have it ready for Sarah to dock." A Dolphin-class submersible was too large to actually be housed within the Blockhouse. Three ports were made available on the left side of the Blockhouse for their conning tower hatch to maneuver into place. But if they had more than two docked at any one time, the Deepworkers were trapped in the central hanger area. "I want the FBI guy up here stat."

"Bill, do we have outside cameras working?"

He switched his monitors to external views and got static on most screens, with the rest just blank. Though one of those blank screens did have an upper right corner showing an ocean view.

"It looks like most of them got busted. But I'd have to guess that these blank ones have their lens covered by something."

"Try rotating them."

A rotational image popped into the corner of each of the blank images along with a display of its direction and position. Rotating five of them made no change to their positional indicator. Rotating the sixth made its screen go to static. The other four spun as directed but did not clear up. "Still blind out there."

"You did your best." Peter rested his hand on Bill's shoulder. "See how many of those static-y guys respond, then pull them in. Let's see how many of them we can get repaired and back out there."

The light to the DeepWorker hanger went from red to green. Peter toggled the intercom switch, "David, stick around down there. We're expecting company at Port..." He looked over to Mike.

"One. Two's already got our escape Dolphin in it."

"Port One. Sarah's bringing an FBI agent down."

"Roger that," came from the overhead speaker. "We got an ETA?"

"She should be pulling in any time now," Judith said and Peter relayed to David.

In about half the time Peter expected, David called back. "She must be here already. The sea doors are open."

"We prepped her arrival."

"Okay, I'm here when she arrives."

"Thanks, David. Get Agent Corsair up here as quick as you can. It looks like Charles Roland, er, Carlos Rondonate, is back."

Chapter Forty-Six

David was waiting at the water lock door for Dolphin Bay One when he caught the blue request light on port Three flash on.

"Blockhouse, this is Dolphin Sarah requesting access to Dolphin Bay Three."

David looked up at the speaker. Sarah had missed her mark again. He mentally organized a series of simulator drills for her when this was over. It was only a hundred feet away from her assigned dock, but she would have had to approach the Blockhouse from the stern instead of its bow.

He pressed the intercom button. "Control, I've got her."

"Don't forget to seal and clear port One, then."

"Roger that, Judith." He activated the purge cycle and moved over to flood port Three. He opened the safety panel and engaged the sea pumps. It took about five minutes for the hanger bay to flood enough that he could open the sea doors without the outside pressure bending them inward. He took that time to insure that port One had fully closed. It was, and the 'occupied' light was on. *They must have an extra escape Dolphin down here,* he thought. *I guess Sarah won't be needing any retraining after all.*

From the camera mounted inside port Three, David watched

as Sarah brought the Dolphin straight up into its bay. Jacob's electronic eye triggered the sea doors to seal themselves when her conning tower was fully inside. As the indicator flashed green, David activated the pumps and cleared the bay of sea water.

"Sarah," he said as the two passengers emerged into the Blockhouse. "Smooth trip?"

"A slight cross current around one thousand feet, but not too strong. I was compensating when sensors read a Dolphin already in Bay One."

"And you must be..."

"Special Agent Neil Corsair." Wearing a light blue wind breaker over his white shirt and tie, he took David's offered hand. "I need to see Dr. von Scorio at once."

"Sarah, I just got in myself. Could you go up to the cantina and grab a couple of coffees? Make one with cream and two sugars?"

"Agent Corsair?"

"I really need to see Dr. von Scorio right away."

"Then follow me." As they reached the hatch leading from the docking bays, "Thanks, Sarah. Next time, I'm buying."

* * *

Since the control room was four decks above, a lift had been designed into the Blockhouse. Sarah got off on deck Three as David took the FBI man a deck further.

The lack of doors on the lift—people were kept from falling out by the wire gate pulled in front of them before the lift would engage—allowed Agent Corsair to get a good look at the control room as he was raised into it.

"You guys must have over forty feet of computer servers down here."

"We've got about two dozen servers, half of them are backups." David lifted half the gate up and pushed the other half down. "Hey, Jake, where's Peter?"

"He went to get some more chairs," the man directly opposite the opening in the circle of monitoring stations called over his shoulder.

"I'd better go give him a hand," David trotted off to the lower level store room before Agent Corsair could react to his abandonment.

Taking in the room, before him was the computer circle, and a few feet from that was another circle, this time of windows that looked out onto the ocean floor with just enough exterior lighting to see a few feet out into the depths. A squid swam past, one large enough to take up two of the three-foot window panes.

Neil drew his focus back to the people manning the Operations Station. It took him six steps to clear the distance from the lift into the middle of the circle.

"Unless you have an actual question," Jake called over his shoulder, "you're going to have to wait for Peter to get back."

Quiet descended over the control room, except for the noise of the monitoring equipment. But only briefly, as soon the thuds of chairs landing on the floor outside the circle echoed through the chamber.

As he turned, Neil recognized the man he had come to coordinate with. "Dr. von Scorio." He left the circle and extended his hand.

"What brings you down here, Agent Corsair? I would have thought the Navy's equipment would do a better job of tracking whether or not you got him?" Peter gestured at one of the two chairs he had brought up and unfolded. Then sat in the other.

"Carlos has slipped through our fingers too often. Every time I thought we had a handle on him, he's pulled an end-run and escaped. No, I want to be on the scene if there's even a chance he's still alive."

"Peter," Bill called over, "the active remote cameras are back."

"David, see what you can do for them? Bill, keep working on the others and see if you can get them back." Peter looked over to Neil, "I have a feeling we're going to need as many as we can get."

"So you haven't been able to get eyes on the scene since Carlos torpedoed the empty canister?"

"No, the explosions must have scrambled the signals of some of our ROVs and debris covered the optics of the rest. I've known David since college, he'll get them working again. Then we can search the wreckage."

"Strange." Everyone looked over to Bill at his console. "I'm starting to lose internal cameras now. Could the Navy be doing something to disable them?"

Neil was out of his chair heading for the lift. "Where?"

* * *

"Dr. von Scorio, get down to your maintenance area immediately. With whoever has medical training." Neil lifted his right fist from the intercom button, then knelt down over the body of the man who had welcomed him onto the Blockhouse. "Call for help. He's breathing, therefore not in cardiac arrest. No bleeding I can see." He found a fire blanket on the wall, pulled it from its bright red box and covered David to protect him from shock. There was nothing more he could do until help arrived.

It was a painstaking few minutes' wait, but Neil used the time to investigate the scene. A wrench lay on the floor next to the unconscious submersible operator. Further inspection revealed a can of spray paint missing from the orderly rows stacked in a nearby glass cabinet. The can lay on the floor under one of the benches. A drop of black paint hitting the floor made Neil look up. Directly above the drop was the room's camera. As he had guessed, it had been sprayed black with paint, still dripping from the camera lens.

He turned as he heard two people coming through the hatch. Judith dropped to one knee to begin examining David, who winched as she probed a knot forming on the side of his head. "Lay still, David," she placed her hand on his chest as he started to rise. "Follow my finger. Good. Now, other than your head."

Neil grabbed Peter by his shoulder and pointed at the disabled camera. "Carlos is on board."

Chapter Forty-Seven

Three sleeping quarters, sleeping quarters larger than what he had been using on the *Suelo Defensor*. *These Americans even waste the space they build for themselves*, he thought as he moved on to the end of the corridor and opened the hatch.

"Now I have something to work with." Inside the triple-sized room were workbenches lining all the walls with various fabrication tools on them and hand tools racked on the walls behind them.

On the far side were mounted cabinets, clear plastic cabinets. One of them had cans of spray paint stored within. He opened it, grabbed the first can and shook it. Not a lot of paint left, but enough for here. He climbed up on the bench directly under the room's camera and proceeded to empty it of its paint before tossing the can onto the floor. "Now I will be able to keep away their prying eyes."

He turned back to the tools rack, pulled the largest pipe wrench he could find off its hooks and smacked it against his left hand a couple of time. Then he back-handedly swung the wrench against one of the 3-D printers sitting on the workbench. Thousands of its plastic pieces scurried across the floor. "Yes, this will work nicely."

After he had laid into the two remaining printers, their control computer, and a machine lathe, he spotted a bin of small camera ROVs. Some damaged, some with ocean debris covering their optics. But none of them were going to survive his wrench, as he took a two-handed grip on it and brought it down on them. Over and over.

"Hey, what're you..."

Carlos swung his wrench around and struck the intruder against the side of his head. The man politely dropped to the floor without uttering another word. Carlos spun back to the paint cabinet and extracted a couple more cans. Cans he decided that were still full. He had many more rooms to explore and many more eyes to blind.

Chapter Forty-Eight

"We believe his main plan was to torpedo one of the fully loaded travel canisters and spread radioactive waste all along the Eastern Seaboard." Neil walked up and down the corridor outside the infirmary where they had brought David for treatment. Peter leaned into the far wall with his arms folded in front of him as the FBI man continued. "We've thwarted that plan. But he means to take down this Waste Gun of yours. So, what will he target next?"

"Nothing permanent can be done to them from inside the Blockhouse. Throw them out of alignment, drop them to the seabed, but nothing we can't quickly restore."

"No, you saw the damage he did in your maintenance room. He'll be looking for something spectacular. Something that sends a message." Neil stopped pacing in front of Peter and looked the engineer in his eyes. "Where do you get your power from?"

"We use one of the newest civilian thermonuclear reactors. It takes up most of the lower level of the central spar, down on deck two. Right above the Deepworker waterlocks."

"Those are single use units with a sealed radioactive core. But breachable with explosives. And Carlos seems to have an abundance of Semtek."

"Semtek?"

"Military grade plastic explosive. And each of your Dolphins are nuclear powered. That gives him three more reactors."

211

"Two. We only have our escape Dolphin and the one you came down in."

"But Sarah, your pilot, said two of the ports were already occupied when we got here?" Neil's eyes opened wide and stopped his pacing. "Can you seal off your submersibles? Keep Carlos from getting into them?"

Peter spun around and pressed the wall button for the Blockhouse intercom he had been standing next to. "Jacob, seal all the doors on Deck One. I want no one to be able to get to any of the submersibles."

"Right away, Peter."

"That should keep him down here with us. But it also means he knows you did that." Neil pointed to the intercom speaker. "How many people can you spare for a room-by-room search? I think we can rule out using your internal cameras." Neil pointed at the hallway camera with the paint-covered lens.

"Is he likely to blow the reactor if he's trapped with us? He'd die also."

"No, Carlos isn't self-destructive. He's willing to sacrifice others, but not himself. I don't think he'll blow it until he has a way off. He's going to have to find a way to release that lockout you placed on Deck One." Neil started heading for the stairs to take him up to the control room. "We'd better get that search organized."

* * *

"Jacob, Harry; set as many of the systems to auto as you can. We've lost all the cameras, but I need you to keep looking. Find out what condition we're in.

"Bill, Mike; I need you guys to do a room-by-room search of Deck Three."

Agent Corsair took over the instructions, "Carlos has been taking out your internal cameras and we need to find him. Find him fast. If you do, do not engage, he's armed. One of you keep an eye on him while the other gets back here to control and let..."

212

Agent Corsair pointed.

"Jacob Helman, sir."

"Let Mr. Helman know. He'll get a hold of Dr. von Scorio or myself, without using the intercom. You can do that, Jacob?"

"Yes, sir." He pulled open a drawer below his counter and handed everyone an earplug. "In fact they can contact you directly with one of these. Just tap the plug and say who you want to talk with."

"All the better." They began inserting them in their ears. "Damn, these things are uncomfortable. This is the first time I miss the government-issued ones."

"It's why we don't normally use them, sir."

Agent Corsair tapped his earpiece. "Peter."

"Last names, sir. The system is designed to recognize everyone by their last name."

"Dr. von Scorio."

Peter added, "Last names only. No titles. Jacob, is Agent Corsair listed as guest or Corsair in the system?"

"I was going to put down FBI Dude."

"Corsair, will do. No titles, remember," Peter instructed.

"Thanks!" Neil continued, "Carlos won't be using his explosives inside the Blockhouse until he is ready to escape. But that doesn't mean he hasn't left any nasty surprises. Use caution when opening any hatches. And don't waste a lot of time investigating each room. It's the man we need to find. Let's get going."

Neil placed his hand on Peter's shoulder as they made their way to the stairs, "Dr. von Scorio, I'll join you in a bit. I need to have a quick word with your operators."

"Okay, I'll start astern and work forward."

"Good, I'll see you there." He walked back over into control room circle, bent down and began whispering to Jacob.

Chapter Forty-Nine

"Most of the hall cameras here on Deck Three seem clear."

"Acknowledged. You're coming in clear on our monitors. Corsair, Scorio. Do you copy?"

Peter tapped his earpiece. "Helman. What have you got, Control?"

"Carlos must have left Deck One as soon as he wreaked maintenance. Bill and Mike aren't finding any trace of his movements. All the hall cameras are working fine."

"It could be a bluff." Peter heard in his ear. "Where is that FBI agent? What's taking him so long to get up here?"

"Carlos probably figures we're tracking him by destroyed cameras and is staying out their view. Though he could have found what he wanted in Maintenance and left. It's mostly living quarters and recreation, anyway. O'Donnell, you continue the search of Deck Three, in case he's still there. Danzig, you join von Scorio on Deck Two, where he has more opportunities to do some real damage. Corsair out."

"Corsair. Just exactly where are you?"

Peter's inquiry was greeted with silence.

"Helman. Is Agent Corsair still up there with you?" Peter turned around and walked back to the stairway leading down to Deck Two and waited for Danzig to join him.

"No, he left a couple minutes after you guys did. He told me to give him five minutes, release the seals to Dolphin Bay One, then seal them back up behind him. He said he needed to search Carlos's boat. Just now was the first I've heard from him since reactivating the lockouts."

"Had any luck?" Bill came bouncing down the stairs two at a time.

"The cameras have been blinded down here, if that's what

214

you mean."

"Then I guess our boy has to be down here." Clearing the last step, Bill turned towards the reactor spare parts room.

"Been that way. It doesn't look like he's touched anything in there. Even the spare core is fully moderated, not even warm. I was just headed down to the reactor when Jacob called."

Bill turned to proceed down the corridor, stopped for a moment and gestured for Peter to proceed him. "Shall we?"

When they were designing the Blockhouse, they thought about a remote lockout on the room, the way they had designed the system for Deck One. But it was decided that in case of a catastrophic system failure and everything got locked down, it was more important to be able to get power restored. With power, everything else was survivable.

Peter placed his hand on the wheel controlling the door mechanism. He pushed slightly and found the door still secured. He spun the wheel, pushed the door in and swung it to the side.

"Bill, check everything. We don't know what he may have done." Peter walked over to the computer monitor that showed the setting on the reactor controls and started mentally checking off all the settings.

Finally he shook his head. *I can't remember all these things.* "Helman. Pull up the checklist on the reactor and confirm with me the settings."

"They look good from here, boss."

"Carlos could have tampered with our interfaces. Let's run through them together."

After about five minutes, they determined that all the controls were optimally set. As he got up from the chair he had sat in when they started, Bill came around the far side of the large cylinder occupying the center of the room.

"Everything looks physically intact. We could use that Nuclear Tech the Navy loaned us to do a more thorough inspection, but I can't find anything wrong. Maybe Carlos didn't get in here?"

Peter looked over at one of the four cameras mounted in the

ceiling of the reactor room. "No, he's been here. Let's see if we can get some of that paint off so Jacob can keep an eye on things here."

The paint hadn't completely dried, so the lens were quickly cleared. Though the two men's finger nails would take a bit longer to clean.

"Helman."

"Yes, Peter?"

"How's your view of the reactor room now?"

"Pretty good, but number three's image is slightly fuzzy. We'll have to use some cleaner on it when this is over."

"Good. Keep at least one camera active down here. If it goes out, let us know immediately."

"Sure thing."

"Any word from Corsair?"

"Nothing since his last instruction."

"Corsair." Peter waited fruitlessly before trying three more times. Getting louder with each one. "Where is he?"

William Danzig simply shrugged.

Peter was slightly out of breathe as he tightened the wheel on the reactor room's door. Both men turned to go to the next room, a janitorial closet. They took one step forward, then independently turned to each other and said in unison, "The air!"

Peter continued the observation. "He's been at the environmental controls."

They ran past the next six rooms to the end of the hallway. "Jacob. Jacob. No, that's not going to work. Helman."

"Control here."

"Check the atmospherics. Something not right down here."

"You're right, CO2 is increasing. The fans are still running, it looks like the scrubbers are offline. I can't seem to correct the problem from up here."

Bill got his hands on the door's wheel and spun it open. A small amount of smoke drifted into the corridor with the distinct odor of ozone. The smoke inside the room was light enough for the two men to find the air pump that ran the returning air through the carbon dioxide scrubbers. The pump's housing had been dented, dented enough that the fan blades' rotation had been stopped. The fan motor had burned up in an effort of keep the constricted blades turning. Instead of blowing the returning air through the scrubbers, the pump was effectively blocking the return air from them.

"Helman. Cut power to the Environmental Control room." *We can't work on a powered system.* He turned to Danzig. "Get a new pump out of the repair locker and ready it for installation. O'Donnell."

"Yes?"

"Get down here to Environmental Control as fast as you can," Peter ordered while he walked over to the scrubber's circuit breaker and pulled down the lever that de-powered the unit.

In the bench below the circuit breaker box, he pulled a padlock from its drawer and slid the loop though the holes in lever and box, locking the lever in the off position. When he moved the grounding device over the pump, he could still feel the heat of the burned out motor coming from it. "Bill, don't forget gloves. This thing is still pretty hot."

Chapter Fifty

"Locking me out of my own sub? Not a very good idea, controller boy." Carlos spoke to no one in particular as he molded about two ounces of Semtek over each of the brackets holding the door's rods in place. He connected the six charges with detacord and stuck the radio detonator in the right upper mound of grey putty.

Figuring the stairwell would be a safe distance, he avoided the spot of dripping black paint under the hall camera and retreated up three steps. Enough to get him out of the corridor, away from the blast.

Thunder reverberated off the wall of the corridor as the metal loops holding the door restraints, and a piece of the bulkhead behind them, were pulverized into pieces too small to see. The door swung inward as continuous shockwaves travelled the corridor for more than a minute.

Even with the camera blanked, Carlos knew they would know where he was after that much noise. "If I can have a little luck, they will be passing out by now," Carlos vocalized his thoughts. "Already, the air down here is getting harder to breath. But I can wait things out in the sweet air of my *Suelo Defensor*."

He stepped over the remaining door frame and onto the deck of his modified Dolphin. He climbed up the conning tower, opened the bubble hatch and made his way down into the science suite before closing the hatch again.

He took a large inhale of ship's air. "Yes, that is *mucho bueno!*" He grabbed the ladder leading to the control room and slid down the outside of the rungs. *I might as well have a snack while I wait out those eco-destroyers.* He walked back into the food area.

It wasn't a large kitchen; this was a submarine after all, albeit one that could stay under for weeks at a time. It had a refrigerator, hot water rehydrator, a wall-mounted microwave and a small table with two chairs. One that was currently occupied by a man resting his right elbow on that small table supporting the Glock 9mm he was holding. He turned the barrel of the gun at Carlos as he entered.

"Carlos Rontonate, if even that is your real name, I've finally found you. I am Neil Corsair, Special Agent of the FBI. I've been looking forward to meeting you for some time now. Please consider yourself under arrest." The man rose from the mounted chair without wavering the gun a micron off Carlos' chest.

Carlos allowed his hands to drift upwards while turning his eyes to find something to throw at this interloper.

"You keep an immaculate galley, Mr. Rontonate. Though I did have to put your cutlery away, in that locked drawer under the microwave. Shall we go back up to the Blockhouse control room?"

"That might not be prudent. The air within your Blockhouse should be fairly ripe about now." Carlos dropped his hands and crossed his arms in front of his chest before giving the man a little smile.

"Keep those hands up." The man touched his left ear and said, "Scorio." After a few seconds, he repeated himself, then twice more. "Okay, what have you done?"

"I could not release the pollution you wanted to throw back into Gaia, so I will release the radiation of the reactors you have placed down here on her ocean's floor. It will drift up to your coastal waters, your politicians will get my message. Especially Senator Marquart and his lapdog, Simmons. Ha! They thought they could control me, Gaia's servant. They will see how wrong they were. You all will see how wrong you are. I will bring you all under Gaia's domination."

Then the world exploded.

Chapter Fifty-One

"Scorio." Neil tried one more time after applying his handcuffs to his unconscious prisoner and the bolted shaft of the galley table. Still no results. "What was that operator's name, Help? No, Helman." Once more he reached for his radio contact and called out, "Helman."

"This, is, Helman," came the parsed response.

"What's going on out there?"

"Sit, tight, repairing, scrubbers." Neil could hear the shortness of breath from the man who should be sitting in front of a computer console.

After a quick check of Carlos' pockets—there was a radio detonator in his shirt pocket, a gun in his left lower leg pocket and a can of black spray paint in the right one—Neil headed back out of the sub.

He had to catch his breath when he pushed open the observation bubble. "Scorio."

"Corsair, sorry I couldn't answer earlier, we've been a little busy. We've got a new recirculation pump installed so the air should start going through the CO2 scrubbers again. It'll take about a half hour to restore carbon dioxide levels back to normal, but if you remember to keep breathing slow and deep, you should get through it."

"Scorio, I've got Rontonate. Can you spare anyone to come down to Dolphin Bay One and help me move him to the control room?" He climbed back down into the air of the Dolphin and closed the hatch. His breathing was easier down here.

"We're done here. We can be down there is a few minutes."

"Thanks. I'm in the submarine he was using."

As he stepped off the ladder onto the science suite of the ship, a nasty thought occurred to Neil. "Scorio."

"We're on our way."

"Rontonate had a multiple frequency detonator in his pocket. He may have rigged your facility with plastic explosive. You need to begin a search for grey putty that has something sticking in it, possibly multiple mounts of the putty connected by wires."

"Mike's on his way to your location. Bill and I will start searching. Any clue where to start?"

"Your nuclear reactor. Rontonate said he planned to release the fuel components to contaminate coastal waters. "O'Donnell."

"Mike here"

"Just come on in when you get here. I'll be in the galley." Neil dropped the seven feet, holding the ladder for control, and went to check on his prisoner.

Rontonate's feet began to stretch out as Neil reentered the galley. Stepping over them, he gave the man a shake on his shoulder before leaning against the far cooking counter. He crossed his arms in front of himself as Rontonate shook himself back to consciousness and pulled on the steel restraints holding him under the table.

Rontonate finally gave up trying to break the steel chains when he discovered they would slide up the central post of the table and allow him to achieve a sitting position.

"Comfy?"

"We shall see." He smiled at Neil, then leaned into the cuffs so he could pat his right shirt pocket, whereupon his smile vanished.

"I think you're looking for this," Neil held up the radio detonator. "And I have your gun, too. They've got the damage you did repaired. The air should be cleaned up in a few minutes. Then you, my friend, are going to join us in the control room until the rest of my team gets down here to extradite you to the surface. Now, what's your connection with Senator Marquart?"

"You will have to talk to Alan Simmons about that. He is the one who has been giving me Marquart's money. I don't know what they want, but their money funds the war. Yet it will not spare them from Gaia's wrath."

"FBI dude?" Neil heard along with the upper hatch clanging shut and boots hitting the control room deck. A second later, Mike O'Donnell peeked into the galley.

"Mike, wasn't it?"

"Pete said you needed some help. So this is the guy that's been causing the trouble. I never got to meet him when he worked for us." Mike squatted to look the terrorist in his eyes. "I heard he was a fair handler of our submersibles." Mike stood back up. "So what do you want to do?"

"We have to get him securely up to the control room, away from those submersibles he's a fair handler of. So I can radio up to the *Halsey* for backup." Neil bent down and opened the cuff holding the handcuff around the table support pole, then wrapped the open cuff around Rontonate's other wrist. He helped him to his feet as Mike blocked the door leading off the Dolphin.

"Okay, there's two ways we can do this, Rontonate. You can walk, or we can carry you. But if we have to carry you, you'll wake up with another headache. Do I make myself clear?"

"I will walk. But this is not over."

"Mike, get up to the hatch. Move it, Rontonate."

O'Donnell climbed up to the science station and opened the hatch as Neil and his prisoner waited in the ship's control room. Mike then climbed out of the sub and waited. Neil motioned Rontonate, with his gun, to climb the ladder.

Taking the lift to the Blockhouse control room, Carlos offered Neil no resistance. They just walked in silence except for the few times that Mike tried to break that silence. Neil's focus was on his prisoner and what he would do to escape. But Rontonate didn't try anything. That made Neil nervous.

Once in the control room, Neil sat Rontonate down in one of the safety chairs Dr. von Scorio had mounted to the floor when he had first arrived. He undid the left cuff around Rontonate's wrist and secured it to the post holding the chair to the floor. Then he stretched his prisoner's left arm around the other side and used his other pair of handcuffs to lock that arm to the central post.

Everyone was recovering with the purified air. "Helman, can you get me a line to the surface? To the *Halsey*?"

"Sure thing," answered the other operator.

Harry, wasn't that his name? I'll eventually get them all straight. "I need to get the rest of my men down here."

"Then we had better send one of the Dolphins back up. The Elevator is still out of service and all the docking bays we have down here are full at the moment," Jake responded.

"Sarah can be up and back in under an hour," Harry offered.

"Set things up and get the *Halsey* on the line. I need to talk to Special Agent Fellows."

"Sarah," Jake broadcast over the intercom. "Run down to Dolphin Bay Three. Take your Dolphin back to the *Halsey*. Agent Corsair needs you to pick up some of his buddies..." He looked over at Neil and held up one, two, three, then four fingers in succession.

"Three." Neil turned back to the radio and issued instructions to his men.

"You'll be picking up three more FBI agents to bring them

down here."

They turned away from their monitors to look at the thud coming from just outside the control center.

"I'm not picking you up," Neil said as they saw Rontonate had pushed himself out of his chair and was sitting on the floor. "And neither are you." Harry sat back down under the push of Neil's hand.

Carlos scooted his legs and body away from the post his hands were bound to, until he was stretched out on the floor.

"If he wants to take a nap, let him. We have work to do. Mr. Helman," Neil rested on his extended arms before a bank of six monitors showing the interior rooms. "Can you replay the footage on each of the rooms that this guy has blacked out?"

"Sure." He rolled his chair on its track over to the sensor controls. Within a few minutes, a list of rooms appeared on the lowest of the six monitors in front of Neil. "These are the rooms where the cameras aren't functioning. You can select each one by typing the number associated with the room," he pointed at the screen, "this number here. Then move the timeline bar just like you'd do watching an internet video. You should be able to take the image back twenty-four hours, if you need to."

Neil pulled a chair from the center of the circle along its track and sat in front of the bank of monitors. Within minutes, he was feeding rooms to Dr. von Scorio for his team to search.

"If we have Carlos in custody, why not use the intercom channel on these things, so I don't have to relay every instruction?" Peter walked up behind Neil.

"Intercom channel?" Neil turned to glare at Jacob Helman.

"Yeah, if you ask for the Intercom, the computer will tie you into the entire structure. Did I forget to mention that?"

"By the way," Peter looked around the room. "Where are you keeping him?"

Chapter Fifty-Two

Sarah flooded Bay Three after she finished her system safety checks and opened the sea doors. She dropped down ten feet and closed the doors again, activating the pumps to purge the bay she had just vacated. She backed her Dolphin away from the Blockhouse and began her ascent to the surface. "Sarah to Blockhouse. I am clear and heading to the *Halsey*. See you guys in an hour."

There was no response from the Blockhouse, but they were busy, and she did have a hazardous trip to complete. She didn't even notice the momentary blip on her sonar screen that vanished as she sped upwards.

* * *

"He's gone!" Agent Corsair was kneeling beside the chair holding the empty handcuffs that had held his prisoner to it. A piece of wire was lodged in one of the key holes. "I should have kept him in that chair. He must have had a hairpin. Once he got on the ground, he could pull it from his hair and work the locks."

"Peter," Jacob cried out. "The sea doors on Dolphin Bay One are opening."

"There's nothing we can do to stop him now."

Agent Corsair ran up behind Jacob and spun him around. "Is there any way to close that bay other than its hatch?"

"No!"

"Rontonate, blew that hatch before I caught him."

Everyone jumped to monitoring stations. "Air pressure in the base is increasing."

"Cameras are still out."

"I can still get the sea doors closed," Jacob said. "Assuming he didn't rip anything off in his escape."

"Mike, Bill, I need a visual on Deck One. It could be flooding."

"On my way," said Bill through the speaker system.

"Mike, do you copy, Mike?" When there was no answer, "Judith, if you can leave David, Mike's not responding. I need you to help Bill search for him."

"Dr. von Scorio, let's not waste any time. These guys can handle things here. We can help search. Where was the last place you sent him?"

"To check out the docking bays."

* * *

"Damn this water is cold," Neil exclaimed as he stepped into the waist-high flood filling the lowest deck of the Blockhouse.

"I've got the sea doors closed. There should be no further flooding. I'm turning the water pumps on now," Jacob said over the intercom.

"We can't stay in here too long," Peter added. "It's well past the temperature where we could develop hypothermia. If you start feeling tired or start shivering, get out immediately."

"I'm already shivering. But if Mike's in this, we have to get him out now!" He pushed forward, going back and forth down the hall towards the open hatch at the far end. Hoping, yet not wanting, to find Mike's body.

Neil stopped shivering after a few minutes as he became accustomed to the water temperature. But as the level started to drop, an uncontrollable bout of mini-quakes racked his body.

Peter saw him begin to shake all over. "That's it, you're out of here. Get warmed up." He led the FBI agent back to the stairs as they passed Bill and Judith. "We got about half way down the hall. Get out at the first sign!"

"Roger that."

Peter led Neil up two flights and into the rec center on Deck Three. He pulled a couple of blankets out of one of the storage closets and wrapped the cold, wet agent. Then he went to the galley to get a couple bags of hot chocolate to facilitate their warm-up.

"Drink this," Peter said handing the hot bag to Neil.

"Peter," announced the overhead speaker.

"Go ahead, Jake."

"The pump in Bay One is overheating. It just packed up."

"Get ready to switch in the pumps in Bays Two and Three. Bill, Judith, are you still on Deck One?"

"We were just about to come up. No sign of Mike yet."

"Before you do, open the hatches on The other two Dolphin Bays." *None of those pumps were designed to handle that much water.*

"Roger that. But you have to get some hot drinks ready for us when we get out. I'm glad we don't dive these waters."

"I'm heading back to the infirmary after we get out of here. I need to check on David. I can get a hot toddy down there."

"I've got a bad feeling about where Mike could be if we don't find a body."

"Carlos' sub, right?" Neil took another pull on his hot chocolate before returning it to his chest, under his blanket, cradled in both hands.

Then he shucked off the blanket, and set his coco bag on the pinball table. Damp but not dripping wet, he headed for the door. "I have to get a message up to the *Halsey*. Then we're going to have to figure out what Rontonate is going to do next."

* * *

"We have no way to know how long he's been mapping out the sea floor here," Commander Wallace said. "He probably knows it better than we do by this point."

"And have dozens of hiding places," Captain Miller finished the thought.

"You've run a search for explosives on their base, Neil?"

"We've gone room by room, Harold. Especially those we know he's been in."

226

"I still need to get down there."

"There's nothing more you can do here. We're clean."

"Unless he's planted something on the outside?"

"Bill and Judith," Peter spoke into the intercom. "Take a pair of ExoSuits and look around outside for anything Carlos may have left."

As Bill turned to leave the control room, Judith called up from the infirmary. "Harry, could you come down here and keep an eye on David, then? He's beginning to stir."

"You have more medical experience than I do."

"Harry, go. She also has more experience than you do with the ExoSuit, and Bill's going to need a buddy out there. If he wakes up, just holler, and I'll be down there."

As Harry left his chair, Peter dropped into it to keep control on communications traffic.

"They're sending a team out to run a hull sweep. Harold, you know that if we let you come down, you'll be an easy target for Rontonate. We have to find him before we can do anything else."

Leo Dayton asked, "If we don't send any more canisters down, what can he do?"

So Peter answered, "We're sitting on two nuclear reactors down here. If he breaks those eggs, he'll make one hell of a hot omelet all along the East Coast."

"If we just brought you up," began Commander Wallace. "That would deprive him of those targets."

"Same problem as bringing my guys down here, Commander. We'd be sitting ducks for his torpedoes. Assuming he didn't go back to base after the *Hamilton*, he still has two more."

"We also have to assume he's overhearing this conversation," Martin Hughes added. "After all, he knew when to attack the last canister we said we were sending down."

Neil switched off the radio and spun his chair away from the console. "Martin's right, we can't make a committee decision with our plans. Rontonate will overhear anything we discuss." He turned to Jacob, "I'm assuming you're using the security suites Marine Workers Inc. installed in the equipment you bought from them."

"We didn't see any need for enhanced systems. We planned to stay as publicly transparent as possible," Peter answered. "Pretty much letting anyone listen in on what we were doing. If fact, we have plans for an internet channel, live-streaming our firings.

"Meaning, even if we encrypted the signal, Rontonate can decrypt it, since he'll have the same set of encryption keys."

Neil went quiet for a moment. About two minutes. Then he spun back to the radio and opened a line to the *Halsey*. "Martin Hughes, are you receiving me?"

"Loud and clear."

"First of all, everyone is alive and accounted for down here." Peter started to speak, but Neil cut him off with a finger to Peter's lips. "We can't locate Rontonate's stolen submarine, all our camera ROVs are out of commission. The communication suite down here is not equipped with encryption technology, that means anything we say can be heard by our problem." He paused for a moment before continuing. "I'm thinking we should try talking with him. See where he's at on this scenario. Can you find some direction to solve our problem?"

"I don't really follow, ow! Just a second."

"This is Captain Miller, son. I understand the tight spot your problem has you in. I know you're blind down there, so we will approach your problem from multiple angles. As long as you can keep talking with him, we can find you a solution. Be advised we will hold off sending any people into harm's way until you say so. Because I know you won't be having barrels of fun while you're down there."

"Roger that, Captain Miller. We will be waiting for any answer you can give us."

Neil switched off the radio and turned to the others in the control room. "Martin is a thorough agent, but sometimes can be a little slow. Captain Miller caught on. But in the mean time, I'm still worried about Rontonate's plans. He means to crack our nuclear reactors. How well designed is this habitat?"

"I designed it to survive ocean quakes, twice the water pressure we are working in and collisions." Peter pointed upwards. "But I never expected to be attacked by military ordinance. The reactor core would survive, but I doubt we will."

"And it's the core Rontonate's after. And if his torpedoes won't do the job, he must have another plan. I sure could use Harold Fellows about now, he's my explosives expert. Jacob, you're the electrical guy down here. You're coming with me."

"I don't know anything about explosives!"

"No, but I'm betting you had a hand in the installation of your reactor room." Neil rose from his chair. "Rontonate uses Semtek, exclusively, it's like he has a warehouse of the stuff. Semtek needs to be detonated electrically. Since the stuff can be molded to look like almost anything, we're going to have to look for a trojan circuit."

"Let me grab the specs." Behind the banks of servers in back of the room was another bank of file cabinets. Jacob opened one of the drawers and extracted both an eReader and a paper binder before heading to the stairs leading to the reactor room.

"Dr. von Scorio," Neil said as he started down the stairs behind Jacob. "Start Rontonate talking."

"About what?"

"Anything; his manifesto, how he likes his Dolphin, what he had for lunch yesterday. Anything!" His voice was fading as he made his way down to Deck Three. "Just keep him on that radio."

Chapter Fifty-Three

"Peter. Judith and I have found some extraneous material under the hull of the Blockhouse out here and on the anchor chains."

"Keep them on the intercom circuit," Agent Corsair said

over the speaker. "Rondonate shouldn't be able to tap into that one."

"You can isolate it using the icon labeled Secure." Jacob also responded through the speakers.

"You have a SECURE channel?"

"Secure as in internal use only, Agent Corsair." Peter said. "Can you guys get off this circuit so I can talk with Bill?"

"Tell him to look for any stick-like objects or wires coming out of the stuff he finds. If there is, pull it out."

"Bill, did you and Judith copy that?"

"We've already started. Following the wires have lead us to a whole lot more of them we hadn't seen earlier."

"It looks like," Judith added, "he was planning on cutting our anchor lines. With all his charges being located under the Blockhouse, I suspect he wanted to force it to rise off the ocean floor."

"Make sure you find all of it." Peter leaned against the back of his chair. *Carlos has been a busy boy down here.*

"So, what have I missed?"

Peter jumped out of his seat at the voice. As soon as it registered as David, he was across to where his friend had just emerged from the lift and wrapped him in a bear hug. Harry walked off the lift and around the two of them to resume his communication's station.

Peter brought David up to date as they returned to the control room circle.

"Judith," Harry called over the intercom. "David woke and insisted on getting up."

"With his temperament, you're not going to be able to keep him down. At least get him in a chair for the next couple of hours."

"I'll try."

Having overheard the exchange, Peter guided his college chum to one of the observation chairs and almost pushed him into it. "I'd tie you into that chair, but it would probably be as effective as it was for the terrorist."

"I feel fine. Ow." David moved his head to the side.

"Really?" Peter gave the knot on his friend's head a finger thumb.

"OW! Stop that."

"Then stay in that chair. Judith's orders." Peter turned back to the monitors. "Agent Corsair, can you spare a moment and clean off the reactor room cameras, so we can see how you're doing?"

The blackness of the image on camera 155, the one over the door of the reactor room, started blurring with little bits of lights breaking through the blackness. Then the remaining blackness started swirling as a view of the room began to emerge.

"How's that?" Peter could see Neil as he dropped off of something—probably the stool they kept in the reactor room— and stepped back so he could be seen by the camera.

"Better."

"It's amazing what a little degreaser will do. I'll get to the others in a few minutes. I need to get back to helping Jacob. This is the first time I've seen Rondonate booby trap one of his circuits."

Okay, now for the hard part. Peter picked up the microphone, switched the radio back on, and said, "Carlos, Carlos Rontonate. We know you can hear us. We want to talk. We want to find a way out of this situation. Please, what do you want?"

Peter waited an eternity of two minutes before trying again. "Carlos, we know you are out there. Please, I'm pleading for our lives. What can we give you? What do you want?"

After another two minutes, Peter was just about to key the microphone again. He stopped himself when he heard, "I want nothing!", on the overhead speakers. "You and your kind have defiled Mother Earth for too long. She is who demands retribution. She demands you stop raping her, killing her children, and defiling her beauty. SHE demands. I want nothing."

He's talking, Peter internalized. "What does she want to let us out of this situation?"

"You have taken the minerals from her bosom. You have

used those minerals in unnatural ways, then discarded them like they were so much trash. And now you want to fire that trash back into Mother Earth with your gun, your Waste Gun. This project must be stopped. The generation of nuclear waste must be stopped. The rape of Mother Earth for the resources to generate that waste must be stopped. You must learn to live on the resources that she gives freely to every living creature she houses."

"That's a tall order. How do you propose we carry out your wishes?"

"Her wishes, not mine. It is not for me to decide how you accomplish what she demands. You will either find a way, or we will eliminate you as a problem. Mother Earth can survive just fine without humans."

"But right now? What do you want us to do, right now?"

"I want you to send a message to the people in Washington, the people who think they are in control, especially those who thought they controlled me."

An explosion rocked the underside of the Blockhouse. The stern port section rocked up slightly before settling back down.

Peter dropped the microphone and tapped his earpiece. "Intercom. Bill, Judith, what's going on out there?"

"Open the holding pen. I've got Judith, but a piece of the anchor line broke off and cracked her suit."

"Those suits were supposed to be unbreakable," Peter commented to himself.

But his connection to the intercom circuit was still open. "I guess they never put one in the middle of an explosion."

"Get her aboard. I'm coming down." Peter turned, but before he could take a step, David's hand was on his chest.

"You have another job to do. Keeping that lunatic talking. I'll go down and help Bill. I owe Judith that much, at least."

"But you're supposed to be resting."

"The only way you're going to keep me here is if you put me out. So, get back there and placate that madman." David turned and trotted over to the lift.

Peter grabbed the mic. "Is that what you want? To kill us?

We offered you a position in our family. Oh, I know who you are, Mr. Charles Roland. I thought you were going to fit right in, be an asset to our effort. Help make Planet Earth a cleaner and safer place. Judith did nothing to harm you, and you've repaid that by trying to kill her. IS THAT WHAT YOU WANT?"

"You're not floating free? That explosion should have severed all your anchor points, disconnected you from the bottom. Tink. I must find another way to raise your reactors to the surface. Tink."

Peter held the mic in front of his mouth, unkeyed and unmoving for a minute. *What was that extraneous sound?* He looked over to the underwater listening system. Nothing. They normally didn't use it, so he had to switch it on. "Tink." *Every thirty seconds.* "Tink."

"Peter," it was David over the speakers. "Judith is alright. Bill got her in before the crack in her suit could split open. I wouldn't recommend using this one again, though."

"Tink." *It's Mike, it has to be Mike. He's on Carlos's ship and is banging away their location.*

"Everyone get up here to the control room now!" he said into the intercom before talking to himself, "I have to find a way to get word up to Leo and Captain Miller."

Chapter Fifty-Four

Carlos slammed open the hatch to his aft storeroom and grabbed his stowaway by his collar. "What have you been doing?"

Mike knew he could make one last sound, threw the wrench he'd brought from the Blockhouse when he smuggled himself aboard Carlos' ship against the side of the hull. It rang gloriously one last time, louder than any of the ones he had dared do before. "They'll know where we are now."

Carlos singlehandedly lifted him off the deck and threw him towards the door. Mike got his arms over his head just before he crashed into the inner bulkhead. They would bear the cuts they had saved his face from.

When he came to again, Mike's hands and feet were zip-tied as he sat in one of the chairs in the Dolphin's small galley. He ached to rub the painful knot on the backside of his head. Carlos stood against the counter, tapping the wrench Mike had brought in the palm of his hand.

"Now we are going to talk about what you did when you invaded my *Suelo Defensor*." He gave his hand one hard smack and stopped.

"I just came down here, fixed myself a sandwich and put on a movie. Great film, but you have lousy..."

The palm of Carlos' hand wracked the side of Mike's head. "I do not have time for your false valor. What did you sabotage, what systems did you mess with?"

"Buddy," Mike spit onto the floor. "I didn't have time to touch anything. I barely found this hidey hole before you came in. But boy, the Navy sure knows where we are now."

"We shall see." Carlos grabbed the center zip tie, and pulled hard enough to make the two around Mike's wrists dig slightly into his skin. Half carrying and half dragging, Carlos pulled him into the control room and threw him under the ladder to the science suite, where Carlos could see him as he climbed up.

"Do not touch anything. Do not even move," he called down as he took the seat in front of the Dolphin's sensors. "I can always flush you out a torpedo tube."

"You ain't got one, big mouth." But Mike knew he didn't need one. There were hundreds of ways Carlos could kill him down here.

A bright light pierced its way through the observation bubble. Carlos jumped from his seat and dropped down the ladder, barely missing his captive laying on the deck. Mike had been trained on Dolphin operations and knew Carlos was activating his engines.

"Looks like they found us."

Without taking his eyes from the sub's guidance controls, Carlos swung a kick into Mike's ribs. "*Silencio.*"

Carlos dove the sub off the walled ledge he had been hiding in. Pings from the sonar unit above them sounded louder and more frequent with each passing moment.

"Maybe I will just drop you off at your Blockhouse." Mike could feel the sub turn left. "They will not dare drop their "barrels of fun", if there is a chance those barrels will destroy what they seek to protect."

"You can't hide here forever. Even a Dolphin runs out of supplies in about a week."

"*Suelo Defensor*, she is the *Suelo Defensor*, she is the Defender of the Earth. She is no Dolphin," he spat the last out onto the deck, just missing Mike.

"Okay, fine, but you can't hide forever."

"Shut up," he aimed another kick at his captive. "I do not plan to."

"Can I at least sit in the pilot's chair? This deck is really cold."

"Fine. Stay out of my way and do not move from that spot."

The Dolphins that Mike trained on were designed to be manned by a minimum of two people. One in the science seat and another in the pilot's seat. To run one solo, Carlos had to move between the two stations and wasn't able to take advantage of the comfort the chairs allowed. Mike wormed his way over to the pilot's chair, then grabbed the armrest and pulled himself into it, accidently brushing the control to activate the port side lights. Knowing full well if help didn't come in time, Carlos would kill him for doing so.

235

Chapter Fifty-Five

"Sir, there's a glow coming from the Blockhouse habitat." The young ensign called out from his monitoring station. As Captain Miller approached, he moved the ROV closer to the underwater structure and finally under it.

The Captain leaned over the sailor's shoulder and stared at the monitor showing the camera's feed. "That's Rontonate's submarine alright. Good work, son." He stood up, called over to the assembled FBI agents, "Agent Hughes, we have him again. The bastard is hiding under the Blockhouse."

"That means we can't drop depth charges on his location without destroying the blockhouse," *Halsey's* XO informed the FBI agents.

Agent Hughes turned to the XO. "Don't you have anything we could drive him out of there with?"

"We never developed a scenario for driving someone out from under an object that deep in the open water while protecting the object."

"Well, there's no point in secrecy now. Get Agent Corsair on the radio," Hughes asked.

* * *

"He's just sitting down there. We have eyes on him, but there's nothing we can do without endangering all of you."

"Thanks, Martin." Peter cut the link to the surface as he saw Jacob motion to him. The electronics guy pointed at one of the monitors. It showed an enlarging image of the Blockhouse from outside.

"Peter, you need to see this too. I've got one of the ROV camera units functioning again, one on the outside." The image followed the hull around and homed in on the light coming from the Dolphin parked below them. "And now we have eyes on Mr. Terrorist."

"Harry, lock out the controls for the Dolphin bays. I don't want him getting back in," Peter quickly added.

David snuck up behind the three men huddled over the computer monitor. "He's sitting under the DeepWorker pens."

They turned to look at the intruder. "Just what are you doing out of that chair?" Peter asked his friend.

"I feel fine. Just look where he's sitting. I could drop my DeepWorker right behind him and he'd never see me coming."

"Then what?" Neil asked. "None of your vehicles are armed. His is. Were you planning to ram him?"

"In a sense." David turned to look his friend in the eye. "Peter, you designed the DeepWorkers to carry the travel cylinders, heavily-loaded travel cylinders. You gave the DeepWorkers more power than anything else ever built. Even greater than a Dolphin's. I could grab his sub from astern, lock onto his motors with my claws, blocking his turbines, then push him to the surface."

"Not in your condition," announced Judith, who was grabbing David by his arm and trying to head him back to the chair he had just vacated.

"Judith, leave off!" He shook off her arms. "I'm fine."

"No, you're not," Harry began. "Listen to your crazy idea."

"No." Peter broke in. "No, it could work. I designed the Deepworkers as our workhorse, an underwater forklift. It has five times the power of any other vehicle in its class. It would be more than a match for the prototype Dolphin Carlos stole."

"And I have to go," David pressed. "I'm the best pilot you've got."

"On one condition," Peter held up his hand to forestall Judith's objection. "I'm going with you. If anything goes wrong, I'm the best one to fix it." He turned to Judith, "I'll keep an eye on him."

Chapter Fifty-Six

"Just like old times," David threw over his shoulder as he focused on running through his pre-launch checklist and systems warm-up.

"I think we've got a little more riding on this run than any we've done before." Someone knocked on the canopy, breaking Peter out his pre-launch focus. He looked up to see Agent Corsair shaking a small box. He disengaged the plastic safety case surrounding the canopy release switch and allowed it to hiss open. "What's up?"

"Bill attached a Semtek, an explosive charge, to your sample retrieval arm. If all else fails, smash that arm against the hull of Rontonate's ship, then release the arm. He said you could do that. Then get as far away from him as you can before pressing this." He handed Peter a small black box with a single red button in the middle. "That's the trigger. Be as far away from Rontonate's craft as you can get before you press it."

"You guys normally carry explosives?" David asked from the pilot seat.

"No, but the guy left so much of it here. It's only fair if we return some of it to him." Neil smiled as he responded.

"Let's hope it doesn't come to that." Peter placed the box in the personal bag on his right and velcroed it shut.

"Now get out-of-here," David said, "so we can get going."

Neil stepped away and down the three steps that led up to the DeepWorker. Peter closed the canopy again. As the light above the bay's hatch indicated that Neil and Bill had secured the bay hatch, David activated the pumps to remove the air and fill the chamber with sea water. The whole process took about five minutes.

While he waited, Peter activated the display of their remaining camera so he could make sure their quarry hadn't moved from his position.

David had configured the DeepWorker to be neutrally buoyant; she floated within her hanger when the water doors opened. He slowly lowered her out of the bay and made a small turn to line up his craft with the stern of the other ship.

Once they were at the same depth as the Dolphin, he engaged his motors at minimal speed and slowly crept up on the other ship. At about half their maximum range, David began to deploy his cargo claws.

At that moment, the water surrounding the Dolphin's jets began to swirl.

David grabbed for the housing of the tubes. The left claw managed to lock on, while the right bit half way over it. The Dolphin had begun to move.

"Peter, emergency lockdown. We can't let him get away."

"Roger, David." A small electrical charge was routed through the joints of the lifting devices, in case of an unstable load, and would stay locked until someone came along to manually open them again. "Those claws aren't opening again."

"He's pulling us with him."

"We can't jam his tubes at this point, our other arms aren't as long as the claws. Looks like it's time to test out this baby's engine strength. Gun it, David!"

David pressed the throttle fully forward. Peter could feel the resistance as they pushed against the other ship. But both crafts began to pick up speed. David dropped down slightly to get a better angle, then began the long climb to the surface. It was working. The Deepworker's power was overwhelming the engines of the Dolphin and they were going where David directed.

For about five minutes.

The Dolphin steered first to the right and then to the left, trying to break off the claws that held her. David compensated, and they held.

Peter watched as the water coming from the Dolphin stopped, then reversed, pulling water in to force the craft backwards. They could feel the other ship pushing against them, but the engines of the DeepWorker were more than a match, and they kept on course for the *Damocles*.

The dolphin tried a spin to break the hold, but with her wings extended, it was not as quick a rotation as David's cylindrical DeepWorker could do. David gave Rontonate an extra couple of spins before forcing him to straighten out.

"I always wondered what they meant by riding a tiger by the tail."

"He was getting ready to leave before we got there, David." Peter sat back in the rear seat. "Why?"

"To get away, of course."

"He had to know the Navy would keep tracking him once they got his position. And that they couldn't do anything while he was using us as a shield. No, he's planning something."

"Peter, we've got him. He's not going anywhere. We're taking him straight to the surface and to jail."

"According to Agent Corsair, he's still got two torpedoes and who knows how much plastic explosive."

After a period of quiet time and as they came to within 150 feet of the surface, Peter had a nasty thought. "David, don't those Dolphins have a sample retrieval hatch for their front arms?"

"Yeah."

"What if Carlos knows about it and uses the hatch to place an explosive charge on one of his retrieval arms?"

Before David could respond, an explosion wracked the bow of the DeepWorker. Once the shaking stopped, Peter ran a visual scan of his monitors looking for leaks. "No pressure loss," he called up to the front seat.

But as he said it, he looked out of the front window. The right claw arm had broken off. The claw remained attached to the forward ship, but had broken off at the mid-joint. The left one was still hanging on, but the joint was bent at a severe angle.

"Carlos is applying lateral thrust again." David tried to compensate for the maneuver, but the arm snapped under the stress.

David put the DeepWorker into a fast dive to avoid colliding with the oncoming submarine. Without the drag of pushing the Dolphin, his fast maneuver allowed them to pass under the sub by a few inches.

The other ship sped forward and turned more abruptly upward, widening the gap between the two of them.

"We can't let him get away. Ram him. Push him up to the surface, David. Burn out our engines if you have to, but don't let him get away."

David reversed his dive and brought his submersible up. He aimed at the midsection on the underside of the hull, slowing his speed to control the contact. He moved his remaining arms to the side. As the ships contacted each other, there was still enough force to snap off the remaining spars of the claw arms. David gunned his engines. With the ships oriented like they were, the Dolphin pointed mostly upward with a northern angle and the DeepWorker pointed upward with a southern angle, David began to slide towards the stern of the Dolphin.

"Peter, use the auxiliary arms. Try and jam his rotors when we get close enough."

Peter activated the three remaining arms and pulled their joystick controls across his lap. Before they got anywhere near the stern, he slapped one of the arms against the hull of the other ship and released it from the DeepWorker. As they approached the jet tubes of the other ship, Peter tried to jam each of the sampling arms into them. The first one slid in, snapped off inside the tube, and redirected the flow of expelled water, sending the Dolphin off at an uncalculated angle. But the second one missed going in the tube, simply snapping off outside.

"Get below him." Peter called out. "I've got a sonar lock for you." As David dropped the DeepWorker another ten meters, "Turn about. Come up under him and let's push him up. As far and as fast as we can."

Then it occurred to Peter what Carlos meant to do. "Keep him level. We have to get him level. Don't let him get his nose pointed directly up. His torpedoes are mounted on his wings. He has to use his entire ship to aim them. We have to keep him from

241

firing on the *Damocles*. A big enough explosion could rupture all those canisters she's carrying and spew their contents all over the Eastern seaboard like he planned in the first place."

David brought his DeepWorker around, dropped his depth another meter, then pointed his own nose at the bottom of the fleeing submersible. "Let's hope this girl is as tough as you promised."

He set the engines for full and punched into the midsection of the bottom of the other ship's hull. The two craft straightened out and began to move upwards. Peter watched as the Dolphin angled her wings so she would fly up to vertical. David compensated by applying more power to his port side, the side pointed at the other ship's stern.

It was slow going until they reached 10 meters. Suddenly Carlos shifted his wings into a dive posture. He caught David by surprise and got away from the smaller craft. He dove a couple of meters, turned his submarine around and launched one of his remaining torpedoes at the DeepWorker.

"Emergency Dive," Peter said what David was already doing. Had he put a conning tower in his DeepWorkers, the torpedo would have slammed into it and exploded their craft. It ran inches above their heads.

"It looks like he's making an attack run on the *Damocles*," David called over his shoulder.

"Keep diving, as fast as you can."

"But he'll kill our friends."

"Just do it. Trust me, he won't get the chance. Peter opened his personal bag, pulled out the detonator, counted out ten more meters, "I'm sorry, Mike," and pressed the button.

The shockwave pushed them a bit deeper, but it was nothing like the one Carlos had earlier unleashed on them. 'We got far enough away,' Peter said internally. "Take her up, David. Let's see if there are any survivors."

"Mike?"

"I hope so, I really hope so."

Chapter Fifty-Seven

Mike had tried to stay in his seat, hopefully blocking Carlos from seeing that he had switched some of the lights on. Something outside was pounding the boat. He fell and rolled towards the galley. When he saw that Carlos hadn't noticed, that he was too busy working the ship's controls, fighting whoever was pounding the ship, he slipped into the galley and began looking for something to cut the zip-ties with.

As he opened a drawer with eating utensils in it, an explosion outside the stern of the ship bounced many of the items out and onto the deck. Two of which were steak knives. Mike chose one of the latter and began sawing at the plastic between his wrists.

The teeth of the knife were a bit large and not spaced the best for cutting plastic, so once he had his hands free he searched for something else to cut loose his feet. The sub jolted as he found a pair of kitchen scissors in the bottom of the drawer. *As long as he keeps fighting whoever's out there, he's forgotten about me*, Mike internalized. *And that suits me just fine.*

Staying low, hoping he could do something to interfere with his captor's plans, Mike made his way back to the control room. There hadn't been many non-lethal objects he could use to attack Carlos with, so he had a large plastic storage bag to try and suffocate him. *Oh, for a frying pan right about now.*

He had just gotten behind Carlos and stood up, when Carlos swung his chair around, pointing a combat knife at Mike's stomach. "I have no more time for you."

As he lunged forward with the knife, an explosion rocked the stern of the vessel hard enough to drive even the seated Carlos to the floor. The knife—yes, Mike's attention was focused on it—spun under one of the work stations.

243

Water began rushing into the control room. With the ship still more or less level, that told Mike the lower decks had already been flooded. He climbed into the conning tower, and when the water—not as cold as he had been expecting—reached his waist, he began hyperventilating before holding his breath. As the water filled the observation bubble, he triggered the explosive controls and jettisoned the hatch. He blew out a bubble, watched which way it went, then followed it up, hoping the surface wasn't too far away.

As he cleared the conning tower, a hand grabbed his shoe. A kick quickly dislodged it and he swam as hard as he could. *My lungs didn't crush under pressure. That means I must not be too deep. Light, I see light. I just wish I could hold my breath as long as Wong can.* He pushed himself as hard as his lungs would let him. The light from above grew. His lungs ached to breath, CO_2 was building up in them. He blew a little of it out and kept going. Finally the light exploded, he broke through the ocean surface to the air supply above.

Chapter Fifty-Eight

"Permission to come aboard, Lieutenant Radcliff."

"Permission granted, Special Agent Corsair." Neil thought he heard pride in the boy's voice for the correct sign and countersign. "Captain Wallace is waiting for you in his conference room."

"Grant the same to the rest of these civilians. They don't know the drill. Where are they keeping the prisoner?" On their way up, word had come down that the *Vella Gulf* had pulled both Mike O'Donnell and Carlos Rontonate out of the water. Carlos was unconscious, but in stable condition and Mike was threatening to deck the next sailor who tried to put him on a gurney.

"He's in Sick Bay. Aft and down two decks."

"Thanks. Inform the Captain I'm checking on him first. And there's another submersible about to arrive." Neil didn't wait for the rest of the Nuclear Recyclers crew to emerge from the Elevator that had brought everyone up from the Blockhouse. Instead he took off, almost at a run. "Rontonate got away from me once."

"Sick Bay," he shouted at the officer he almost collided with as he slid down stair rails for the second time.

The young man instinctively pointed down the hall. After Neil had taken a step in that direction, he tried to stop him. "Sir, you can't be down here."

"FBI," Neil threw over his shoulder. "Check with your Captain." He never even broke stride. He almost ran into two other crewmen before he got to the unsecured hatch.

He pushed it open to find the medic pulling himself off the floor, steadying himself on the central gurney in the room. A gurney without an occupant.

Neil pulled the young man upright. "Where's your patient?"

"I was leaning over him, checking the dilation of his eyes when the world exploded." He massaged the back of his head. "I'm just now waking up."

Laughter, he remembered one of the sailors he bumped into gave a slight laugh as he passed him.

"Call Captain Wallace. He's got a terrorist loose on his ship." He was out the door before the other man could react to his orders.

The corridor was empty when he got to it, but he sped back to where he had bumped into the second of the two men. Both were wearing blue Navy coverall, both were headed forward. But only one had the goal of getting off the ship. "How would he do that?"

Then the answer came to him. The Nuclear Recyclers' ships. He had been trained on them, knew how they worked. Neil sped up the stairs two at a time. As he dashed across the deck, he had to shove aside several crewmen who tried to restrain his madcap flight.

"Stop that man." He saw Rontonate, still in Navy coveralls, begin climbing down the ladder to the Dolphin parked below.

A large sailor decided to get between him and wherever he was trying to get to. "Out of my way, FBI." He took a step to the left and ran around his right side.

Rontonate was already half way down the ladder as Neil looked over. The terrorist stopped long enough to give the FBI man a little wave and began sliding the rest of the way to the open hatch of the submersible.

Neil dove off the *Vella Gulf*, grabbed Rontonate on the way down. The two of them just missed hitting the Dolphin. They sank about a meter into the Atlantic. After a brief struggle, Neil put a choke hold on the squirming terrorist until he calmed down. Then kicked his way back to the surface.

As he broke through, he could see men starting to congregate where he had jumped from. A few of them had drawn pistols pointed in his direction.

"Tell Captain Wallace, I have his escaped prisoner," Neil hollered up. Most of the guns lowered to a resting position.

"I'd play this easy if I were you, Rontonate. Yes, I want you alive. I have a lot of questions, especially after our last talk. But dead or alive, you're not getting away again." Then he yelled back up to the ship, "Can I get some help here?"

Rontonate was still squirming as several sailors rappelled down the side of the ship and helped Neil pull his prisoner back aboard.

Epilogue

"I'm telling you, Bob." Senator Marquart sat behind his office desk entertaining the new Senate Majority Leader, Robert Marley, whom he had shepherded into the position. "This is the time to shake things up. The way the FBI has bungled that eco-terrorist investigation... Well, we need to privatize crime prevention in this country, the way we did the prison system. Capitalism will find ways to make our lives safer."

"Then you haven't heard? I don't think the information is classified. They caught the guy, Carlos Rontonate, I believe. The President personally congratulated Agent Corsair and his team. He even went so far as to offer Nuclear Recyclers a contract for the disposal of the Department of Energy's hazardous waste."

"My aide just delivered a memo from Alan Simmons," the Senator picked a set of papers up from his desk, "saying that recent terrorist attacks have crippled the company. They don't have the remaining capital to get up and running again."

"Probably not, but it seems that they got Lloyds of London to insure the tests. They're collecting about a billion dollars to rebuild."

"Still, look at how long it took to catch the guy responsible. No, we need organizations that are more nimble. That can develop and use new techniques faster than Washington bureaucracies to stop bad guys."

There was no knock on the Senator's door. FBI Supervisor Alan Turner, flanked by Special Agents Neil Corsair and Martin Hughes, pushed past two of the Senator's aides and marched in.

"Senator Marley, please leave us," Turner ordered.

The tone in the FBI man's voice made the Majority Leader jump out of his chair and head for the door. "I'll talk to you later, Richard."

As soon as the door closed. "Richard Marquart, I'm placing you under arrest for conspiracy to commit terrorist activities against the United States."

"You can't do this."

"We already have the deposition of your co-conspirator, Alan Simmons. Please make us take you out of here in handcuffs. The press is waiting outside."

The End